DARK POOLS

DARK POOLS

ALEXANDER DUCHARME

Copyright © 2024 Alexander DuCharme

The moral right of the author has been asserted.

Apart from any fair dealing for the purposes of research or private study, or criticism or review, as permitted under the Copyright, Designs and Patents Act 1988, this publication may only be reproduced, stored or transmitted, in any form or by any means, with the prior permission in writing of the publishers, or in the case of reprographic reproduction in accordance with the terms of licences issued by the Copyright Licensing Agency. Enquiries concerning reproduction outside those terms should be sent to the publishers.

This is a work of fiction. Names, characters, businesses, places, events and incidents are either the products of the author's imagination or used in a fictitious manner. Any resemblance to actual persons, living or dead, or actual events is purely coincidental.

Troubador Publishing Ltd
Unit E2 Airfield Business Park,
Harrison Road, Market Harborough,
Leicestershire LE16 7UL
Tel: 0116 279 2299
Email: books@troubador.co.uk
Web: www.troubador.co.uk

ISBN 978 1 83628 024 8

British Library Cataloguing in Publication Data.
A catalogue record for this book is available from the British Library.

Printed and bound by CPI Group (UK) Ltd, Croydon, CR0 4YY
Typeset in 10.5pt Garamond Pro by Troubador Publishing Ltd, Leicester, UK

For All of my A Team

PROLOGUE

Dark Pool, *n*.
A private forum for trading financial securities anonymously.

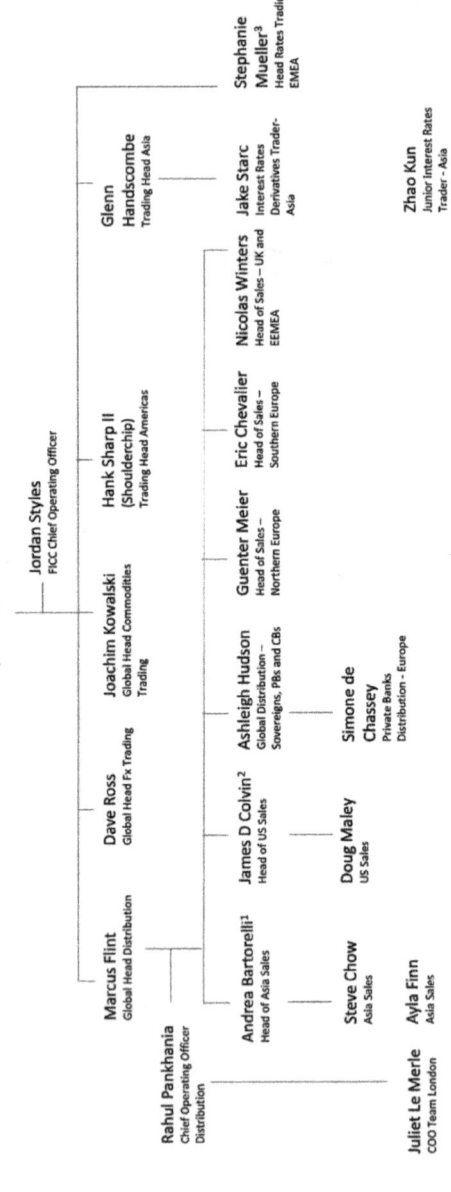

ONE

What is your life about, anyway?
Nothing but a struggle to be someone,
Nothing but a running from your own silence.

The mist was lifting. Slowly. Inevitably.

Marcus Flint (English, late forties) observed the distant waking activity across the valley while monitoring, unperturbed and semi-detachedly, the buzz of emails dropping on top of each other on his mobile screen. He found the chilled but faint breeze refreshing and cleansing rather than uncomfortable, as he reflected, somewhat contemptuously, on why the Teiflaubach waters and its valley took the longer, arduous route to flow into the Meiringensee rather than run directly, and geologically more aptly, past where the Weisenberg chapel now stood.

He had been through the Americas traffic. Tokyo was coming to a close, delivering calm, deferential, elaborate but inconsequential updates on business. The place was totally unprofitable, but the costs had been hidden in with the wider Asia region, and he enjoyed his annual trip there too much to shut it down.

Most of the current flurry in his cc box was from Singapore and Hong Kong. He took care not to open any, no matter how enticing the header. His instincts were well honed to spot anything that could be a problem – regulatory, reputational – and, most importantly, to avoid being implicated for any blame. In any case, he largely trusted the guys from his time there – they would come through on his private number with any delicate issues. He noted, though, that the cc folder was starting to receive more traffic – maybe it was just the new guys with some heightened insecurities.

The buzz of his inbox gave way to a ping – the Continentals were in. He tolerated their texting, or rather he had to; as global head he needed to show his cosmopolitan diversity, and not be open to an accusation of English exceptionalism. It gave them a feeling of intimacy. It left him with the uncomfortable sense of village intrusiveness.

London would arrive soon, and the calmness of Asia would descend into a Trojan battlefield of egos, as he, like Zeus, chose which of his mortal underlings to favour.

He moved across to settle on the wooden bench where some warm and dry cushions had just been placed, but the armrest was cold and damp from the dew. He closed his eyes and folded the nearby blanket across himself. He needed to respond to the New Yorker 'Shoulderchip'. He shut his eyes – a few minutes' meditation would help.

A double ping disturbed the focus on his breathing. He looked at his watch – 6.30am in London. Emma. What had he forgotten? Oh yes, Ollie needed to select his foreign languages for next year. He deleted the message on the recorded work line – he understood why Emma texted on both phones, but he was having enough of his private life being recorded.

He took out his iPhone and tapped 'Spanish and Sanskrit – speak later. Mx'.

Urs Waelchli (Swiss, mid-sixties) placed the tray on a white metal table and tugged shut the glass doors behind him. Dressed immaculately in his jacket/chinos combo, with perfectly creamed dark hair, he strolled across to the Englishman holding two coffee mugs. Although tall and slim, bordering on lanky, he walked with a firm upright posture, purposeful but not rushed.

Despite the rattle from the closing doors, Marcus didn't turn to acknowledge him. He needed the coffee, perfected over the weeks to his taste and strength – a tenacious mix of Columbian and Kenyan beans, and served, unlike in his first few days, straight from a mug rather than through the over-the-top palaver of a metal pot poured into a china cup.

Marcus kept his eyes shut as Urs approached. Neither particularly wanted to talk to the other. Both felt obliged to.

"Good morning, Marcus. Not enjoying the view?" Urs had only the faintest trace of his Germanic Zurich accent. He had boarded at Charterhouse when his mother and younger siblings escorted his father for various ambassadorial postings.

"Shoulderchip is being an arse." Marcus lit his once-daily cigarette, or, to be more precise, he lit his once-daily, when sober, cigarette.

Urs took a sip and took in the view across the valley. Marcus waited for Urs to reflect on his response. Within that silence, he could sense Urs' hidden disdain for him, the concealed superciliousness that Urs probably held for all his clients, a repulsion flawlessly disguised behind a warm, welcoming façade – one that came with a life and career of serving, not questioning. He had felt Urs' contempt clearly grow with his stay, but it wasn't something that particularly troubled him.

Finally, Urs spoke. "Why do you bother now? Let him be?"

Marcus took another sip. He looked up at Urs, dressed, as always, like a Savile Row tailor going for a Sunday lunch.

What a rigmarole, like the china cups – who bothers to wear Prada chinos in the mountains? His mind shifted back to Shoulderchip.

"Nah, he's a cunt. He's trying to run me over while I'm away."

"Let me guess. He's saying the numbers would be a lot better under him. Pierre won't buy that. He's expecting you back soon. Anyway, not a good look trying to shaft you while you're recuperating."

"Plus, the team are supposedly unhappy. Etcetera, etcetera. You think I trust Pierre? He'd change things and chuck me out tomorrow if he thought the revenues would look better. All he cares about are the numbers and having a nice 'collaborative tone'." Marcus raised one hand, wiggling two fingers to denote speech marks. He made a conscious effort to exhale away from Urs, but the faint breeze swept the dying cigarette smoke back across their faces.

The coffee and cigarette were having an effect. The cheeks relaxed a little and a hint of a smile formed across his face. Even uncombed, unshaven, and half hungover, Marcus could do silent charisma.

"What do you think, Urs, Spanish or German?"

Urs shrugged blankly.

"Ollie has got to pick his foreign languages. All the Swissies speak English now, don't they?"

"Well, not everyone."

"I mean the ones that count."

"Well, I don't know."

"I'd like to know your opinion, Urs." Marcus raised his volume slightly.

"Spanish then." The conversation had already told him the answer to give. "Doesn't he get to pick two?"

"Latin or Sanskrit. Both useless. Emma said Sanskrit."

Urs was relieved to hear the sound of the doors opening behind him. Muttu Murali (Sri Lankan, mid-thirties) smiled across the lawn at the two men. A broad smile, so broad that perhaps he wasn't even smiling at them at all, but at the beautiful view across the valley behind. The same smile each moment, each day.

"Herr Waelchli! Your mobile rang twice. I didn't see the number."

Urs didn't need another invitation to sneak away, to get away from the smell of last night's whiskies and off-quota cigarettes, and the sight of the unshaven, English, dishevelled lump slouched across the bench in a wine-stained gown and worn suede slippers.

He made his way back to the villa, towards the doors by which he had come, into the back entrance of the restaurant or 'dining room' as he called it.

Above him was the grey cliff face of the outer wall with the teal-blue shutters precisely bordering nine rectangular windows in a three-by-three pattern, which had spent the last 127 years admiring the views across to the Bernese Alps. Neat square stone-grey slabs cornered the walls, each placed with immaculate stereotypical Swiss accuracy. On top lay a lightly inclined chocolate-brown tiled roof. Iron-railed balconies had been added to the higher two floors. Behind Urs, a neat lawn peppered with shrubs and large pots blended into the Alpine trees. A solo path wound its way past the side of the house where Marcus sat, to the terrace at the front of the villa, where a little tributary path set off towards a gate into the dark woodland foraging through the hills and trees.

Once inside, Urs could see Marcus talking to Muttu through each of the three large windows of the dining room; Marcus, whose fine Derek Rose pyjamas were unable to add any sheen to the hungover blotch against the manicured lawns, and Muttu, still smiling vividly and nodding in that circular South Asian way that they had tried to mimic so many times. Chopin's 'Piano Sonata No. 2' played quietly in the background.

The villa stood at 1,100m. A steep drop led to the Teiflaubach flowing below.

Urs could just about make out the start of their conversation.

"Hey, Muttu, I found this little book in the library last night about the history of this villa – you know, about the Traxler guy."

"Yes, sir, the hotel was unrivalled for its luxury at the time, and the highest service levels that we have sought to emulate."

"Ah, cut the crap, Muttu. He built it as his family home initially. Guy made a stack of money constructing those Alpine railways. Josef Traxler was his full name, seven kids as well, impressive, though not sure why he needed twenty rooms. Anyway, it seems finance wasn't his thing – made some bad investment decisions. He needed a wealth manager like your boss!"

"Ah, didn't realise, so the hotel was a conversion from a family home?"

"Yep, needed to replenish his bank account, but the guy had a wherewithal to build a funicular up from the Meiringensee. I guess that was fairly unique at the time and you're right – the place was considered the place to go. Apparently, his missus was also a super cook, Florence, no doubt like yourself."

"We try our best, sir."

"There is a picture of him in the book, in front of the villa playing some fucking Kuhreihen on his alphorn. Can't see you and Urs entertaining the guests with that!" Marcus chuckled to himself. "And the guy still had time and energy to go cavorting with a local barmaid."

"Does it say that in the book?"

"Ah, come on, you know what I'm getting at. Should have kept his dick in his pants, or at least kept quiet about it, especially with a feisty missus. I heard that thing again last night. All the locals talk about it. It doesn't sound like it's playing any alphorn though, more like singing…"

"Oh, I really don't believe in such things, sir," Muttu interrupted him, "just local village talk. Nothing very exciting happens here. He just fell off the ladder fixing the shutters. The noises you hear are just from the wind rustling through the trees only, nothing more outer-worldly than that."

"Well, whatever, the Germans obviously didn't care, taking over the place in the war."

"I imagine it's a great place for recuperating soldiers, sir."

The voices tailed off with Muttu's contemplative tone as Urs entered the hallway.

He recalled how the Traxler brand had faded as a hotel after the war. Eventually, it was sold in the '60s to Banque Collardi, who were attracted by its close location to Zurich. It was converted into a conference centre and a place to entertain wealthy clients of the bank.

One such client, the Aljawahiris, a Middle Eastern family based in the Emirates, were so enthused by its view and location that they bought the villa in the early '90s and converted it back to a discrete private residence. They were also, frankly, rather enthused by the tax-efficient structures proposed by the bankers to their family office, which allowed them to move their money into real estate across various geographies ultimately through a trust based in Mauritius. The Aljawahiris 'rented' the villa for a nominal amount through a Swiss subsidiary of the trust. Their banker also advised that one of the trustees be a Swiss national. Such was the personal and financial value of the arrangement to the Aljawahiris, and motivated to solidify the discretion of their private banker who had gained such a deep insight into their affairs, that they rewarded their banker, in addition to his employment remuneration and bonus, with a private hidden allocation of shares in the trust and hence an indirect share in the villa. Urs had been that banker.

Various Aljawahiris spent a few weeks to a few months at the villa, moving with the seasons between Traxler and their other residences. For reasons of discretion, privacy and security when the villa lay empty, and to undertake general housework, they brought across their own staff from the Middle East. Urs' contacts within the local canton bureaucracy meant their presence was barely noticed or questioned. The Aljawahiris businesses were largely above board, and those that weren't stayed firmly below the radar of any authorities.

That was until Ishmail, one of the scions of the family, was mentioned in a report into the Turkey-Iran cash-for-gold scandal that allegedly sought to bypass US sanctions.

Although Ishmail was a very peripheral figure in the report, his name had been on a database of Fox News, from a time he had been involved in a scuffle outside a Manhattan restaurant. This aroused the interest of a junior journalist, Meghan Moretti. The reporter tracked Ishmail down to Villa Traxler, where Ishmail was spending a lot of time drinking vodka, smoking weed and writing Arabic love poetry. After feigning an interest in the great ancient poets al-Qais and al-Mutanabbi, Meghan took her cue from 'today is for drinking, tomorrow is for more serious business', and suggested that she and Ishmail would perhaps gain more poetic inspiration within the memory foam of his Tempur mattress.

Two days later, she filed a report, more fiction than fact if truth be told, linking sanction-busting, money-laundering, Middle Eastern business interests and tax evasion with Swiss secrecy – all buzzwords at the time. Nevertheless, this made everyone, from the Aljawahiri elders to the local canton administrators, unnecessarily uncomfortable.

At the time, Urs was looking forward to his retirement in four months and had been transferring his clients to younger, supposedly more dynamic, managing directors at the bank, more interested, in his view, in making money rather than observing true client service. The Aljawahiri family office, code-named Ochre at the bank, was, however, not interested in engaging with a new, untested advisor at this delicate time. They were also keen to wash their hands of any publicly known Swiss assets.

His bank insisted that Urs delay his retirement a little until the matter had blown over. Urs, devoted to his clients, could not refuse. To be honest, Urs, seeing a major retirement trade, could not refuse. He offered to take Villa Traxler off their hands, through a transfer in the Mauritius trust, in exchange for a much less ostentatious but nevertheless supremely well-located chalet he owned near Grindelwald. He was also able to place seven of the junior Aljawahiris in interesting jobs with investment banks, consultancies and internet start-ups across London, Paris, Zurich, and San Francisco.

A few weeks after the Fox News story, Ishmail disappeared, leaving the verses of Rumi to be whispered by the trees. The family said he had moved to Beirut, but unpleasant rumours surfaced that his body lay buried below the undergrowth on the banks of the Teiflaubach next to the villa. Urs, of course, was happy for the investigators to search the area – clearly, he would espouse that someone's imagination was playing games with the historical myths around the first owners of the Traxler. He pointed to the unblemished reputation of his client over many decades and noted passenger records showing that Ishmail had left in a private jet to Cyprus. The Swiss authorities decided there was nothing further to look into and Urs was paid CHF 500,000 across various accounts for his assistance by the Aljawahiris.

Urs used the money to refurbish Villa Traxler and convert it back into a hotel, targeting the most discerning customers whose needs he had got to know so well. So, rather by chance, he had realised a retirement dream. The Aljawahiris staff left and went back with them to the Middle East, but one member of the team had caught Urs' eye, with his dedication to client service and discretion, very much in his own frame. It also happened that he had initially flown in on a private jet and had no papers to be in Switzerland. Urs decided to keep him as his first recruit to the hotel team – his name, Muttu Murali.

Urs entered the chocolate cave of the cigar room and was met immediately by the coalescing smell of cigarettes, cigars, late-night cognacs and other herbal flavours deeply entwined within the fabric of the burgundy-red carpet and coating the wood-panelled walls and bookshelves. He found his phone on the side table where he had cleared the previous evening's whisky tumbler. He knew who had called and why and summoned his decades-experienced 'yes-means-no' tone.

"Good evening. This is Urs Waelchli. I am sorry to have missed your call. How are you, and tell me, how is the delightful Mrs Li?" Urs raised his tone and intonation to maximise his enthusiasm.

He was not flustered by the unfriendly aggressive tone of young ambition and arrogance on the other side. Urs, the son of a senior diplomat; Urs, the retired senior partner of Banque Gaumet et Cie; Urs, one of most well-connected individuals in Switzerland and maybe the world; Urs, owner of probably the most desirable hotel in the Alps. No, Urs, with his perfectly creamed dark hair, the dapper dresser, had dealt with many climbers looking to make a name like his many times before.

"Yes, we received your email, and I have just this morning

spoken to our guests, and it seems they will be here for another three to four weeks. Very honestly, we would love to have Mrs Li's family here, but, you understand, I can't ask our current guests just to leave. We want people to feel they are at home, not in a hotel.

"Early April can be a lovely time here. We still have some snow on the higher peaks, plus the temperature can start to get a little warmer and the days are longer.

"Yes, absolutely, we understand Mrs Li's busy schedule." Urs was not irritated by the tone but had to strain a little on the strong Cantonese accent. "I have already been thinking of some ideas. An acquaintance of mine has a wonderful modern villa in Wengen with a spectacular view of the Jungfrau. It would be perfect for you. It is a little smaller than the Traxler but perfect for a few days. The catering and service will be done by my team at Traxler so you will notice no difference.

"No, no, don't worry, the guests here have fallen in love with Muttu and are just as happy with his dishes, so there will be no distraction for you on that front. The rest of the team are free, and as soon as the Traxler is available, we will transfer everything and everyone across. I can mail you details of the property.

"Or we can look for something near Engelberg, though Mrs Li's father wasn't so keen on the Bollywood crowd. Having said that, Muttu has introduced other guests to the charms of Shah Rukh Khan. Further away options are Zermatt and St Moritz. They are also wonderful places.

"Please let me know. The villa is yours unless I hear otherwise. We are waiting for you."

He put the phone down. The piano sonata had moved onto the more calming and romantic barcarolle. He was sure they'd come – there was no time to find anything else. He just needed to make sure that Marcus would be out. He went back to his office with a view into the valley.

* * *

Slowly but inevitably, the morning sun yawned across the hills, embracing their verdant curves. Icy peaks were lighting up in the distance like victory beacons, even though their sheltered slopes remained stubbornly and defeatedly grey. Dark, dormant woods, rising from the banks of the Teiflaubach and engrossed in their mysteries and horrors, cast an impenetrable shadow across the waters below, shrouding the eddies ebb and flow, engaging in an unseen battle for space and form. And the daily confrontation between the lights and the unlit had started again and would end again with, even on the brightest and warmest days, much of the darkest spaces totally untouched.

TWO

We do not know a truth without knowing its cause.

Marcus took a few steps to the front of the villa, took in the view across the valley with the mountains beyond the drop below and, as he often did on such mornings, felt the self-congratulations of a man who had earnt this whole vista to himself; a man, at least outwardly, able to face and overcome whatever issues crossed his path. He stretched and yawned aggressively. Even in this solitude, in this mood, he needed and wanted to be seen and heard, even if only by himself.

He sat back on the bench and flicked through his earlier emails. One had caught his attention from the head of trading in Asia, Glenn Handscombe (Australian, early forties). Glenn had joined three years ago, brought in by Pierre to 'shake up' the region. This had primarily involved replacing the existing traders, good or bad, loyal or not, with his 'own guys', and constantly criticising Marcus's sales heads for not winning enough client business.

Marcus had been cc'd on the mail and, from what he could see without fully opening it, it concerned a local bullying incident. Marcus hesitated for a second but couldn't resist taking a look – in any case, the topic may come up on a subsequent management executive committee 'Exco' call and he didn't want to be blindsided.

Strangely, Pierre was not copied on the mail. The matter would seem important enough. Perhaps Handscombe had already informed him. There was certainly a chance, though, that he was keeping things deliberately under the radar – Marcus wondered why he had been cc'd. Handscombe probably figured Marcus would have found out anyway from one of the sales managers and he could show he was being open and collaborative by informing him directly. The bullying allegation was made by a junior trader, Zhao Kun (Singaporean, mid-twenties). Zhao Kun was a pretty serious and level-headed guy, a PhD from Stanford, and it would have taken quite something for him to raise his head above the parapet in this way. He had also been working on some interesting and innovative interest rate algorithms that had been creating some much-needed local excitement (and in some cases, envy).

The complaint was against Jake Starc (Australian, late twenties), an interest rate trader that Handscombe had known from his previous employer. Starc had been bought out from MM Capital, the hedge fund, at some substantial compensation package and sign-on bonus, and had needed a full-on tantrum from Handscombe, with Pierre, to bring his fellow Aussie in. To be fair to Starc, he had had a couple of decent profitable years on the desk, executing some opportunistic relative value plays. To be also fair, so had all the other interest rate desks on the Street and who had, in all likelihood, delivered even better results. Nevertheless, he had helped to boost the local revenue numbers and that is what Handscombe and, more importantly, senior management cared about.

However, Starc undeniably had an ego and arrogance that stretched some distance beyond his grade and pay packet. He felt within his right to 'rough up' whoever chose not to show sufficient deference. He had had various shouting fits at the sales guys, even threatening to beat up one of the Hong Kong team after work over a fairly innocuous, low-value, trade booking error. Things calmed down swiftly when Starc learnt that the young salesman, Steve Chow (Hong Kongese, late twenties), was a taekwondo champion, though that didn't stop Handscombe and Starc hammering Marcus to reduce Chow's year-end bonus.

Marcus recalled his last social bonding session with Handscombe and Starc in Singapore, a night of giant chilli crabs followed by cocktails at the Fullerton where he was staying. The local team had drifted away as their voices had gotten louder and the conversation had moved onto the standard 'who was making more money at which bank', 'who had been fired for whatever breach' gossip, before descending into the normal Aussie-Pom banter that was lost on the Singaporeans. Suitably freed of the local company and inebriated, Starc moved onto a few one-liners about the Chinese. Marcus smiled the first of these off, before detecting a deeper unpleasantness to the humour. He'd go along with the odd stereotype, but he was conscious of Starc's volume, the public location, and the bank's diversity policy, and made a signal to Starc to change the tone and topic. It also genuinely wasn't his thing, and Starc and Handscombe noted it. Things went quiet, at which point Marcus bid his farewell, but was still within earshot to catch, but ignore, Starc's parting comment – "Ah, you Poms are so fucking stiff."

It seemed that the Zhao Kun incident had been resolved through a caution for Starc via HR, which almost certainly meant that Starc would be pushing for Zhao Kun to be on the next cull list, or at best the one after, and the division would lose a decent young talent. Still, trading wasn't Marcus's area, and he had his hands full with Shoulderchip on the other side of the world.

It was nevertheless surprising though that Pierre hadn't been copied on the mail. Marcus felt there was potentially some political future value in the saga and made a mental note to find out more from one of his local guys the next morning. Maybe he'd also find a reason to call Zhao Kun directly.

He thought about calling Emma. No, he'd get the US issue sorted first.

Juliet le Merle (Canadian, late twenties) welcomed Marcus Flint's name announcement on her mobile with the glow others would reserve for a Brad Pitt or a Penelope Cruz. She rushed her payment for the medium latte and muesli yogurt and stepped into the rain, her hands too full to open her umbrella. Torrents of commuters gushed and brushed past from one of the flooded exits to Bank tube as she fumbled to press the answer button.

"Hello, Marcus, how are you feeling?"

"I'm OK. Are you in the office?"

"I'm by Bank, five minutes away, getting drenched and run over by the crowds. Nothing like the Swiss countryside, I guess?"

"I need you to get me something." Marcus spoke faster notably to demonstrate both how busy he should be and his senior authority. "I need the last three years' revenue data for North America, cut by team and product, but can you amend it so that those large one-off elephant trades from two to three years back are amortised over duration. My guess is that will show business growing both last year and this year by about 20%."

"Well, if we are going to amend the reporting system, I'm going to have to run it by Rahul. He's around."

"No, I'm not asking you to change the system. This is analysis! You know this is what you're good at, otherwise I would have just gone to the numbers guys. Don't worry, I'll speak to Rahul. Can you get that to me by midday?" Marcus wanted the report quickly so he could not only nip things in the bud with New York, but also before anyone stickier and less malleable than Juliet started asking why he was 'manipulating' the internal reports.

"Sure, Doug was asking for something similar yesterday."

"Doug Maley?"

"Yeah. I said I'd get it to him today before New York gets in."

Marcus reflected for a second. Fuck. Maley has been siding with Shoulderchip. Wait a minute. Maybe Shoulderchip is putting him under pressure, but surely Maley would have alerted him if that was true, and he hadn't seen anything from Maley in the last couple of days. Maley throwing himself in with Shoulderchip would make sense. He had been after Colvin's job for a while. Shoulderchip must have promised him something. Did he care? Damn right he did. This was total disloyalty. He'd have him out in the next cull round, next quarter, but hold on a second, could that be what Maley wants – get out and cash in his deferred bonus. No, Maley would certainly be after the promotion, and he's been sucked in by Shoulderchip. Well, he's going to learn that crossing Marcus isn't the right way to go about anything.

"Hey, Juliet, get me the numbers first. Let me take a look and then you can forward." Marcus waited a second. "You're doing a great job, by the way. You know Rahul won't be around forever. He'll want bigger things and I've got you in mind for that role. Keep it up."

"I'd love that, but, you know, Rahul has been in the job for ten-plus years – he covers a lot of stuff."

"Yeah, I know but you can do it."

Juliet, drenched by the rain but thoroughly warmed by the compliments to her future career, sped towards the office. Marcus had already forgotten about any such career promise, but the image of Juliet's blonde hair, high heels, and short skirt lingered in his mind momentarily.

Time to call Emma.

* * *

Emma Kapoor (British, early forties) pulled into the drive after school drop-off. The morning drizzle had stopped, and the sun started peering through the clouds. The extra rain had dragged more traffic and more irritation onto the south-west London residential streets, the large Range Rovers and BMWs with their peroxide mums competing with the white vans of plumbers and builders, naked egos versus naked envies, on their way to gyms, coffees, or to meet with each other for yet another loft, garden or basement construction. Through this land of ill-disciplined rhinoceroses, she had driven her genteel Mini home, harassed but unscathed.

Like the lifting sun lighting up the driveway tiles, her mood brightened with the sight of Marcus's name and photo entering her morning with its humming on her mobile phone breaking through the Radio 4 News.

"Hello, Marcus, just a second, I'm literally just opening the front door. How are you?"

"I'm good, Emma, yes, feeling good this morning."

"Why do you never use FaceTime? I'd love to see you and what it's like where you are."

"You know I hate those video calls – feels like I'm at work, and I really don't want you to see me like this. You might stop fancying me."

"I won't do that. Anyway, do you not want to see me? I had my hair trimmed two days ago."

"I see you in my mind all the time. Send me some photos, and of Ollie too."

"He's been asking when you're coming back. What are the doctors saying?"

"They think soon. I saw another guy. Didn't really have any more on diagnosis other than just a bit burnt out. They're the best in the field. Just need to rest – no work, no alcohol, no cigarettes – just good food and fresh Swiss air."

"And I hope you're doing all that, Marcus."

"I am, darling – you know Urs – keeps a tight rein. I think another three to four weeks and I should be out of here."

Marcus moved the conversation on. "Did you get my text on Ollie's language options? You know you're better positioned to decide on these things."

Marcus didn't have much new to say on his health and may have slipped up on the questions about his drinking, work, and the cigarettes. He knew Emma was very sensitive to his voice tone when he was hiding something. Emma, of course, noted he had moved the subject on. After asking about Ollie, he had steered the topics onto feigned interests in her family, friends, and the neighbours whom he wouldn't recognise let alone care one iota about.

So, she told him about her sister; things not going well with her husband. Emma had offered to talk to both of them or look after the kids so they could get away for a few days. And the conversation continued until they both knew she would have to get ready for her yoga class.

"Oh, Marcus, I didn't realise the time. It's nearly quarter past. I need to get ready and go to yoga. Can I call later?"

"Sure, of course, call whenever, maybe when Ollie gets in from school."

Emma put the phone down. Clearly, he wasn't keen on talking for too long with her. Clearly, something was wrong, but why wouldn't he tell her? Was he worrying about making her anxious? What was wrong with his health? Surely, he must realise not telling her was making her even more anxious, and yet he was saying he'd be back in three to four weeks!

* * *

Muttu was returning across the lawn back from a delivery van.

"Have you seen my laptop, Muttu?"

"Yes, sir, I think it's in the library – shall I bring it across?"

"Yeah, Urs was looking at something for me. What's for dinner?"

"*Karahi Gosht.*"

"*Karahi Gosht* – with lamb, right? Your version is something else. How do you get that smokiness?"

"Black cardamom, I believe, sir, and I also add *Kashmiri mirch.*"

"*Mirch*? Chilli – like paprika. You know your spices?"

"I spent some time in Kerala after Bangalore. It seems you know your Indian spices too, sir."

"Ah, I have some connection with Kerala too. Actually, leave the laptop there. I'll get changed first."

Marcus got up. He flicked up his Spotify app, put on the earphones, and started to stutter aggressively to the music of Prince's 'Sign 'o the Times', before bellowing some muddled lyrics defiantly across the valley about men not being truly happy until they died, but why?

THREE

Tomorrow, and tomorrow, and tomorrow
Creeps in this petty pace from day to day…
Life's but a walking shadow…
That struts and frets his hour upon the stage…
full of sound and fury,
Signifying nothing.

My Darling Emma,
I know you'll be perplexed at receiving this letter.
It's difficult to know where to start with these things. I know I haven't been totally open about my stay here in Switzerland and my condition, and I realise this must have been causing you some anxiety. I suppose I haven't been able to bring myself to tell you the full story face to face. Frankly, I haven't had the courage. I should have gone through this much earlier. Perhaps I had hoped to avoid this eventuality, that things would resolve, that life could somehow go on with nothing needing to be said, but you see over time the weight of life starts to bear heavily on our minds and bodies until it begins to crumple us. Those paths and decisions that once seemed right, or not fully considered, their repercussions play inside our minds with their stresses, the guilt, the fear of the truth being exposed, tearing us from the inside.

You'll have plenty of questions so please bear with me till the end and you'll know everything.

In life I've pretty much always managed to get what I wanted, but the one thing that has escaped me from the start is peace. This time, these weeks and days, here alone in Switzerland, have helped me to reflect on everything and to try to decide what I should do next. I arrived with what I thought was a physical and maybe mental problem, but the real problem was spiritual, going to the core of how I became who I am. Emma, we all have our stories, our contexts, and I'm not seeking to excuse myself, but I do want to share a little of mine if only to help explain some of what I am going to say.

As I say, as a child I got everything that could be bought, but little else. I don't mean to sound ungrateful, but my childhood wasn't a 'peaceful' place – a child with no affection, no direction, no red lines. I boarded while my parents married, affaired, separated, divorced and remarried in various orders. I could barely remember the names of stepfathers, stepmothers, step siblings, but when you get bought everything you ask for, how do you complain, how do you get attention?

You know all this but maybe what I haven't told you is that when you get what you always want, you want more – a different excitement. So inevitably, I started to get drunk at parties and ultimately ended up taking drugs – first soft, then hard. I flunked my O Levels and was put on warning in the sixth form. My dad's attitude was I'd sort it out and it was kind of OK.

All that laissez-faire attitude resulted in was my going all-in; from being an irregular participant in the drugs market, I became the school's primary supply chain until I was caught and expelled. Thus, arriving at my dad's country pad, I finally got his attention.

For someone who had been gifted anything I needed with a monetary value, I hadn't, at the time, appreciated the two most valuable things in my possession. The first, I think, would come to anyone who has had to survive a childhood with no love at home – he or she seeks a pseudo-love by becoming friends, or at times buys friendship, with virtually everyone he or she meets. I just learnt to get along with almost anyone to the point that I would even get invited by friends on their family holidays, which frankly also suited my inattentive parents. This was all good until some of the middle-class parents got a sniff of my drug dealing – once somewhat hypocritically when one of the dads was placing an order through his local lines!

The second, and even more valuable thing, was my dad's contact list.

The last thing he wanted around him while he spent his inherited wealth on divorces, mistresses, society parties and poker, after all these years, was his eldest eighteen-year-old son. Having said that, though, compared to my mother, I actually believe he cared. She took zero interest in where I was.

So, he got me a job at a City broker, Bonham Morays, and a flat just off Eaton Square. Dad was at Harrow with both Bonham and Moray, and I started trading UK government bonds. After a couple of mergers, we were taken over by TDT Capital as they sought to get a foothold in Europe. So that's how I ended up in banking at an American investment bank – totally by chance.

Peter Bonham retired, but not before he moved me across to sales. Clearly, I wouldn't have cut it as a trader with the US guys so focused on my quarterly numbers, but he had spotted my talent to get along, and noted that many of my school chums had started taking positions with various asset managers and, in particular, a couple were with the larger hedge funds. In those days these guys would give business to who they liked, or who did them favours, you know, like a ticket to Wimbledon, a little delivery of the best stuff, an evening out with an aspiring model – you can see how things worked. Our compliance team was dim and trim and that's how TDT liked it.

The final skill I needed to climb the corporate ladder, I learnt from my new American boss, the guru of office politics. Have I mentioned his name before? Frank Underwood. House of Cards' *Underwood – couldn't make it up. My sales, driven by favours and old contacts, paid his and my bonus, and in return he showed me how to work the corporate machinery, so I went on to become head of my rates desk, to head of European rates sales and a rather young managing director.*

Our New York masters liked their numbers big and getting bigger. Before the era of LIBOR scandals and FX rates rigging, and exposure of chat rooms across different houses, we didn't let any social conscience get in the way of a good trade. Some guys like Sanju didn't like this world but I had never grown up with red lines. I excelled.

Anyway, I became head of UK sales across all fixed income products and, by the way, was getting rich in my own right. Then Underwood got poached by Morgans and asked me to go across with him. And with hindsight, I wished I had done so, so today I wouldn't be where we are now. I didn't. I stayed at TDT.

The guys in New York sent across another American to be head of Europe – Dietmar Offenbach. I think he was chosen simply because his name sounded European. He only lasted fifteen months but he wanted to put his stamp on the place, which meant 'getting rid of the deadwood'. The London atmosphere was getting truly unpleasant. By now some of Underwood's political nous had rubbed off on me, and my sales numbers were more of threat than a boost to Dietmar's bonus, and maybe, probably, I was getting a bit cocky.

Anyway, Dietmar the Shit put me on the next cull list. It was a bit out of the blue, and I kicked up a fuss with the old-timers. Dietmar wasn't done and played the compliance card about the mis-selling of some trades, as if we were some heavenly angels. Things got ugly until Giles Moray, by then UK chairman, got me a transfer to Singapore.

Despite all the aggro, the guys gave me a pretty decent send-off party. Dietmar said some lovely words – makes me vomit thinking about it. I don't remember what, or how much I had had to drink, or what I had smoked, but the one thing I do remember is being introduced by Sanju to his attractive lawyer girlfriend. And as you've said many times, you didn't even notice me.

FOUR

Only when the tide goes out do you discover who's been swimming naked.

Marcus read the letter again from the start. He did this each time he edited or redrafted. Was there anything missing? Was it too much? Would she skim-read or take it all in in sequence. Emma was a lawyer. She would read quickly and then reread forensically. He didn't want her to skim but it was something he couldn't control. She wouldn't be expecting a letter; she'd dive through quickly, and then go back. Too much side detail was better than gaps.

He leaned back into the black leather again. His laptop looked too small for the oak table. A jury of books gazed down on him, staid and still on their shelves – leather-bound classics that no one had touched, recent Booker Prize winners, books on politics mingled with philosophical works in English and in German, guides to Swiss mountains and lakes with their meandering walks – all looked down on Marcus curiously, and possibly accusingly. A large window shed enough light across the clean, dark, and polished library surfaces, to provide Marcus a hint of his own reflection.

He looked intently at the laptop. What was he trying to say, to achieve? Clarity? Comprehension? Closure? As a minimum, context? Maybe he needed those as much for himself; maybe he would only achieve those only for himself. He had asked Urs to read through the letter and tell him what he thought but had got nothing back.

Urs entered the library with a simple, solemn, judge-like expression.

"Tell me what you think." Marcus spoke with an impatient, almost aggressive, tone.

Urs' solemn stare stayed solemn. His silence stayed silent.

"Have I missed anything?" Marcus's tone lowered. His irritation stayed raised. Marcus looked towards the window. Urs stood behind him. Outside, he could hear the cooing of pigeons. Inside, the still quiet of a deliberating courtroom lingered. "Well?" asked Marcus again with a more patient calmness.

"Well, I think, perhaps I will let you know once you have totally finished your first draft. Then I will know exactly what you want to say. How long do you think it will take now?"

"Another couple of weeks and I'm done." Marcus turned around to look at Urs but got nothing but an expressionless face. He knew it was a loaded question. *All he fucking cares about is when I'm leaving so he can get the next lot in.*

"So, if I may, I'll leave you to continue your work." Marcus had turned towards the window, leaving Urs to speak to the back of his head.

Marcus heard Urs leave. He shuffled round to face the laptop again before slamming it shut. "Fuck him," he mumbled.

* * *

Urs stepped outside to get some air. Respecting the client was something second nature to him but Marcus had really started to vex him. Still, he would be leaving soon. Two weeks, he said. At a stretch, that would be three.

How could he be expected to comment on Marcus's personal letter to Emma and, beyond that, what an arrogant and entitled tone – it was common amongst his guests, but nevertheless grating.

He recalled how their relationship had evolved over the years, and Marcus's unexpected call a few months back.

They had first met about twenty years ago, having been introduced by Peter Bonham, for whom Urs had been a wealth advisor. Urs remembered Marcus as a pleasant young man, not necessarily the brightest, but enthusiastic, unquestionably ambitious, seemingly hard-working and he was clearly being mentored and supported by Bonham. Urs had taken Marcus out to dinner. He was keen to get Marcus's father onboarded as a client. After a few drinks, Marcus's brashness had become more pronounced. Urs put that down to youthfulness and the investment banking culture and, overall, he had enjoyed the evening.

Their paths crossed again four or five years later. TDT Capital had taken over Bonham Morays, and Marcus had become UK sales head. He had certainly become more stressed, more political, and keener to remind all and sundry that he was now in charge of the UK team and only just past thirty. This time, Urs was the potential client. But for Marcus, it was patently more about the trade, about making money, than the relationship.

TDT Capital had developed a number of structured investment products using derivatives to deliver enhanced yields for wealthy investors. These had been back-tested over various durations, to show how well they would have performed through different economic conditions and were proving popular for distribution by many of the private banks. Urs had been invited to a product review meeting by Marcus and his team. Although it was Marcus who spoke the most, infusing his quick and loud delivery with contemporary buzzwords, it was blatantly evident to Urs that Marcus knew little of the detail of what he was selling, and pretty much didn't care to know. It was also plain that his answers could politely be described as unconsidered; less politely, as blatant untruths. The back-testing durations for one thing had been selectively chosen. Urs could sense the raised eyebrows behind his poker-faced team members. Perhaps it was the sale-at-all-costs culture of the American bank, but he couldn't reconcile the Marcus of then versus the enthusiastic and relatively pleasant one he had met just five years earlier.

Urs sat on the Product Approval Committee at Gaumet, responsible for deciding which investment products ought to be shortlisted for recommendation to their client base. Urs simply didn't have confidence in those proposed by TDT and didn't even bother to present them to the committee for discussion.

A couple of weeks later, he got a call from Marcus to see if any of their products had received approval.

Urs set off on a spiel about the rigorous analysis that Gaumet et Cie undertook, how very few structured products they placed on their platform, the nature of their discerning clients and…

"Cut the crap, Urs. I hear Morgan's Precious Metals Range Accrual is on your platform."

"Well, my understanding is that their structure has less downside risk in unfavourable markets."

"Is that right? Well, I can tell you that most of the Geneva banks prefer ours. Have you considered the potential upside?"

"Yes, we have. Absolutely. Look, we take very few of these certificates on for our clients. Of course, we will consider anything new you have to show us, but these decisions are not mine personally but set by our committee."

"Yeah sure, Urs. Well tell your committee this is not the best way to win my father's business." Marcus put the phone down.

Urs' intuition had been well founded. Over the next twelve to eighteen months, the TDT products fared poorly, and the limited downside protection meant that many investors lost substantial sums. TDT's reputation with the private banks took a big hit and would take a long time to repair.

The next time Urs heard from Marcus was about four years later. He had moved to Singapore.

Underwood, Marcus's boss, had been replaced by Offenbach, and it was certain Marcus would be forced out, but it seems a guardian angel had stepped in and Marcus was moved to Singapore, where TDT were supposedly looking to grow their franchise.

Urs had now become European head at Gaumet and had been assigned a new salesperson from TDT in London, so was surprised to get the call from Marcus based in Asia. This was a much smoother Marcus, relaxed in his new surroundings and the Singaporean heat.

"Hello, Marcus. What a nice surprise to hear from you."

"Hi, Urs, good to hear your voice, and belated congratulations on the promotion. Well deserved, and I suspect keeping you very busy."

"Yes, there is a bit more travel, but, you know, we have a great team so it's really no great extra effort."

"Well, it only becomes a great team with a great manager to recruit and mentor them."

Urs wondered if Marcus had been getting some coaching. Perhaps he was being primed for a bigger role.

"You're in Singapore now, I hear."

"Yes, it's been about three years and now I'm in charge of the region. Listen, Urs, I'm sorry about the way I spoke last time. I was under a bit of pressure but that's no excuse."

"I have no recollection of it, Marcus." Urs felt it best to confine their previous conversation to a distant past.

"Well, in that case, would your clients have any interest in some triple A CDO tranches, super yield for the rating?"

"You know TDT products still have a weak reputation here."

"Well, we could white label them under Gaumet."

"Except everyone knows we don't structure our own CDOs; they'll ask who's behind them."

"Tell them it's Morgans." Urs could hear Marcus scoff and sense the conversation going downhill. Marcus seemed so flippant about, what's the word, fraud.

"I have a new sales guy in London from TDT. Isn't he going to get upset with me talking to you?"

"Oh, don't worry about him. I'm only joking about the CDOs. I was ringing to say sorry for last time and wanted to invite you out to dinner next time you're in Singapore, or I get across to Zurich. Would that work?"

"Sure, Marcus, but it's really not necessary."

A few months later, Urs was in Singapore and had a spare evening. He met Marcus, whose conversion to charismatic smooth operator was pretty much complete. They ate at the Swiss Club and Marcus entertained with a couple of excellent Australian wines. Marcus had brought along a couple of junior members of his team to provide Urs with more contact points within TDT in the region. One, he recalled, was a charming and stunningly beautiful salesperson, who had recently moved to Singapore from Kerala. Her name – Caitanya Iyer.

After that, their paths crossed at the odd industry event, once when both were passing through JFK Airport, and as both had become global heads and the relationship between TDT and Gaumet had become closer, so Marcus had taken him out for dinner a few times in London and Geneva. At their last dinner, Urs had announced his retirement and his plans with Villa Traxler.

Marcus had taken a keen interest, and, sure enough, he called last November, saying he had been diagnosed with some health issues, was overworked, and needed to take a break, and could they meet in a couple of weeks in Zurich.

Urs' chain of thought was interrupted by seeing Muttu crossing the lawn towards the garages.

"Hey, Muttu, I just got an answer from Marcus: two weeks, maybe three."

"OK, sir. I will get things ready."

* * *

Rahul Pankhania (British, early forties) asked for some ranch dressing to go with his salad box and picked up a mango yogurt pot. Other than that, his lunch was much the same as it had been the day before, and the day before that: same place, same time. He had a weekday window between 12.00pm and 12.30pm that he kept free of meetings before the regular global conference calls started, with New York waking up, and Singapore signing off.

It was time to clear his head and get some air. The salad bar was just the right distance away and was relatively quiet and well stocked. Mostly, he would go on his own and avoid engaging with anyone other than a short call to his wife at home. His team, as well as the rest of the trading floor, had also learnt to let him have his space at this time. A couple of years ago, he had got into the habit of skipping lunch, as a reduction in his team due to cost-cutting, combined with an increase in workload due to waves of regulation, had left little time other than a rushed-at-your-desk breakfast, and a vending machine chocolate bar in the afternoon. His work ethic, driven through a combination of pressure, anxiety and ambition, took its toll. One Friday evening, he fainted, which led, after a few medical visits and a number of tearful discussions with his wife, to a restock of priorities and a greater discipline of his day. For these thirty minutes, he would leave his work phone in the office.

He flicked through a couple of text messages from Sonia – a date for a parents' evening and availability for a dinner date. He dialled her – she'd be waiting – though the conversation, like the lunch, would have the similar daily ingredients.

"Hi, Sonia."

"Hiya, Rahul. How's your day going?"

"All good. Usual winter hassle with the trains this morning…" Rahul broke his sentence. "Hey, Sonia, really sorry, I'm going to have to call back. I've got another call coming through. I know it shouldn't happen on my personal phone, but I need to take it. Speak in a minute."

"Hey, Rahul. Have you got your lunch?"

"Hello, Marcus. How are you?"

Rahul knew why Marcus would be calling now – Marcus knew this was Rahul's lunchbreak time and he'd be out of the office, and both could be open on their personal unrecorded lines. They had been working together since Marcus had returned to London. Rahul had been with TDT Capital a couple of years prior to that within finance, having been with a couple of the Big Four previously.

Following his promotion to global head of sales, Marcus felt a need not only to make changes within the division, but also to exhibit to the world a more impressive set of CVs amongst his directs. Rahul, a natural sciences graduate from

Cambridge, MBA, CFA, chartered accountant, fitted the bill better as his COO than the long-standing incumbent.

When Rahul got offered that position from Marcus, he was utterly in awe of his new multimillionaire high-earning boss and set his heart into the role. He got to know Marcus's other direct reports, the regional, country and product heads, and over time started to recognise the dynamics of contacts, greed and survival that defined their lives and their successes, whilst he spent his days on the processes and governance overlay that allowed them to operate and get paid a multiple of his, not poor but relatively sufficient, salary.

He also got to know Marcus, or at least Marcus of the office, as very much a 'keep the plates spinning' sort of guy. There would be plenty of talk of client breakfasts, lunches and dinners but very few actual meeting call reports filed. No one would really know which clients Marcus was seeing but everyone had learnt not to challenge him. Marcus would be ruthless in stamping out anyone who he perceived as a threat to his career, or, indeed, anyone who made a comment that brushed against his ego, no matter how innocent the observation.

At one sales review, Marcus had been relating how he knew a senior portfolio manager at a hedge fund, and there was an opportunity to double TDT's business with them. A junior manager commented that the said portfolio manager was another father at his daughter's school, but who had not mentioned there was this senior connection between the two firms. It would be great to see him in the next meeting together with Marcus. The meeting never happened, and the junior salesperson was placed on the redundancy list at the next round simply for the perceived slight of appearing to challenge Marcus's relationship.

On the other hand, Marcus would strongly protect and promote those that stayed loyal to him and his ego, at least as long as it didn't clash with any of his wider interests. Part of Rahul's job was to ensure the bank ran within its controls and policies, which occasionally led to run-ins with salespeople and traders, who would also get agitated with Rahul's deep but nerdy intellect. Marcus always supported him.

A couple of years back, Rahul had been trying to get the credit hedge fund desk to provide an update on their quarterly forecast, but they had not been returning his calls. Marcus needed to consolidate the numbers across all his teams and asked about it during their weekly catch-up.

"Is Bruce the only one outstanding with his numbers?"

"Yes, I've chased a few times, Marcus."

"You need to get on your feet, Rahul, wander over there; these guys are too busy all day with clients to answer the phone, making money, and the exercise would do you good." Marcus was relaxed and enjoying the little tease. Rahul was very conscious he wasn't a revenue earner in sales or trading and despite being Marcus's direct report, often felt a second-tier member of the trading floor to those 'making money'.

"Well, actually, I did go across last time." Rahul spoke with a measured pace. "I wasn't sure whether or how to bring it up, and I'm not so bothered but you should know that I found this note on the desk." He handed across a folded piece of paper and recalled how Marcus's face turned ashen as he read the scrawled note. 'Rahul the Panki called' with a drawn smiley face.

Marcus got up so quickly that his chair crashed into the drawers behind. "Come with me."

Rahul had never seen Marcus walk so determinedly across the floor. There was a loud buzz of activity as the markets had been volatile all that week. A couple of the credit hedge fund sales guys were standing up, leaning across the partitions, shouting orders and prices at the traders. Others were poring over their Bloomberg terminals talking to clients.

Marcus was still a few metres away from the credit desks but spoke loud enough to be heard by them. "Hey, Chanders, can I have a word?"

"Hi, Marcus. Hey, bud, the markets are really busy right now; can it wait until close?" Bruce was in the middle of a transaction and placed his hand over the mouthpiece.

"No, Bruce, I'd like your attention now and the team too." Marcus's tone was calm, but his demeanour reflected the storm that was to come.

"OK, guys, close out what you're doing. What's up, bud?"

"I think the team know this, but, just in case, I wanted to introduce you to Rahul. He's our chief operating officer." The sarcasm in the voice was clear. Rahul was standing a few paces away.

"Yeah, we know Rahul."

"It seems Rahul has been trying to get hold of you."

Bruce's face was starting to display the tension of the conversation but couldn't comprehend what Marcus was so concerned about. The credit traders and other nearby sales guys lowered their voices to hear what was going on.

One of Bruce's team, a young sales assistant, butted in to help out his boss. "Sorry, Bruce, I left a note on your desk that Rahul came by looking for you, but I should have brought it to your attention."

"Hey, Marcus, Rahul, dude, the markets have been super busy and…"

Marcus interrupted him. "I have that note right here. Perhaps you'd care to read it."

Bruce looked at the note. Now his expression was serious and fully attentive. Bruce hung up on his client. "Hey, Marcus, listen, it was just a joke within the team. We shorten everyone's name. Look, you call me Chanders for Chandler, right? Hey, Rahul, dude, I'm sorry."

"The fucking point is, Bruce, guys, that I'm not fucking getting the fucking joke." Marcus uttered each word, stressing every syllable, and was as good as shouting. The whole trading floor had quietened – the din of volatile markets had completely disappeared but for the faint typing of the odd keyboard.

Bruce spoke again, keen to protect himself and his team. "We're very sorry if you took offence, dude. I know my guys. There was no racist intent and nothing like this will happen again. It was just innocent humour to lighten the day, the last couple of weeks have been…"

Marcus interrupted him again, speaking firmly and clearly, "I'd like you and the team in my office at four thirty, because I'm still not seeing the fucking humour and I'd like to know what the fucking punchline is. Dude!" before strutting back to his office and slamming the door shut.

Within a week, Marcus had fired the desk head and three of the team. Nothing further was ever said about it again, though Rahul did occasionally wonder if Marcus was really protecting him or protecting himself and the bank. Rahul could potentially have taken the note to HR or a lawyer and either been paid-off handsomely or effectively become untouchable within TDT, but he hoped that Marcus valued his integrity and loyalty rather than seeing him as someone blindly naïve, and that Marcus's actions were genuinely well intentioned and principled.

Over the years that they had been working together, Rahul had felt his importance grow within Marcus's world, as regulatory change and controls had become more important within the industry. Rahul's was the first line of defence role and, perhaps, Rahul took this on too diligently, but it meant, at times, also preventing Marcus doing something that, in his interpretation, could be seen as a compliance or controls breach.

Rahul had felt a tension start to build up between them, at least until the start of Project Epsilon nine months ago.

Epsilon had started off as an internal review of various structured deals and investment products that TDT had sold many years ago. Then the FSA became interested and asked to review some internal documents. That was followed by requests from other various US and European regulators. Marcus and Rahul had been involved in the initial stages, but with the external regulatory intervention, both had been taken off the communication distribution lists.

Marcus had grown visibly irritable and stressed, which Rahul assumed was because Marcus had been a reasonably senior salesperson at the time of the period for the review, and, further, Marcus hated not knowing what was going on. However, he was well connected, so Rahul also presumed he would have other channels to hear how Epsilon was progressing and, ultimately, be protected.

It came as a surprise when Marcus announced he would need to take a couple of weeks off, as doctors had suggested he was overworked. Marcus may have been a driven workaholic early on in his career, but Rahul certainly didn't see him as 'overworked' now, and even if Marcus was stressed, he was astonished that he would want to be away from London at this time – surely that would be worse.

That was around three months ago. As far as Rahul knew, Marcus had not come back to London and had stayed in Switzerland during the Christmas period. He was still actively looking at emails, so it was not as though he had disconnected himself from TDT. They had spoken every couple of weeks and Epsilon was noticeably at the forefront of his mind.

"I'm good, Rahul. I'm looking to get out of here and back in two to three weeks. There is only so much Swiss mountain air a man can get."

"Good to hear, Marcus." It was the first time Marcus had indicated anything positive about his plans.

"So, I better know what's going on."

"You mean about Epsilon."

"Well, let's start there."

"The whole thing is, as you know, pretty hush-hush. They've been collecting brochures, client communication, term sheets and back-testing illustrations for those products. I've seen a couple and, look, by today's standards, I think it'd be fair to say they were weak."

"Misleading, even."

"Misleading, even, by today's standards."

"Hindsight is wonderful, Rahul. So, assuming they infer a breach, that would mean what? A hefty fine?"

"My read from my old finance pals is that we're reserving for a fine – the amount is, as yet, undeclared. It depends if the regulatory fines cut across from different jurisdictions, but it'll be big certainly."

"Fuck!"

"But the real issue is if we get direct legal action from clients. Who knows then what that cost could be. It could be significant. Have you not spoken with Pierre?"

"Hmm." There was a pause. "No, I haven't spoken to Pierre. What does he say?"

"Oh, nothing to me, Marcus. I just thought you'd get more from him."

"No, I haven't spoken to anyone. The doctors have advised to keep off the stress. In any case, probably not a good look asking questions about that, right?"

There was another pause.

Marcus continued. "And then they'll want blood. Who approved it, sold it, right?"

"I think we're getting a bit ahead of ourselves, Marcus. All of those things were approved by the product committee, by compliance. I can't see TDT firing everyone. And, in any case, hardly anyone is around from that era."

"Oh, I think TDT will want some public executions. I was around."

"Come on, it was committee approval. There won't be anything that implicates individuals – who said what to whom. You're just stressed. Nothing to worry about on this front, I would say."

"You remember that case about Schmidt. Jailed for twelve years. Rotting somewhere, and this is worse."

"Marcus, come on, mate, break out of it. Look, in case you're wondering, I'm reasonably sure they've listened to the tapes and found nothing. And they must have trawled our emails – I guess there was nothing there. I don't know how far back they are going. A lot of people would have left, so difficult to dig out their emails, see who approved what. May even have been deleted, and there was some email archive exercise that lost a lot of TDT's records, at least here in London. I shouldn't be discussing that, but, mate, I think it should be OK."

"Cheers, Rahul. I'll let you get back."

Marcus put the phone down.

FIVE

Let your plans be dark and impenetrable as night,
And when you move, fall like a thunderbolt.

Marcus poured himself another glass – an Albariño de Fefiñanes – his third. He didn't eat together that often with Urs, but both were unwinding today. It was a mild evening, so they decided to lay out a table on the patio. The sun had dipped but there was enough comforting warmth from the parasol heater.

The evening lights gathered in specks below them, mountain roads stringing them together, like a galaxy with a dense centre of towns and villages along the banks of the Meiringensee. As Marcus munched aggressively on the olives and canapes, Urs took a more pensive approach to both the food and the wine.

He was looking forward to Marcus's departure and back to a time when guests stayed for two to three weeks and morphed into a new set before they became truly irritating. There would be new interactions with people from different backgrounds, and new opportunities to learn and entertain.

"He really is a good cook that Muttu, turning these simple blinis into real delights."

"You're right, and he'll keep feeding you until you break

for the next course." Urs paused, hoping Marcus would get the hint. "We have a super steak tonight – the animal probably hasn't travelled for more than five kilometres to get here."

"Not a bad place to spend your final days before getting chopped up. Don't worry, I have a pretty decent appetite."

"Yes, I see you're in a fine spirit."

"Yep, I had a good afternoon."

"Let me guess. New York has been put firmly in its place."

Marcus looked across at Urs and both allowed themselves a small smile.

"So, tell us, Marcus, about the fun you've been having." Urs seemed genuinely interested to know and Marcus was very genuinely keen to share.

"Well, Juliet and I worked through the 'numbers' before sending them across to New York. Shoulderchip is right; they're down, or at least flat, over the last two to three years. Issue is that we used to do a lot of multi-year trades and register the whole profit upfront in our reports. I've been thinking for a while that we should really be accounting them more accurately, you know, amortising them over the trade lifetime." Marcus let out a resisting smile towards Urs.

Urs raised both eyebrows. "Indeed, a different and a smarter, more correct perspective, but naturally, with all the pressure of work, it's probably not been an issue top of mind, and not to forget it had the, shall we say, benefit of artificially enhancing the profits and bonus pool in those first years."

"Er no, Urs, we work very hard for our bonuses and part of what we get paid for is clearly about how we present ourselves." Marcus smirked knowingly.

"So, with your new approach, apart from boosting this year's numbers, you get the benefit of counting the same production again for that important end-of-year bonus discussion – how wonderful, Marcus. Now, tell me, who gets to control the numbers?"

"Well, Juliet is in the COO team, so her, I would say. Look, Rahul will kick up a fuss but that'll be in a few weeks. He's preoccupied with other stuff, and frankly, it's the right thing to do and this approach should have been done earlier! Anyway, this is just a starter to the main course."

"Very good, I see."

"Juliet sends the numbers report to Maley and cc's me. And you know me. I'm a collaborative sort of guy. I did exactly the right thing. I forwarded it to Pierre, suggesting that he congratulated Shoulderchip, Colvin and team on a great set of ongoing results!"

Marcus took a moment to acknowledge Urs' silent, lip-clinched nod, too enraptured in his anecdote to discern the obvious disdain, before continuing.

"So, this Pierre email goes to the US management team and lands just before they get together for their morning meeting. Oh, man, I wish I could have seen Shoulderchip's face. He is obviously forced now to talk about how the sales numbers are up year-on-year and praise everyone."

Marcus took a glug of wine, looked across at the hillside lights, his self-glow shining sweetly amongst them all. "As expected, Pierre also cc'd me, so I call Colvin. Apparently, Shoulderchip's voice totally creaked during their meeting, but being an arse, he couldn't stop himself looking across at Colvin and Maley, saying he didn't know where Pierre got his numbers from, and we should just double-check."

"It was certainly a bit below the belt, no, Marcus?"

"Don't worry, I suspect Shoulderchip won't feel anything down there. *Santé.*" Marcus raised his glass, unable to resist a little snigger at his comment, at Urs who responded likewise.

"But there is more."

"I thought there might be. There is, undoubtedly, the issue of Maley's perceived aberration in loyalties." Urs raised his eyebrows in rhythm with the intonation in his voice.

"Hmm – exactly. And I'm not sure only perceived." Marcus leant back and turned towards the villa. "Hey, Muttu, bud, bring us up a decent red, will ya, maybe a Cab Sauv – Napa Valley."

"Muttu, we may have an Abreu in the cellar," Urs interjected.

"Nah, nothing so flash, Urs. We'd need to decant it and I'm ready to get drinking now."

"Sure, I can see that. So, tell us about Maley?"

"Right, you'll like this, Urs, it's right up there with our values. A few years back, we had a really good young sales guy in New York – super connected, family fucking loaded – Jonti Brown, been MD a few years but wanted out to go and try his hand at wine making in California.

"And so, in one of the redundancy rounds, he puts his hand up, but naturally wants to take his accrued bonus, not a bad sum, filthy rich, you know, but why leave money on the table? Maley wants to squeeze a couple more years out of him, but I'm like, come on, guys, let him go, we'll get him to hand over his connections. Anyway, Jonti really appreciated that of me, and a couple of years back, I'm in San Fran and he invites me over to taste his wine."

Marcus pushed his chair back again and turned towards the villa, "Don't be long with that red, Muttu, this story is getting me thirsty!" before glancing back at Urs.

Urs stared back, quietly folded his fitted checked blazer tighter, and pondered on Marcus's tales; none of them surprised him now. The air was getting cooler, and he too would welcome the warmth of a fuller-bodied red. The faint breeze was just strong enough to momentarily lift Marcus's thinning, fine brown hair, which, despite its slow growth, was starting to look untidily long now.

Marcus continued. "So we're onto the third bottle and Jonti says, 'Shame you weren't around for my leaving do, great night, up at my place in Darien, Connecticut.' Apparently, Shoulderchip had had a little too much bourbon and was starting to try to get cosy with one of the interns, before Colvin, teetotal, does his thing; brings Shoulderchip's wife up into the conversation and insists on driving him home. Shame. I think I could have done with that sort of scandal now." Marcus mused contentedly at the thought of really taking Shoulderchip out of business.

"'To be fair,' Jonti says, 'can't blame him, she was super cute,' and starts flicking through some photos on his phone. He's rushing through these photos to get to ones near the end with her in the pool with a couple of sales guys, none of them with any kit on, and Jonti is right – she looks very nice, and there is a bunch of people in the background watching and cheering, and there, Urs, in one of them, there is this guy, ginger, looking blank and a bit worse for wear, doing a line on the poolside table!

"I look at Jonti and I'm like, 'Wow, that's obviously Maley, right?' Jonti looks back as if surely everyone knows about Maley's little habit; well, everyone, it seems, except Colvin, and Shoulderchip, and me. There he is, in front of the whole team, doing fucking coke, and I mean, this is just a few years back, not in the Wild West days. So, as I said, Jonti is not exactly a fan of Maley's, and he is about to forward me the photo, and I'm like 'No, no, no, this conversation never happened.'"

"You don't want to have to deal with it."

"Exactly and, you know, Maley, for all his faults, he was one of our best sales guys. He delivered the numbers."

"Until now – needless to say, that anecdote has become more interesting." Urs rubbed his chin and spread his index and middle finger across his lips, before resting his chin in the cup of his hand, with the solid expression of someone now fully familiar with the upcoming plot.

"Please, sir, how about this wine?" Muttu arrived, carrying a bottle of Ridge laid across his forearm.

"Pour us a glass and give it a bit of air, Muttu."

"Of course." Muttu spoke English with a slow, South Asian, considered accent like the well-travelled professors and businessmen of that region, but was always keen to try out any new expressions and colloquialisms. "And both of you would take your steak rare, as per normal?"

"Correct."

"Just wipe the animal's arse and bring it to the table, as one says," Muttu continued, knowing his repetition of Marcus's line would generate smiles coming with his Sri Lankan intonation.

"I hope you will avoid using that unpleasant expression once Marcus leaves, Muttu." Urs was unable to hold back the anticipated smile.

"Of course, just having a little fun." Muttu poured three glasses of wine into the specific Cabernet Sauvignon Riedel glasses, including one for himself. Marcus had really embraced Muttu and insisted that if he and Urs were having dinner then Muttu also joined.

Marcus knew Urs had understood the rest of his story, but that he also wanted to hear the conclusion. "You see the problem, or opportunity if you want to look at it that way, is that Jonti had shared the party photos with a number of his ex-colleagues, and I doubt that Maley incident was a one-off. Frankly, I've been amazed it has never come up. Pretty sure Colvin didn't know. He would have told me. So, when I sent the numbers to Pierre, I said they were great but that we needed to have a chat.

"Pierre gets the mildly sinister request and calls me about

half an hour later – private line, naturally. I told him that I'd had a couple of calls – one from a friendly headhunter, and then directly from a pal at a competitor bank. I made up some bull that Maley has been sniffing around for another job as head of Americas' distribution. I made out that we should have known he was a departure risk, and maybe Shoulderchip did, but Colvin hadn't said anything. Just slipped that in. Anyway, there were rumours on the Street that he has doing coke. I stressed to Pierre how obviously shocked I was, and again, how I doubted whether Colvin or even Shoulderchip would have known that, but the recruiting bank where my pal worked, and the headhunters had done some due diligence and it seems that not only was it true, but that there were plenty of photos around with him doing lines in front of our teams. So, they are not proceeding with any offer but felt they should just let me know discreetly. I made a couple of calls myself and it seems it is true. Frankly, I said to Pierre, I was amazed that any of the guys with a grudge against him hadn't brought it up already but it's undeniably an issue – an armaments factory waiting to blow.

"Look, if Maley wants to do whatever in his spare time, fine, but brazen drugging in front of the troops, in my view, not on, and that was Pierre's take too. So well, that's Maley's career over." Marcus looked across at Urs and raised his glass.

"Really nothing you wouldn't do to get your way, Marcus." Urs spoke with such a flat Central European modulation, he gave no clue as to whether he approved or held Marcus in the highest contempt. *All for a slight to that ego*, he thought.

"Yep, I called Colvin," Marcus continued, with no care as to what anyone really thought, just pleased with what he had achieved.

"Colvin is one for high integrity, evangelical type, absolutely no idea what's going on, hates the idea of drugs.

Fuck knows what he's doing in this industry. He'd be hopeless if his old man wasn't a senator. First, he couldn't believe what I said about Maley, but must have gone to check with someone. He calls me back after ten minutes, saying he's going to get rid of Maley, has spoken to HR, and unless I had any objections, he'll speak to Maley this morning. I just said obviously it was his division and his decision, but it seemed to me the right course of action, and clearly, no need to discuss the source of our information. That would just make things messy. So Maley is no longer with us, marched off with his cardboard box, and as of yet, no further emails from Shoulderchip."

"Very good," Urs continued with the same flat tone.

"Yes, don't you think? Now let's enjoy this delightful steak."

The three men dined, bantered, and chilled with the evening. They moved from one bottle of red wine to the next, and then one more – Urs and Muttu managing their pace – Marcus consuming without care or effect.

The temperature dropped suddenly and steeply, as was the norm for the time of year. The men were warmed by extra layers, the brandies, the patio heaters and their jovial repartee. Muttu had wrapped himself in an additional shawl, enveloping his sturdy frame firmly in a style reminiscent of the Himachal foothills. He smiled diplomatically as the Englishman and the Swiss mocked each other and their stereotypes. As per previous such evenings, a good section of the conversation was devoted to Muttu's liaisons with the local ladies. Muttu would laugh along with his teeth gleaming even whiter at night, against his dark skin.

"He can cook, and he is an exotic mystery to them." Urs would make the point each time.

"Yep, and lively in the sack, I suspect," Marcus slurred with a glint. "It's true, though, you're a true scientist with the food."

"Sir, yes, a chemist," Muttu confirmed.

"Why don't you come to London, Muttu? Let's open a restaurant, you know the English would love it."

"Hey, stop. You're trying to steal my staff," Urs intervened with a jocular hold of Marcus's elbow.

"I'm happy here, sir."

"Come on, you've been all over the world. Why not a spell in England? And you'll meet more great and exciting people like me!"

"Sir, I cannot say I've lived all over the world. Just Sri Lanka, India, as you know, and then Dubai and now here."

"And did they like you there? Come to England and be a chef – they'll love you."

"Stop, Marcus, or I'll start talking about the weather," Urs joked.

"Well, I don't know about being liked or not liked; in Sri Lanka, we had a civil war, so naturally some people didn't like you. In India, you could get mocked for your accent, but everyone is different so the question of being liked for who you are gets a bit blurred. In Dubai, I was a servant and was definitely treated as such, so again unclear if and who really likes you." Muttu had largely stayed silent for the evening but now spoke meditatively and peered into the darkness of trees that framed the outline to the villa. The two others listened intently and dwelled quietly on his words.

"You see," Muttu continued, "here in Switzerland, they tell you whether they like you or don't like you, straight to your face – 'We don't like you' – and I like that. Now in England, I feel I would not have a clue on this point; some will warmly like me, some will warmly pretend to like me, and others warmly hate my guts, and the final group would be cold but actually be OK with me as I am. I think life is easier when you know how things stand."

"Indeed," Urs confirmed.

"Hmm, a chemist, you say, Muttu. Maybe you're right, but many are right to reserve judgement. Do we ever really know each other, and who can tell what catalyst will change us into somebody else? And on that note, I shall finish this glass and perhaps another in the library." Marcus got up and headed into the villa.

Muttu looked across at Urs with a vague questioning stare. "Don't worry, you didn't say anything of note, Muttu."

SIX

Float like a butterfly, sting like a bee –
'Your' hands can't hit what 'your' eyes can't see.

He sat in the library and read that letter again, alone with a solitary lamplight; the exuberance of the early evening wine had sunk into silent brandy. He poured and downed another glass, sat back, and let a tear roll untroubled across his face. One more glass. The tears came thicker. Did he care? He did what he had to do. He took opportunities when they came – anyone else would have done the same – guilt was for the stupid. No but yes. He cared about the hurt caused, he cared about what was coming and he cared about the ending. He ruminated in the brandy glass. He had been there enough weeks, worrying about how things would evolve, searching for some answers, and finding nothing but the vacuousness of Swiss mountain air.

Another glass. The tears stopped. Marcus shut the laptop and turned off the lamp. The villa was silent. Urs was happy to let him switch off and close the place down. Muttu had likely gone into town to meet one of his ladies. Marcus sat in the stillness, the cold emptiness, the faint light of the moon insufficient for the taciturn tomes to judge his expressions of guilt or innocence, of remorse or defiance, of fear or flippancy, drunk but still sensitive enough to inhale the vapours of the cognac mingled with the aroma of polished leather chairs.

The tears gave way to anger as they often did on nights like these. Anger with what? It didn't matter with what. The psychologists and counsellors kept delving into his childhood – wasting his fucking money – it had been forty years since he was a child. He was angry now, angry about the future, angry about what he couldn't control.

He needed the light from his phone to walk into the hallway. On his left was the reception desk with an idle desk lamp and two idle office chairs. Behind it, a small room was the receptionist office. In front was Urs' shut office that looked onto the front drive, from where Urs could easily step out to welcome new guests or say goodbye as they loaded waiting taxis to leave. Ahead was the dining area with its glass front onto the veranda, where they had eaten earlier. To his right was a grand staircase jutting straight up before dramatically taking a right angle turn onto the floor of guest bedrooms. In the dim phone light, clinging to the high walls, he could just make out the odd portrait of a Swiss grandee, long gone, and old paintings of various Swiss mountain vistas through different seasons; vistas that had virtually remained the same through the test of time.

Behind the staircase, invisible from reception, on the left and attached to the dining room, were the kitchens. They were accessible through a small driveway that came up behind the villa against the hillside. Marcus did not know what lay behind the staircase to the right but suspected they were sleeping quarters for staff as Muttu often stayed at the hotel. Urs had a living area and bedroom on the top floor, separated from the rest of the building. A small lift on the side of the library allowed access from the basement to the second floor but needed a code to access Urs' third floor. There must have been another staircase also for Urs at the back of the villa. Marcus wondered for a second how Urs must live, what he cared about; he had never seen Urs meet friends or relatives in all the time he had been there, or talk about any hobbies, or shared any of his views.

Next to the lift was a door through to the small cigar room and a fire exit but also to a small staircase down to a floor below. The thick burgundy carpet of the reception area gave way to marble tiling on the descent into a cooler basement. Marcus toyed with the idea of going straight up to bed but then took the stairs down. At the bottom, a glass door opened into a gym that stretched below the dining room and kitchen. With the phone light, Marcus could see a little doorway that led into a pool area. The slope of the hillside had allowed Urs to extend the pool through some transparent insulation flaps outside and create an infinity effect across the valley. Urs had offered to keep the pool filled and heated for Marcus, but the cost had been too prohibitive for him. Marcus thought about Ollie and Emma and how much they would have loved that pool. He hadn't mentioned it to them.

Marcus pointed the light towards the gym. Past the loose weights, the machines cast gargoyle-like shadows across the walls and floor. A couple of rowing machines and exercise bikes faced off against the treadmills. Scattered pedestals paid host to empty water cannisters. Some clean folded white towels had been left for Marcus on a bench next to a punchbag, with a small pile of A4 papers and a pair of boxing gloves.

He walked up to the punchbag, clenched his right fist, and hit it hard. It rattled in its fixings on the ceiling, disturbing the death-like silence of the villa. The bag swayed back towards Marcus. The darkness and the brandy meant he hadn't achieved a clean hit, but Marcus piled in again with a flurry of punches, left and right, mouthing whatever swear words came into his head, as the synthetic protagonist swayed backwards and forwards, with Marcus oblivious to the minor skin grazes across his knuckles.

Marcus's eyes watered up again. He held back. Crying was a lack of control. Boys don't cry and all that. He laid into the punchbag again, harder, longer, so that he needed to pause for breath. The brandy and wine started to rise through his stomach. He didn't want to vomit there in the gym. He stopped for a second, sat on the bench and picked up the phone, spraying a beam light across the wall and floor.

He picked up the pile of papers and sifted through to find a picture of Shoulderchip, Hank Sharp II. With a name like that, what the fuck did he have a chip on his shoulder about? A thin rope knotted to the punchbag ceiling attachment dangled with a small clip. Marcus fumbled with the piece of paper with Shoulderchip's image, until he managed to clip it in front of the padded leather bag. Marcus put the phone down – its light now pointing towards the ceiling. He aimed hard at the bank's senior executive's stock photo of Shoulderchip. The paper face crumpled from the first blow. A thin streak of blood from Marcus's grazed knuckles splattered a red hyphenated line across Shoulderchip's face. The blows came harder, with the face ripping apart. The phone light went off. Marcus grabbed the tattered remnants of paper, crushed it in his palms and threw it violently across the floor. Beads of sweat rolled down his forehead. They mingled with the now-obvious tears. However angry he had been – it had now been emptied against a piece of paper. He sat back on the bench and groped in the dark for a towel.

That's where Urs found him asleep, and not for the first time, the next morning.

SEVEN

The hardest thing to see is what is in front of your eyes.

Emma Kapoor checked the phone by the side of her bed. There was no message from Marcus. She hadn't heard from him now for three days; the gaps between calls had been getting longer. When he had left London, he would call at least daily, sometimes twice, and now he would just get irritated if she rang him just for a chat without a reason. And just as Ollie had started asking more and more about where his dad was, Marcus seemed to have been progressively getting less and less interested in them – Ollie and her.

She felt so helpless not being able to share Marcus's pain and comfort him, especially after everything he had done for her. She recalled the Thursday evening just over three months ago.

"I'm just going to pop into the garden for a quick fag, Emma." Marcus had been drinking all evening; first a couple of beers, then a bottle of wine, and then some brandies.

"Marcus, I do wish you'd quit smoking again. It's just getting worse by the week. Why don't you have some water and go to bed?"

"Stop nagging me, Emma. It's not what I need right now." Marcus got up to go to the garden door.

It had been the same response every time she had brought up his smoking or drinking. "I can't even talk to you anymore, Marcus. You get so irritable with me. I just feel there is something wrong. It's one thing getting hammered at client events, but you never used to drink at home like this."

"Oh, for fuck's sake, Emma, just stop! I'm going for a cigarette."

"There's obviously something. I need to know what it is, Marcus. Is it me?" It wasn't the first time she'd asked that question, but she could still sense her voice shaking with anxiety.

"No, it's not you."

"Is it work?"

"Everything is fine." Marcus spoke in a totally emotionless tone.

"Please talk to me, Marcus. I want to help." Emma struggled to control her tears as Marcus went into the garden, shutting the door behind him.

Every time she tried to find out if something was wrong, he would just stare at her blankly, then answer with the same passive 'everything is fine' when clearly it wasn't. He'd be uptight and irritable when he got home from work and then would just start drinking. Emma knew there were some investigations going on around some historical transactions at work, as there had been some commentary in the press, but Marcus hadn't said anything about that. However, in all the years she had known him, it was the first time she had seen him so stressed, or even stressed at all.

A few moments later, Marcus came back and sat on the armchair across from her.

"You're right, Emma. I need to tell you something."

Emma's heart filled with trepidation. She had no idea what to expect.

"The doctors have asked me to take a rest. You know I've been getting those headaches and chest pains and not been sleeping well."

"Darling, why didn't you tell me before? I keep asking." Emma leant forward to hold his hand. "And they've said that in the previous medicals, so I'm pleased you're taking it more seriously, finally. I'll take care of you. It'd be nice to have you at home. Have the doctors said anything else other than a rest?"

"Actually, some time away would be good."

"Sure, Ollie will be on holiday in about four weeks. Why don't we go away for some Christmas sun?"

"I don't think I want to wait that long."

"Well, I could ask Jemima to see if she could take care of Ollie, and we could go away, maybe in a week or two."

"Look, I need to see some specialists. There is a place in Switzerland that's been recommended by that guy, Urs. Remember him? We had dinner with him a couple of times, the private banker at Gaumet. Well, he runs a boutique hotel now. I'll be staying there. It's near the clinic and a great place to relax."

"What do you mean? You've already decided what you're doing!"

"Yeah, you stay here and look after Ollie. That's best. I shouldn't be away for more than a couple of weeks."

"But, darling, I'm your wife. You haven't told me anything. You must have been thinking about this for a while. How can you spring this on me like this?"

"Listen, I know. I should have said but let me see the experts and as soon as I know more, I'll tell you everything. I'll be back before you know it. As you say, it's Ollie's holiday soon and maybe we can do something then too."

"Can we just talk about it a little more, Marcus? What experts? I'd like to be with you."

"There is a clinic that the doctors suggested. They'll do some tests. Urs also knows a couple of guys there. I'd love to have you there, but they suggest it best I'm on my own. I don't want to be worrying about Ollie with you away too."

Emma tried to find out more, but Marcus didn't add anything, and it was clear that he wanted to go alone.

Two weeks passed, but Marcus said the medics had told him he needed more time. Emma assumed he'd definitely be home for Christmas; there was no way he would miss spending time with Ollie then, or with her. But again, he said the medics had advised against coming back too early. And now it was already March.

She hardly got any more information about his illness or the treatments. She didn't know who these medics were, and he gave no details about his condition, saying it would only concern her. She was his wife. She felt a right to know. He had mentioned the Kusnacht practice but gave no details about any diagnosis or treatment other than to rest and maintain a healthy lifestyle. She looked at the Kusnacht website. She looked at the addiction and mental health therapies but couldn't relate anything to Marcus. He assured her that he had given up drinking and smoking and spent time daily in the gym, but she could definitely hear the lingering hoarseness of a hangover and nicotine when they spoke in the mornings.

At times, she would think it wasn't so much he wasn't telling her because he didn't want to worry her, rather more that he didn't want her to know; that there was something else. She would force herself to dismiss any such thoughts. He had been her rock – why would he mislead her? A couple of times she had thought about leaving Ollie with her sister and flying out to see him, maybe surprise him, care for him – surely that's what he would have done for her – but when she had suggested coming out to visit him, he had been firmly brusque against the idea. She couldn't understand why, and it was her curiosity as much as her concern that was distressing her.

She wondered if Marcus would be asleep. She started to text him. No, it would just irritate her when he didn't respond. And if she called and woke him up, that would annoy him. He was an hour ahead. It would be 11.30pm. She resisted the idea of dialling her sister. She knew what her sister would say – she had never really liked or trusted Marcus since their marriage and, in any case, it was late. No, it would have to wait until the morning. Emma laid down, closed her eyes, and focused on her breathing.

A few minutes later, she got up. There was enough light from her bedroom to see down the corridor and walk to Ollie's room. She could hear his breathing, and see the outline of his dark brown wavy hair against the white pillow, peacefully asleep. His face seemed so much darker when he was sleeping in this low light. She knew Ollie was much closer to her than to Marcus and they had become even closer since Marcus had left. She wondered how that would change as he entered his teens and adulthood and as he looked up to his father. She kissed Ollie on his forehead and went back to her bedroom.

Suddenly, she felt that pang of loneliness, the feelings of emptiness that had returned and started to become more frequent, like they had been a decade ago. She had no idea what triggered them now, but something in her instinct felt wrong, unresolved, and uncomfortable. Her heartbeat started to rise and with it came a light-headed confusion, the solitude turning to fear. The same fear from those years ago. She sat down closed her eyes and breathed slowly.

Emma picked up the phone and went downstairs, past Ollie's room, past Marcus's silent study that overlooked their garden, past her own hobby room, and beyond the stairs leading to the loft and another spare bedroom. Downstairs were two reception rooms and a large kitchen area with an island that faced a dining space and seating overlooking, through a wall of glass doors, onto the patio. The old Victorian house in southwest London was far too big for them, even with Marcus at home. They had bought it just after they married but had not been able to have any more children. Sometimes she would think about it, sometimes guiltily, but never really sadly.

Emma made a cinnamon tea and took it back upstairs. She peaked again into Ollie's room. The same question drifted through her mind as it often did at times like this. Was she a good wife? She did everything she could for Ollie. Was she a good mother? Would Caitanya have been better? Caitanya. Caitanya, or Tani as Marcus called her. Why did she come in her thoughts so often? She had been gone so long ago. Why did Marcus sometimes still mention her? She stretched out her hand and clasped empty air, as if catching an invisible fairy, before throwing the bad doubts away.

She put the lamp on in the hobby room, sat down, and started to look at the news on her phone. This room was her space. She sat in the old comfy button-back armchair covered in a mustard fabric lodged on wooden legs, taken from her mother's house, and grandly positioned by a window overlooking the garden. The thick curtains to her side comforted and protected her. There was a matching footstool. On one side stood her guitar, a music stand, and a small electric keyboard. It had been a while since she had had time to strum or play anything. A bookshelf contained a varied selection of legal files and publications, again untouched since she gave up work. A couple of shelves contained books she had read on aeroplanes and holidays, books by Allende, Rushdie, Garcia Marquez, and Murakami, with their mystique and mystery, and older books, classics: Dickens, Brontë, a *Romeo and Juliet* she studied at school, and a tattered copy of *L'Étranger* in

French. She wished she had time to read more. And paint. One shelf had some canvases at various stages of completion, in acrylic and watercolour, next to paint tubes and boxes, and a tidy pile of brushes. Across the room was a small mahogany desk with a black leather swivel office chair on wheels. A pile of magazines were stacked in one corner – *Tatler*, *Vogue*, *Condé Nast*, with a couple of issues of *The Economist* and the *FT's How To Spend It*. There was an old radio/CD player. A small line of CDs, mainly classical, with one exception: 'The Hurting' by Tears for Fears, leaned against the player. She tended to listen to the radio more. On the other side was a photo of her with Ollie as a toddler, taken in San Gimignano in Tuscany. In the centre was her shut laptop.

She took it onto her lap and opened a couple of news sites but there was nothing of interest. She still had half her tea left. She opened the photo folder. She flicked through pictures of their previous holiday in Dubai, last October half-term. Most were of her with Ollie by the pool or at the water parks. Marcus spent most of his time working and even went to meet a couple of clients. As she rolled through the albums, she quickly started reminiscing about the days before parenthood, before her marriage to Marcus, and started flicking through old photos, with only a light gossamer of guilt, of her time with Sanju.

On the side table by the armchair stood her wedding photo with Marcus, her sister and her mother. They were all smiling, but she could see the concerns in the eyes of her sister and mother. She looked closely. She looked at herself in the photo looking towards the camera, and she could see in her own eyes questions as to whether she was really marrying a person she loved. She cared deeply for Marcus, but love – she was still asking herself that question now.

EIGHT

Humid seal of soft affections, tend'rest pledge of future bliss,
Dearest tie of young connections, love's first snow-drop,
virgin kiss.

They had been family friends – her father worked at the same surgery as Sanju's. Sanju was three years older and other than when Sanju's family spent their whole summer vacation in India, which was about every third year, his family would come and spend at least a week or two with her family at their place between Grasse and St Paul in Provence.

Emma's grandmother was French and her old house, all buttery Provençal stone, was in a hamlet sat on a small hilltop, with orchards that rolled down the slopes merging into the blues of the distant sea. Emma's parents treated it like their summer home, especially since Emma's grandfather had passed away. Emma had also inherited her grandmother's wavy blonde hair, wide green eyes framed by light eyebrows, long feather-like eyelashes and full sensuous lips. She tanned easily and, having spent so much time with her grandparents, spoke French fluently in the local slow-paced, melodious dialect. She was equally at home in the heat, space and light of the Mediterranean summer as the dense greyness of winter in south London.

As a child, she had been shy and reserved and her main negotiation style to get things she wanted was to sit sulkily with a well-developed and irresistible pout. This worked perfectly with her father; with her grandmother; with just about anyone else except her mother, her older sister Jemima, and often, to her irritation, Sanju.

For most of the summer, the two sisters would spend time just with each other, joined only occasionally by visiting cousins. Over the years, they had got to know some local boys and girls of similar age in the nearby hamlets, but those *copines* had drifted away as they had entered their teens. By then, Jemima and Emma would happily spend days at the weekly market or chatting with locals at the café or at the *boulangerie*, where they got their daily bread.

A couple of years back, their father had persuaded their grandmother to build a swimming pool to the side of the house, where an old barn was being pulled down. After that, the sisters would pass hours, when the heat allowed, under a canopy by the pool listening to their radio. Jemima was a couple of years older, with dark hair, a slim frame, and was much more outgoing than her sister. She was very much like their mother and could be both protective and bossy towards Emma, as her mother was.

When they were younger and Sanju came, the three would be inseparable as the *trois enfants anglais* in the hamlet. Sanju with his dark hair, deep eyes and glowing skin was a hit, not only with Emma's grandmother, but, indeed, with all the grandparents in the hamlet.

They would also see Sanju regularly in London at barbeques or dinners, but as they got older Sanju wouldn't necessarily come with his parents to their house and, by the time he was in his late teens, they would only see him once or twice during the year and then, if his family came, during the annual summer holiday.

By then, the whole sisterly bond dynamic would change upon his arrival. He would spend most of his time talking with Jemima. This had become progressively more annoying for Emma as they had gotten older, and Emma held her sister largely responsible. Things came to an abrupt precipice the summer Emma turned fifteen.

Jemima was a year younger than Sanju, and that summer the two had spent the whole of Sanju's stay engrossed in conversation with each other, rabbiting in that teenage south London dialect that their parents hated; it was a time before they had started speaking like the other bankers, lawyers or publishers in the City that they were to become.

"Shame that Marr's left The Smiffs, wouldn't have minded seein' 'em again."

"Yeah, some bust-up, right? Not cool."

"Know whatta mean, mate?"

"Reckon you'll see any bands in Oxford, Sanju, bit of a village, innit?"

"Yeah 'course, but, to be 'onest, it ain't that far from home. Anyway, it's only physics; will have loads of time – won't be in the studio drawing pictures all day, eh, Jem?"

"Haha, funny, not, Sanju. Actually, one more time just for your benefit, it'll be 'istory of art. No paintings. You're just jealous it's Cambridge."

"Yeah, 'course I am."

"Hey, fancy coming down to see New Order endda term?"

"Yeah, Jem, that'll be wicked. You'll never guess who I bumped into at the Palace the other night..."

"Tell me... was there meself the other night..."

Emma scoffed silently. She knew Jemima was talking like some cool done-it-all but had only ever been to one Kid Creole concert and had no idea which 'Palace' Sanju was talking about.

Sanju had taken to wearing a long coat and the colour black as often as the heat would physically allow, often with Indian kurta tops, and had cut his hair at the sides and back with his black curls cascading down his face at the front. Jemima was now all hairspray. Emma would look at them, removed and disconcerted, talking and walking through the dusty French countryside as if in some Duran Duran video. Emma had little to add to their conversation, and, with her metallic-brace smile, little to give to the idyllic, romantic scene.

Once when she was alone with Jemima, Emma just couldn't resist venting her frustration, but it just made things worse.

"Didn't know you was plannin' to see New Order, Jem?" she asked mockingly.

"Don't need to tell ya everything, lil sis."

"Are they playin' at the Palace then?" Emma lingered on the word 'Palace' sarcastically.

"You won't know the place. Why don't you join in the conversation – you might learn somefin?"

"Be nice to get a word in edgeways, talking do-di-dah about bands you know nothing 'bout. Oh, I'm going to Cambridge, history of art, actually, much better than Oxford," Emma mimicked a Home Counties posh accent.

"Oh, piss off, Em. Maybe you'd find your tongue if you weren't glowin' into Sanju's eyes all day."

"Oh, whatchu talkin' about now?" Emma realised that the split-second momentary silence, at the shock of what she'd just heard before responding, had given away Jemima hitting her mark.

"Em's got a crush." Jemima stretched out her words tauntingly.

"You're the one monopolising him all day, Miss know-it-all trendy bands." Both sisters sensed Emma's tone being too obviously irritated and aggressive.

"Oh, Em's really got a crush," Jemima repeated with a confirmatory matter-of-fact intonation.

"Oh, why don't you just shut up and get lost?"

In reality, it was more than just a bit of a crush; Emma was totally infatuated with Sanju – his black curls, the smile, the fact he would talk about contemporary music, his clothes, him doing physics which she barely understood, him going to Oxford, him everything. Sometimes Sanju would clear his hair away from his face by curling out his lower lip and blowing it away before it lightly settled back again. This nonchalant act accompanied with a blank stare at nothing would drive Emma into a state of silent ecstasy lost in that cool cuteness.

Emma realised that Jemima had no such feelings for Sanju, but couldn't understand why she was behaving that way, shutting her out from anything where Emma could contribute. With hindsight, she wondered if perhaps she had just been feeling protective towards her younger sister, or whether it was just a bit of sibling rivalry and fear of being locked out if the other two got close. Anyway, they never spoke about it.

Occasionally, when no one else was around, Emma had tried to have a conversation with Sanju about something, anything, but rarely got any further traction than short monosyllabic answers.

Years later, Sanju would tell her he was totally oblivious to all these dynamics and perplexed that Emma would think they were freezing her out. In fact, he used to get a bit agitated that Emma didn't join in with them, but 'hung around behind like a bored stalker' with little or no interest in what they were doing. Maybe it was an age thing. Jemima had similar interests at that time, and Emma would have been too young 'to understand the deep challenges faced by someone of his eighteen years of age' he would tease. For him, his feelings at that time – which, frankly, he hadn't really analysed, but if pushed – were more a brother would have for his sisters than anything else.

For Emma, that fortnight was about new scents, brighter make-up, shorter dresses, and trying different ways to tie her hair up. But nothing. Nothing got noticed or commented upon, at least not by Sanju.

* * *

That day had been particularly hot. The sky was a deep blue, expansive but for a still, white, silky strip of cloud. The light stretched across the fields and orchards, infusing the valley below the villa, extending to a hazy sea on the horizon. It sparkled on the curved roof tiles, peered into every gap and crevice in the old stone walls, crashed against the freshly painted white wooden shutters that had been partly shut to keep the inside cool, and glistened across the pool.

The families had lunched on the shady veranda by the side of the house – a starter of green beans with chopped tomatoes cooked in garlic, followed by herb-crusted lamb cutlets with thin potatoes sautéed in oily onions, with white peaches for dessert. The two dads had polished off a bottle of Cahors and two rounds of espressos.

"Can I offer anyone a digestif? It's a local *liqueur d'abricot*." Emma's grandmother was holding a tall, dusty, label-less bottle, part-filled with a peach-coloured liquid.

"That looks jolly nice, almost dangerous, *Madame*. Would be rude to refuse." Sanju's father was in good spirits.

"*Et toi aussi*, John?"

"Well, I can't let Satish die on his own. Fill me up, *merci, Maman*."

"Would you like to try some *aussi*, Sushma? It's very nice."

"*Non, merci, Madame*. I really can't drink at lunchtime."

"Thérèse?"

"*Pas pour moi, Maman.* I'm driving down to Cannes with Sushma for a bit of shopping and Jemima needs some shoes."

"You comin' too aren't you, Sanju? There's a really cool new ice cream place on the Croisette." Jemima was sitting opposite Sanju. Emma noted how she had not been mentioned.

"*Et tu vas aussi,* Emma?" Her grandmother must have noticed her looking grumpy at the other edge of the long table.

"If I must," Emma muttered, her voice barely audible.

"This brandy is super, *Madame.*"

"And she's got some other decent liqueurs in the cupboard; shame you're returning in a couple of days."

"You know, John, we should have stocked up with a few bottles before going back."

"For our wine cellars!" The two fathers chortled with each other, recognising their 'wine cellars' were nothing more than a couple of racks in the cupboards under their stairs. "Well, why not? We could hitch a lift into Cannes with Thérèse."

"There's space if Sanju and Emma are happy to stay behind. Jemima desperately needs some shoes, so she'll need to come."

"Yeah, why don't you two stay here? It's so hot. You'll be cooler here." Her father had spoken before Jemima could butt in. "There is a *cave* I know, Satish, where we can taste before we buy."

"Haven't you two had enough to drink already today?"

"We'll be sober after the siesta. Us medics know what we're doing. Everything will have passed through the system!"

Emma's mother shook her head semi-disapprovingly at her husband who was chortling again. "Grandma is popping round to Valerie's to collect some figs, so you two will be on your own, is that alright?"

"Yeah, whatever, *Maman.*" Emma feigned total disinterest but inside her heart was racing. She would be alone with Sanju for at least a couple of hours.

After clearing up from lunch, everyone went back to their rooms, except Mr Kapoor, who went into a deep sleep at the dining table, large beads of sweat visible across his forehead and creating a fine delta of tributaries across his neck. They had decided to wait a couple of hours for the heat to die down before leaving. Emma sat in her room, hoping the mothers wouldn't change their plans, that Jemima wouldn't change her mind, that the dads would still go after their sleep had lifted the alcohol, and that her grandmother would stick to her commitment. The next two hours felt like two days.

The old Peugeot spluttered off just after 4.00pm with the old crackling radio churning out Hot Chocolate's 'You Sexy Thing'. Emma's grandmother got ready to go just after, but did Emma a big favour, maybe by chance, or maybe because she sensed what was in Emma's mind, by telling Sanju that the pool had been cleaned that morning and was free of floating leaves and the dead insects that he hated, so would be great to use that afternoon. Sanju nodded and shouted up to Emma that he was getting his swim shorts on if she wanted to join him by the pool.

Emma was in her room, desperately trying to decide which swimming costume to wear. They were in France and the oldies were out but topless would be too much – she had never done that in front of Sanju. She tried on all her options, feeling comfortable to 'borrow' and pair with some of Jemima's accessories. In the end, she wore a red bikini with a partially transparent white beach cover top, tied her hair up in a loose knot, and, with a final squirt of perfume, went downstairs.

Sanju was sitting with his legs dangling over the edge, rotating in the water. He had not been in. She noticed his skin and how much he had darkened in the few days he had been there, and how it had started to peel across his reddish-brown shoulders, and how skinny he looked without his clothes on, and the faint perspiration just above his eyes as he turned his head towards her.

She sat down beside him, about a metre away, and put her legs in the water.

"It's warm."

"Yeah," he replied. "I love it when they've cleaned the wa'er."

"Yeah," she repeated. "And when it's empty, though not when I'm totally on my own."

"Nah. Me neither."

Emma looked away. The monosyllabic responses may have been what she had expected but not what she had hoped. She looked across the garden wall and pointed to some trees on the hillside. "You know, when *Maman* was young, we used to own those fields. They 'ad cherry orchards, peach and apricot trees, olives, all the way down to that road, which used to be a path. Her grandpa would take all his stuff down to Grasse. He met his wife, her grandma, at the weekly market. So different – two gens later, *Maman* met Dad in London at a Canadian friend's 'ouse."

Sanju looked up, interested in the story. He stood up and peered across the wall. "They owned fields all the way down to that road?"

"Yep, and those on the other side of the valley by that 'ouse, but that was all their world and a trip to Cannes was the 'ighlight of their lives." Emma knew that Sanju would get curious about how people used to live but she was still pleasantly surprised at his level of interest. She had made it all up, of course, so had nothing more to add, but he had sat down again, inadvertently closer to her, and now within touching distance. There was silence again as they both stared into the pool, rocking their feet backwards and forwards. It was left to Emma to start a new conversation.

"So, whatchu wanna do after uni, Sanju?"

"Dunno." Sanju continued to stare at the water. "With physics, at least some fings are fixed, at least I ain't gonna be a doctor. What 'bout you, Em, whatchu wanna do?" Sanju finished by looking straight at her, sighing with that irresistible lower lip jutting out, blowing his hair away from his face.

Emma felt transfixed every time Sanju did it. She had a momentary direct view of his face, unencumbered by any hair, his hazel eyes glinting in that late-afternoon Provençal sun, sitting just a foot away, and he had asked something about her: what did she want to do?

What did she want to do? She kept staring, watching the curly locks settle back across his face, uttered the word 'law', and leant across, as if pulled and pushed by some uncontrollable, as yet undiscovered physics force, and kissed Sanju low on his cheek.

She moved back. She froze. She saw Sanju's face – blank, retreating, annoyed, embarrassed, confused. It was only a split second before she jumped into the water, but it felt like hours... She felt the deep warmth of her blush even below the surface of the water. Through the refracted light, she could see Sanju take his legs out of the water and the glimmer of his silhouette walk away. She stayed under the surface and let the water swirl around her. She would write him a note to apologise, to say it was just a joke; to hope they would still stay friends. She would leave it on his pillow. He avoided her until he left two days later. She would cry. She wouldn't see Sanju again until her eighteenth birthday.

* * *

Before the days in which she had lost her husband, before she had lost her child, before the time she thought she was losing Marcus, it was the most traumatic thing that had ever happened or could ever have happened to her.

She felt so innocent then. She wondered what she would have done if the incident had happened ten or fifteen years later. She would have stuck her tongue down his mouth, maybe fucked him there by the pool before Grandma got home. The thought made her smile. She wondered where he was now and how it would feel if she could hold his hand.

She sighed with a melancholic shrug and closed the album laptop, turned off the light, walked past Ollie's room, and went to bed.

NINE

Everyone sees what you appear to be,
Few experience what you really are.

His knuckles still felt bruised, but the grazes had dried into deep burgundy scabs. He had done even less than normal the day before. After Urs had found him, he'd had coffee, spoken to no one, showered, and went for a walk through a thin drizzle in the woods above the villa. He took a bacon sandwich for a late lunch and spent the afternoon slowly going through Emma's letter again. Muttu brought him dinner in his room. He thought about calling Emma. She had texted a few times and it had been a few days since they had spoken, but he couldn't bring himself to do it. By 9.00pm, he was asleep.

He was up early this morning. He made a coffee in his room and took it onto the veranda. The valley was calm – the Teiflaubach lay below like a still grey carpet. There was no one around. He sat in his gown and slippers and listened to the sound of birds, the distant cows with their alpine bells and the early traffic along the banks of the Meiringensee. He lit a cigarette and took deep puffs interspersed with his coffee, enjoying his peace, resisting the temptation to take out his phones until he had finished both.

He moved up to the road that led to the villa, sat on a bench by the side, and peered down the hillside. A few early morning farmhouse lights flickered in the valley. He watched a magpie, alone, appear from above the trees and sweep down the hill above the grass, with its long, elegant tail behind the black-and-white clicking shutters of its wings. Someone had told him that seeing a solo magpie brought bad luck, but he was transfixed as the bird soared above him, bouncing on the air currents, free, but somehow out of place with its monochrome silhouette clashing against the greens and blues behind. It dived suddenly onto the grass in front of him, and he could see it grab a small animal – a mouse – and was just close enough to watch the magpie peck out the mouse's eyes as it wriggled under its claws. With its clackety sound, it picked at the mouse's neck getting to the meat under the fur. The magpie took a couple of small morsels of flesh but seemed more intent on the thrill of the kill than satisfying its hunger, a red speck of blood giving colour to its beak. It looked up towards Marcus as Marcus exhaled his last cigarette breath, before flying off behind the trees. The mouse lay there, still, before other birds arrived and ripped any remaining life in its body apart.

Marcus took out his personal phone first. There were a couple of texts. The first was from Ollie. He had attached a photo of a painting he had done for his art class. He had had his first golf lesson, asked when Daddy was coming home, and said goodnight; more or less his standard message. The other message was from Emma posted just after 11.00pm, also standard stuff about her day. The gas boiler had been fixed. She had renewed Ollie's cricket club. She was looking forward to speaking to him but was off to bed now. Marcus looked at the photo of the painting again. A dark brown track wound its way across a bright burnt-orange dusty landscape. Besides the road was a white restaurant or café, with deep green hills behind and what looked like a castle, also in brown. The colours blended into each other like in a tie-dye print. In front of the restaurant was a small stall selling snacks, with a lady in red and a man holding a child. Marcus reflected on the detail, the story and the bright colours melding into each other. He typed back, saying: 'How lovely, Ollie' and that he would call them later that day.

He took out his work phone. He had gone through his emails over dinner the night before. There was nothing new of note. He read an update from his Asia sales head.

Marcus had known Andrea Bartorelli (Italian, late thirties) for over a decade. They had worked together in London before Marcus had moved across to Singapore, and although Andrea was very much the junior, they had gotten on almost like close friends from the start. It became quickly apparent from their initial business trips to Milan that Andrea was not only well connected within both the financial and professional Italian circles, but also with the politicians, the hereditary industrialists, and the aristocrats. Andrea's mother's family also owned a handful of hotels across Tuscany and Umbria, as well as a vineyard near Verona. Andrea secured Marcus's gratitude when he arranged for use of one of the hotels near Siena for Marcus's management offsite. Andrea was also an exceptionally smooth and intelligent salesperson, relishing in the design of complex product structures. At sixteen, Andrea had signed an agreement that he would have to work externally somewhere for at least five years before he could enter any of the family businesses, but it seemed he had actually taken very well to banking and loved it.

When Marcus left for Singapore, he had half-jokingly suggested to Andrea that if he ever fancied a change of scene, there would always be a desk for him in Asia, but he was truly surprised to hear from Andrea eighteen months later that he was keen to leave London. At the time, the Asian business was not going well, and Marcus didn't have any headcount for a new arrival, but immediately set about engineering a position for him. Although it was never discussed openly, Marcus gleaned from various conversations over the years that Andrea had split up with his Columbian girlfriend, had got involved inadvertently with some unpleasant people in her inner circle, and needed to leave Europe quickly. Within three months, Marcus was able to exit someone from his team to 'create a space' for Andrea. From both a professional and personal perspective, it proved a good decision. Andrea was not only a great revenue generator, his contacts list extended well beyond Italy across the globe, but he also became a loyal and trusted lieutenant. Within a few months, Marcus had promoted Andrea to be a team head, running the local hedge fund desk, and just before Marcus returned to London, he had lined Andrea up as Asia sales head.

Marcus would call Andrea once a week on their recorded work line – a dull review of the business. The more interesting discussions happened on their private unrecorded numbers, a practice banned by compliance, and a breach of which both Marcus and Andrea had disciplined members of their teams on but had chosen to ignore personally. Andrea would still be at work, so Marcus rang once and hung up – the missed call an indicator to call back when free. Andrea didn't take long.

"*Ciao*, Marcus. How are you?"

"I'm good as can be, Andrea. How's life in the office?"

"Man, that fucking Starc is really squeezing our balls, screaming non-stop at everyone. There is going to be a mass sales walkout if someone doesn't sort him out."

"Not much anyone can do. He's Handscombe's boy. I heard he had a bullying complaint being reviewed by HR. Has that calmed things down?"

"Not at all. Maybe worse. Listen, the guy is a crook."

"What do you mean?"

"You know, fiddling with the mark-to-mark, leaking false positions – I reckon he'll do whatever he can get away with."

"Listen, Andrea, if you have any evidence, you need to blow the whistle or you'll also get stuffed, but you'd better be right. I can guarantee it won't stay anonymous."

"I don't have any evidence, but I smell the type."

"Who's at risk of leaving that you care about?"

"*Allora*, Steve Chow for one. He's still upset about his bonus and blames that squarely on us not standing up to Starc. I'm fairly sure he's interviewing, and he'd be a loss. Kun going wouldn't be a good look either. Everyone knows what's happened there."

"Can we get Steve a bigger role? What about looking after the Central Banks initiative? That's already producing results and he can take some credit by year-end."

"That's really Su's area. She set it up and she's doing a great job."

"Yeah, I know, but make them co-heads, find some reason to get Steve involved. She'll be annoyed but get over it. She's too loyal to walk."

"*Si*. Sure, OK, not so fair, but nothing in life is."

"Keep me in the loop on everyone else, Andrea. For Zhao Kun, I can't do anything unless he asks for a move out of Handscombe's world. Frankly, he won't survive the next cull. Can he do sales?"

"Too bright for flow sales and I don't have a space elsewhere."

"I can't do anything now. Think I've pissed off Handscombe too much already. I'll have a word with the treasury guys and see if they can pick him up when he gets put on the hit list."

"Marcus, Handscombe has been asking about Epsilon."

"Fuck, how does he know about that? Has it gone global?"

"I don't think so, but the MAS here have asked for some documents. I shouldn't know that but, you know, hardly anything exciting ever happens here, and everyone likes a little gossip. Handscombe sounded very sympathetic towards you."

"Like arse. He wants to screw me over. If he had any sense, he'd keep well clear. Fuck it. If he wants a scrap, let's let him have it. When was the last time Asia had a full business audit?"

"Been at least a couple of years."

"Is sales all clear on the compliance front, Andrea? I don't want to shoot myself in the foot."

"All clean as far as I know. Look, there'll be some small audit points, they always have to find something, but nothing sackable I wouldn't think."

"Right, you remember Johnson, compliance officer in Tokyo a few years ago; moved to New York. Well, he's about to get the global head compliance role. Owes me a couple. I'll suggest he does an Asia regional audit – look at the marks on the books, information leakage, chat room governance. If there is anything there, it'll be a win for him, and it should take Starc down."

"For sure there'll be something there, Marcus – that guy will do anything to boost his books."

"Let me drop Pierre an email also about our culture and respect for diversity. We'll get HR to do some interviews – make sure Chow and Kun are on the list. No, wait, let's do an anonymous survey. Complete fucking waste of time, but that should definitely sink Starc. Reckon he'll be out in two months. Agreed?"

"Agreed, Marcus. Miss you not being here, bud."

"Listen, Andrea – the Epsilon trades – I don't think we did many in Asia, but we certainly pitched. There'll be some call reports with clients, right?"

"We didn't do call reports in those days. Might be some

emails to clients, pitch documents, and internal stuff pushing to sell them, but unless a client tells MAS they were approached, they'd be very difficult to find. I'd be relaxed."

"OK, good to hear. I'll leave you, Andrea. Let me talk to Johnson and Pierre and will let you know. *Ciao.*"

"Er, one more thing before you go, Marcus. Caitanya."

"Tell me."

"*Allora*, well, you remember Ayla Finn, the Kiwi, great friends with Tani, and was quite cut up when she left us. Anyway, she is going on holiday to Kerala in a couple of weeks. Will do the backwaters so will be there by Alleppey. Is that how you say it?"

There was silence. "I'm listening."

"Alleppey, as you know, is near Tani's family home, so Ayla wants to go there. Don't know why. Maybe to share some stories about their time in Singapore and look at some photos with the family? Ayla has worked out roughly where the family lives, from Tani's description and Google Maps, but not exactly, and ideally wants to call first. Ayla said she emailed you to see if you still had a contact number, and then asked me to ask you rather than pester."

Marcus stayed silent a little longer. "I'll take a look, Andrea," he blurted distractedly before hanging up.

TEN

He who permits himself to tell a lie once, finds it much easier to do it a second and third time.
This falsehood of the tongue leads to that of the heart.

The senior guys ultimately tried to dress up my Singapore transfer as an opportunity to gain international experience, etc., but the reality was that Singapore was a bit of a backwater then, and although I had a job – God knows it was the one thing that had given me a raison d'etre – my career at TDT had stalled. I hadn't been able to land anything else in London and I was pretty bitter about it – all as a consequence of Dietmar's insecurity and feigned concerns and lies about some trades we had sold.

So, there I was. Tripped by lies. Well, there is an irony. Normally, we had been such cosy bedfellows.

You see, Emma, I suspect within a normal childhood when a child lies, the parents point out that that's wrong. The child accepts and never asks why. But even then as he or she grows older and becomes a better liar, first with the small fibs then the bigger lies, and starts to see the potential rewards, often with no downside, he or she could rightly think that truth is somewhat overrated. Then, if like with me, no parent has even attempted to define any such line, you live life without any ethical differentiation between truth and untruth.

I have to say, in my job and life in general, that the comfort of not feeling constrained to the truth has bought me revenue and wealth, promotion and power, loyalty and lovers; and sure, once you got somewhere, you could start to preach integrity and reputation having covered your tracks, so no junior masquerader followed your path to your throne – well, what was not to like? If you stumbled, you doubled down. You saw truth as the loser's curse. If you throw this into a noxious cocktail of greed, ambition, and no care for others, you got the catalyst for unlimited promise.

As in your childhood, you start with the little deceptions, half-truths, harmless exaggerations, then move to misleading stories and finally the blatant lies. Some will fade as fleeting moments, but others stay throughout your life and even beyond your death. Some become more serious through the lens of time. Some impact strangers and others, those closest to you. I have affected them all, without limit, from the simplest to the most complex, and enjoyed the fruits without hesitation.

But truth is eternal, as they say, outlasting us all. Each fib and lie fertilises its burgeoning growth like a melting stream surging into a river, until one day the flow bursts its banks to drown everything that dared to confound it, destroying the loves, the loyalties, uprooting the once powerful trees that represented the fabrics of your life, and guarded the false fluvial fringe.

Sometimes I have seen you tell Ollie off for little fibs; I've wondered why, but today as I face some of the implications of my actions, I see that yours is parental love, the explanation of right and wrong that sacrifices immediate gratification for avoiding the pain later. He will not have the excuse of lack of parental love, and though I mention it, frankly, neither do I.

But equally, he needs to know that there are many that live life like me, who have played with different rules, some with no rules, and others who change the rules midway. Perhaps they all have their stories and motivations. But he will also see how inconsistent judgments are made from different angles – everyone applauds if you squash a cockroach, but you dare not hurt a butterfly. Assassins become heroic freedom fighters, exploitive robber barons are hailed for building their countries, and silent accomplices who make these things happen live in the dark unknown, with their discomforting truth, so often, conveniently tucked away.

But I digress. I mentioned Dietmar getting het up with compliance about some structured trades and complex investment products we had been selling without ensuring that the underlying risks were sufficiently well understood by the buyers. Of course, at that time, that was the way of the world and Dietmar's only interest was to get me out of TDT, rather than any empathy for the investors, but somewhat inadvertently his concerns proved prescient.

Many corporations, pension schemes, local government authorities and retail funds bought these things – they loved the investment returns but didn't understand the risks. Even those that understood bought them as they feared just missing out. The rating agencies lauded them as they didn't want to miss the banks' business elsewhere. Many banks sold them. But unfortunately, many of those investments have gone sour and people have lost savings, companies have made losses, etc.

And now they are complaining. Those buying dimwits are complaining about what they willingly took, and the people that willingly employed them – bigger dimwits – are complaining too, but not about their own recruitment mistakes. And they are complaining to the regulators who wrote the loose rules that didn't bother, at the time, to 'protect' the people, the pensioners, the institutions, etc. for whom these dimwits were working, and the politicians are complaining about the regulators, though were happy to let our businesses grow and rake in our taxes. And they are all complaining about the evil banks. And the bank shareholders who made the juicy returns are complaining about the management at the time even though most of those guys have long left with their bonuses.

That's the truth of it, but various investigations have kicked off internally at our place, and externally by the regulators, looking for an alternate truth, and somewhere to vent themselves. And soon this will be in the papers and TDT Capital will be up there in the headlines. So, our new management will be looking around for scapegoats.

Emma, I want you and Ollie to know that when that happens, that on this, I believe I'm truly clean. I was the salesperson, not the fucking risk manager. Who bought what – I was totally agnostic. They were professionals and they'd take our invite to Goodwood, enjoy the Perignon and trade with us the next morning. But now, apparently, they didn't have all the information to assess the underlying risk. Why didn't they ask? I didn't understand the products myself, fuck it, how was I supposed to judge whether they did or didn't, but that's what the regulations say, and the regulators will look back and say that our processes and controls were not strong enough – you wouldn't believe it but one of the bastards leading the case was in our fucking compliance department at the time!

So why have I been worrying? Frankly, because there aren't many of us still around from that era senior enough to be accountable, and yet not quite senior enough to be able to pin the blame on someone else. I was head of sales: first in the UK, and then later globally, and a lot of this stuff was sold on my watch. I brought the ideas and paperwork to the risk committees for approval. I didn't set the policies or hire the compliance guys that approved them, but they, like me, were just told to boost revenues. If we had objected, we'd be working elsewhere and TDT would just hire or promote someone else to do it. I sound like the victim, and look, I don't deny I've done well out of it, that we've done well out of it, but I was doing what I was told, and everyone knew about it.

And I certainly don't think I deserve what's coming. Not for this.

The regulators are trawling through emails – TDT emails – and client emails and then will be presenting evidence of our wrongdoing. TDT will be presenting its innocence, protecting its reputation, but, of course, without talking to anyone who was actually involved. All of this will be reviewed through a rear-view mirror with no context, and the bank will be looking to settle for a fine which will likely be lowered if some suitable individuals are sanctioned.

And if that was the end of it, so be it.

But TDT have had a few of these cases; we haven't been the cleanest, and each time the fines and sanctions have gotten tougher. If it lands with me, as a minimum my deferred compensation will be gone. They may look at clawing back bonuses they've already paid. Worse, a few days back, I heard there may be a public lawsuit being filed in the States. There is nothing the politicians will want more than to show a bit of populist red banking meat to the ignorant voting sharks. The bank will want to, need to, line up with the politicians and the public mood, especially in the States. They'll spin a story – tell the world it was something in the past, there were some bad eggs and they've cleaned up, so much the better if some Brit with a posh accent is also getting it in the neck. They'll want an extradition, and you can guess how much resistance that'll get from our government – zero. TDT will do some trade with the regulators, some settlement, agree the fine and the sanctions, decide upon whom to pin the blame, like in some dark pool without any visibility or scrutiny.

Emma, I'm clean with this. I want you to know that, and I don't think I'm being overly paranoid about what is going to happen. I needed to come here, to get some air and think it through, and try to develop a plan to protect myself, to protect us, but the net is closing in and I'm running out of ideas. I feel like I'm facing an invisible enemy. No one has been telling me anything about what is going on even though it was my area. And I'm dragging you into it.

But, unfortunately, there is more.

As I say, they are going through every email, every recorded conversation, every document. As things come out about the trades and fines, some other things are getting leaked. Look, banking is not a place for angels. Some things I've said and done are regrettable, more than regrettable. I haven't been totally honest about the whole saga with Tani. Part of me just thought there was no reason to rake up old stories – it was in the past. That was wrong. But now if it leaks, the whole dire episode will no doubt go down very well in the Daily Mail *with all the embellished gory details, but I want you to know what really happened. It's not great but I'd rather you hear about it from me first. It will be out in the public and Ollie will be forced to deal with all that in school.*

And there is still more. Something that should never have happened, something I should have told you about a long time ago, something that shouldn't become public but something I cannot face. Emma. Forgive me. I love you.

ELEVEN

When there are deals to do, business minds get sharper too,
Just as owls can better see the darker it begins to be.

Marcus stayed on the bench and lit another cigarette. Not much was left of the mouse now. He was captivated as the last morsels were pecked off, barely leaving a hint of any stain on the grass, where life had turned to death had turned to nothing but a vague memory.

Soon he would see the cleaning ladies in the old white Volkswagen chugging up the hill and then take a left into the drive to the villa. They would be met by Muttu. Since Marcus had moved in, they would only come twice a week and would be finished by midday, going through the bedrooms, the common areas, the kitchen, and gym. The villa would be largely empty in the winter months, as nearly all the visitors preferred to be closer to the ski slopes. Urs had kept the villa restaurant open to non-guests during the Christmas and New Year period as in previous years – Marcus had initially planned to return to London by then, but then changed his mind, though had been happy to stay out of the way, mainly in his room, during those weeks. After that, most of the staff had left to service Urs' other properties at Wengen, with only Muttu and Urs staying at the villa.

Muttu greeted the ladies with his customary permanent smile. He was very much in charge. As with Urs, Marcus knew little about him. He could see why Urs valued him, but not so much why Muttu was so loyal the other way – maybe he didn't have Swiss residency and so was obliged to be so, but the bond seemed stronger than that. It was rare for Marcus to have any interest in others unless it was of some value to him, but over the past few days his curiosity around Muttu had become more intense. Marcus gave an acknowledging nod to the cleaning ladies but stayed on the bench.

A few minutes later, another Volkswagen arrived, this one yellow. This was the repair and odd-job man, Gilbert, who also tidied up the driveway. Normally he would sweep away the snow and ice and salt the driveway in the winters, and clean the pool in the summer, but there was little to do today, though Muttu was having a long conversation about something with him. Muttu handed him a bag and Gilbert took a spade out of the shed and headed towards the wooded slopes.

They all disappeared until Muttu came out again with a mug of coffee. "Sir, I've asked the ladies to clean Herr Waelchli's room first, and then the library. Is that where you plan to work?"

"Oh, where is Urs?"

"He has gone to Zurich for a couple of meetings and lunch. He left early."

"Indeed, he must have done. Yes, why don't I get changed and have breakfast. I have a few calls to make and can stay in the library after that and be out of the way. Will it be ready in about an hour?"

"I will ask them to do the library first. What would you like to eat?"

* * *

Surender Singh Trivedi (Indian, age sixty-one, as per passport but unknown exactly) had just taken his siesta and was enjoying one of his many daily teas, milky and sweet, in the afternoon sun. He peered across the large pristine garden of his bungalow on the edge of Dehradun, Uttarakhand. The sun and tea worked jointly, but only partially effectively, with his thick jumper, ski socks purchased in Austria, and a Kashmiri shawl to keep the sturdy Himalayan winter chill at bay.

All three Trivedi brothers lived together with their mother and split their time between Dehradun, looking after the elderly lady, and their main residence in Shanti Niketan, New Delhi. The family had moved from their ancestral home in Bareilly to escape the infernal summer heat there. Historically, they had owned small furniture and handicraft factories and some farmland, but Surender, the middle brother, had led the expansion of the business into larger-scale construction and then travel – first, through building a mid-market hotel chain, and then by upgrading heritage properties into boutique hotels. Under his tutelage, the family's fortune and influence had grown substantially, and it was through no small favour to, and a chance encounter with, Marcus Flint. A meeting that, as it transpired, was significant for both of them.

Although respectfully and notionally it was the elder brother, Davinder Singh, who had run the Trivedi group since the death of their father, it was Surender who had the vision and drive to seize the opportunities with extensive financing and political nous to grow their enterprise. The youngest Trivedi, Jitender, had talents that were more attuned to dealing with the rougher business practices of their native Uttar Pradesh, than the global group that Trivedi Enterprises had become. However, the family had made substantial donations to the local political leaders, and this had led to Jitender Singh becoming part of the chief minister's inner circle, which in turn had allowed them to keep some of their less salubrious business and personal activities away from media attention.

Surinder definitely saw his brothers' contribution as notional and their involvement in the business a necessity to keep their mother happy. He was very much in charge; the Don, he liked that; the original, the Amitabh Bachchan.

Three gardeners moved diligently around the lawn; one worked on the grass itself, manually addressing each weed and non-uniform growth, while the other two tidied the beds as they did each day of each week of every month. Surinder Singh glared at them critically, waiting for the faintest error to comment and bark advice as if the one trip to the Chelsea Flower Show and occasional viewings of the BBC's *Gardeners' World* had transformed him into a higher-tier horticultural expert; a Monty Don if you will, ah, he liked that too. He was clearly more interested in them than the business update coming from his accountant-cum-assistant sitting on the neighbouring rattan chair.

A glistening creamy tea rim bordered Surinder Singh's proudly thick, black-dyed moustache. His thinning hair, also proudly black, was spread to maximise coverage. He couldn't be bothered to reach for his glasses to see who the ringing phone call was from, so passed the mobile to the bespeckled accountant, instructing him with a flick of the neck to deal with it.

"It's Marcus Flint, sir."

"Give it here!" He snatched the device from across the accountant like a sibling repossessing a favourite toy. Marcus was Trivedi Enterprises' senior relationship manager for TDT. They had not spoken for around three years, as juniors would typically deal with the day-to-day activities, and Marcus had never called for a social, so Surinder knew it would be important. The excitement of the call made him release a large, noisy fart that had been bubbling since lunch. All parties – Surinder Singh, the accountant, the three gardeners, and various other servants – ignored the gusty noise, pretending it away as an out-of-tune honk from one of the passing trucks on the adjacent Dehradun-Saharanpur highway.

"Hello, Marcus. What a surprise and pleasure to hear from you! I was just thinking about you. How are you?" This was standard Eastern Uttar Pradesh speak – Marcus hadn't crossed his mind since they last spoke.

"I'm well."

"And where are you?"

"In Switzerland."

"Ah, wonderful. You know, us Indians, we think of Switzerland as Heaven on Earth. I still remember that event you took us to in St Moritz – White Turf and Mount Titlis."

"Actually, I'm not far from there."

"Wonderful, and how is the beautiful Mrs Emma and the young lad. He must be now about eleven. The name, what is it again?"

"Ollie."

"Ah yes and does the young lad have any young company, a little brother or sister?"

"No, just Ollie." It was clear Marcus wanted to move off the chit-chat. "Listen, SS, I need to share some developments."

Surinder Singh had observed how any stressful conversation caused Marcus to speak at double speed, even faster than when he simply wanted to sound important and busy, which subconsciously seemed to make him pause to gulp air and inadvertently made him also sound somewhat furtive.

"You may have heard about some structured trades we sold a few years ago and an investigation that some regulators have kicked off in a number of countries. Look, there was nothing abnormal about what we did – all the banks have been selling them as investments and for hedging purposes."

"Yes, Marcus, I had a mail from your guy in Singapore; said you were dealing fully with the regulatory authorities. Nothing to see here, as you say. In fact, I hope so. That young fella tried to sell me some of that stuff five or six years back." Surinder Singh had put the phone speaker on, so everyone in the vicinity could hear and sense the importance of him talking in English to his banker in Switzerland, though fully recognising that it would be lost on the gardeners and probably his accountant too. Still not bad for a furniture maker from Bareilly. If only Pitaji could have been alive to see him.

"Yes, SS, I should have called you earlier. Look, that investigation will go where it goes, but they are diving into all our historical correspondences. Who knows what will come out of the woodwork, and when the regulators and or management will get itchy." Marcus gulped for breath and, after a couple of seconds, released a faint burp, which would often accompany the gulping, quiet this time, but still just audible to the accountant on the speaker. "But that's not of concern to you, though I've been thinking about things, reflecting on this and that, and I'm thinking of doing a reset. You know – come clean – just letting you know. OK." The tone was crisp, seeking to convey control and decisiveness, but the clipped 'OK' felt as much a question as a notification, and a tacit request for affirmation.

"*Acha.*" Surinder Singh turned off the speaker, but the volume dial was still loud enough for the accountant and gardeners to hear the ongoing discussion. He stroked his moustache from the nose outwards then repeated the action a couple more times. The Trivedi family had become renowned businessmen with a global reach; ambassadors for India, admired for staying humble to their roots despite a fleet of premium cars, noted for philanthropic projects ranging from building large temples to the odd school, with a place high enough in the echelons of Indian society to get invites to Bollywood events, and on social terms with senior politicians, and at least at State level, with the local regulators and law enforcers. There would seem to be little of concern with Marcus's call.

The events to which Marcus alluded had happened a long time ago. Even if some pesky journalist, trying to make a name for him or herself, started snooping around, there would be no trail now. Yes, the international dimension may generate some excitement, but they had dealt with a lot worse. He thought Marcus would have rung from his private line but nevertheless was concerned as to whether the call was being recorded. This short deliberation concluded with the release of another fart.

"Of course, I have no idea to what you are referring, Marcus."

"Understood, SS. There is nothing for you to be concerned about. Nothing documented or will be, but you know people may start hypothesising, putting two and two together, what was said and done." Marcus was noticeably starting to lose his gravitas, the sentences were becoming more incoherent and tense, and the gulping with accompanied burping more frequent and pronounced.

"Marcus, I understand you have some issues at the bank with some structured trades which has led to some regulatory investigation but, as you say, that's nothing for us to be concerned about." Surinder Singh leaned away from the accountant and released another fart – this one with significant volume and alpha authority, which happened also to coincide with a loud counter-belch from Marcus – a trans-continental duet no longer remotely confusable with any load carriers on the highway. The accountant held his pose but was unable to avoid a mild squint under his spectacles from the combined physical and, one sensed, metaphorical stench of the conversation.

"Yes, that's it."

"Thanks for letting me know and enjoy the rest of your stay in Switzerland."

Surinder Singh got up, adjusted the shawl over his shoulders, and walked back towards the bungalow, dialling his elder brother as he entered the building, away from the accountant, the gardeners, and the lingering odour. "*Haan Dada*, Marcus Flint just called."

* * *

Marcus stared out of the library window. The morning's wispy clouds had thickened, darkened, and wrapped themselves like a damp quilt around the villa.

Marcus recalled the evening a decade back when he first met the Trivedis.

The Trivedis had been medium-sized clients of the bank in India but had big ambitions to grow the business. TDT had a revolving loan to them that had come up for renewal, but TDT's credit department had become uncomfortable about reputational risks circulating around the family, and business risk from the amount of debt across different banks that Trivedi Enterprises had taken on to fund their growth.

The reputational risk swirled from unsubstantiated rumours, heavily denied, that the younger Trivedi, Jitender, had been involved in the murder of an associate supplier in Bareilly to whom the Trivedis allegedly owed money. Although Jitender had a noted reputation for settling disputes through violence in his extended student days, the police, after a stretched-out investigation, had found no evidence to support the murder charge. Nevertheless, the murdered supplier's family had continued to pursue the case and would get occasional support from young investigative journalists, but the probability of any prosecution had been low even a decade back, and since then the Trivedis' stock and influence had grown substantially. A second allegation concerned the eldest brother, Davinder, again heavily denied, accusing him of the sexual abuse of a number of poor Dalit women around Bareilly, including three cases of alleged rape, where the women had initially filed a police case and given media interviews before withdrawing their allegations. Supposedly, it was rumoured, following some form of threat or pay-off or both. The Trivedis strongly rejected these allegations and countered that they were being maliciously targeted by those envious of their success and, over time, the stories had lost any traction. Even ten years back, the TDT compliance team had felt these matters were more for the local police and, even though they got raised at each review meeting, they were really more focused on the business risks for loan renewal.

Here, the issue was opaque financials, largely due to the unnecessarily complex holding structures for a business the size of Trivedi Enterprises, which aroused natural suspicions. It was not a secret that a lot of the growth that had been achieved, and planned, was on the back of heavy borrowing across a large number of Indian and overseas banks. But the size and exact nature of these loans, value of collateral, and recovery priorities were unclear enough to make TDT's credit department very nervous about any further extension of their credit lines. At the same time, there was commercial pressure not just to build a potentially profitable business with the Trivedis, but also a recognition that should TDT pull out, it would certainly create a domino effect amongst the other Indian lenders, which would most likely result in a Trivedi default, with a knock-on impact to the reputation of the rest of TDT's Indian franchise.

TDT's credit department required a senior executive to meet the Trivedis and sign off any loan.

Marcus Flint had not intended to be that senior executive. Credit approval was not his area of expertise, but he happened to be in India and was on his way back to Singapore. Whereas the relevant TDT's capital markets management had been keen to give the Trivedi discussion a wide berth, Marcus saw it as an opportunity to expand his area of influence and demonstrate his calibre for further promotion. So, despite being upset and very tired following his visit to Caitanya's in Kerala, he made a stopover in Delhi and arranged to meet the Trivedis for dinner at the Leela Palace hotel.

All three brothers were there, charming and charismatic. Keen, one could have said desperate, had it not been for the relaxed veneer, to secure the loan. All four were malt whisky drinkers and a drink and a distraction was exactly what Marcus desperately needed. It was well into the second bottle of pre-dinner drinks, tucked comfortably into the wide leather armchairs, that the discussions moved onto the business relationship, with Surinder laying forward elaborate ambitions and promises of substantial future business to their trusted advisors and partners, read TDT. But even in his inebriated state, Marcus could sense the current status of the business and its finances were unstable. As he tried to dig deeper, under the gaze of a framed old British commander of the Raj, the conversation would inevitably move to the future plans, the global growth opportunities, and the likely potential for future TDT services from foreign exchange hedging, wealth management services, acquisition support, all there for their trusted partners. Exasperated, Marcus finally took the bull by the horns. "Look, guys, I like the plans, but I need more of the here and now to convince my credit guys."

Surinder leaned back. "Marcus, the first human who would have seen a large crab would have instinctively moved away, but the first man who dared to catch and eat a crab would have been a forward-looking fellow like you."

"Hmm, and probably very brave?" Marcus retorted.

"Or, indeed, very hungry," responded Davinder with a wink, to which all four laughed heartily, and by the third bottle and second helpings of Hyderabadi biryani, the deal was verbally sealed. Frankly, Marcus liked the guys and at that point he didn't care too much about the risks to TDT. Indeed, looking back, it was a shrewd – or shall we say, lucky – decision. Trivedi Enterprises grew multiple times over the next ten years and became one of TDT's biggest Asian – even global – clients, with all revenues registered for performance compensation purposes next to Marcus's name.

By the fourth bottle, and Marcus was now being treated to a local *desi* whisky, they had retired back to the lounge. Marcus was definitely feeling the alcohol and took the opportunity to try to get behind some of the personal rumours starting by asking about life in Bareilly, in Uttar Pradesh, where he had never been, but the brothers handled everything deftly, moving the conversation to Premier League football, of which they knew little, or to cricket, of which they clearly knew a lot. Anything that could lead to questions around Jitender's youthful transgressions or accusations about Davinder were handled adroitly with a straight bat that Rahul Dravid would have been proud of.

Marcus's probing took a sudden halt when standing right in front of him, smiling like a lost brother, was Sanju Kapoor, with Emma standing just behind, carrying a young baby. Marcus had not seen them for about eighteen months since they had moved back to England. While Marcus was still assessing whether it was all a drunken hallucination, Sanju introduced himself, his wife Emma, and sleeping son Anshu, six months' old, to the brothers but turned down the offer to join them for drinks. They had come on holiday to India for Emma and Anshu to meet some of Sanju's extended family, and to see some of the country, as Emma had never been to India before. The Leela was TDT's corporate hotel, so Sanju had taken advantage of the discounted rates, but it was rare for anyone from their capital market's division to pass through Delhi, so they were totally surprised to see each other there.

The Trivedis, keen to show their gratitude to the whole TDT family, offered the Kapoors a stay in their most recently refurbished hotel, an old Rajput fort-cum-palace in Rajasthan, and not too out of the way from where the Kapoors were heading. They would be welcome to enjoy the Royal Suite and be treated like Shekhawati royalty. Sanju declined, but the idea seemed too much for Emma to refuse. They accepted, but keen to get Anshu to bed, said their goodnights and left the foursome to continue their drinking.

Marcus had stayed largely quiet during the Kapoor interlude, but seeing the happy family, the gorgeous Emma, and feeling both the alcohol and the renewed pain from the separation with Caitanya led Marcus into a sombre reflection, which wasn't missed by the Trivedis.

"So, what brings you to India, Marcus-ji, surely you haven't come this far to enjoy a biryani with us?"

Marcus needed to drink, but more, he needed to talk. He needed to share the Caitanya story, his loneliness, his pain, his guilt, his fears and because, by now, he had had a lot of whisky, he shared all of them. He spoke far too much for far too long.

By the end of the evening, both bonds had been made and deals had been done.

TWELVE

The mind loves the unknown.
It loves images whose meaning is unknown, since the
meaning of the mind itself is unknown.

Muttu passed Marcus exiting the toilets on his way back to the library.

Of all the unpleasant things about Marcus, the one that Muttu had noted over the many weeks, and found most grotesque, was Marcus's habit of not washing his hands after going for a piss. It felt strange to him that his disgust for this non-act was more pronounced than for Marcus's patent moral and ethical shortcomings, to the extent that he genuinely struggled, should they cross post-urinals, to hide his revulsion and maintain his constant smile. Yet, he did smile, a fluorescent ivory-white halo, jutting through dark, dry, round lips, against the serene darkness of Sri Lankan heat.

He knew that others with their various daily tribulations or traumas would be wondering what he was smiling about. But Muttu also knew the safety of that gleaming broad grin. He would look at the Swiss pines, the mountain peaks, the lakes, the rivers and green valleys, and see the palms, the golden sands, the dense forests and waterfalls of his childhood. Everywhere, he would discover the silence and serenity that drowned out the internal childhood screams of his neighbours, as the library where his father had first met his mother in Valvettithurai was bombed and burned, with those unlucky to have been gathered that day cindered inside. He would feel the freshness of the cold, the cleanliness of the snow in winter, so distant from the flames of his youth. A smile that allowed him to be the servant, that inspired trust and warmth in a world in which he could trust no one, not even Urs who, though like a surrogate father, had given him back some sense, however dark, to his existence.

Marcus had tried to tease out of Muttu, through banter and familiarity, more about him, but got very little. He did some internet trawling as he would often do around a new office colleague, checking if they had some valuable contacts, understanding their financial worth and perhaps any aristocratic history, etc. But he stopped short of employing one of TDT's investigative agencies, perhaps sensing that he didn't really want to know or, having grown fond of Muttu, didn't wish to expose anything that Muttu was clearly keen not to share. He definitely felt there was more to Muttu's reticence than just being a private introvert.

What Marcus did learn was that Muttu was born in Sri Lanka, somewhere in the north, in a town with a long name he didn't catch, beginning with a 'v' like velvet-something. His family seemed highly educated and relatively well-to-do. Muttu was Tamil and must have grown up during the civil war troubles and, perhaps, that's why his parents, about whom he spoke little, had sent him to study chemistry in Bangalore at the Indian Institute of Science. However, even though Muttu had stayed to do a postgraduate, Marcus could find no trace of his name in any of the research papers around the relevant time frame, and the Murali name was simply too common in Sri Lanka to make any headway there.

But how did he end up in Dubai? Why would someone so hard-working, charismatic, and intelligent choose to go and work effectively as a house help. Maybe it was the pay, but that seemed unlikely, and then how did he get to Switzerland, and now as a boutique hotel manager-cum-cook. Marcus knew that Urs had taken the Villa Traxler off one of his clients, the Aljawahiris, and Muttu was one of the first of Urs' recruits – maybe that was the connection, but he dismissed the idea again that Muttu was there for the money. The inability to find any trace had gone from being a minor curiosity for Marcus to a small irritation. Of course, what Marcus didn't know was that along that intercontinental journey, Muttu Murali had changed his name twice, and while Marcus was searching for where Muttu had come from, others were very keen to know what he had become.

Marcus went back to the library. He switched on the espresso machine and took out the tray of capsules, selected a purple Arpeggio, and walked across to the drinks' cabinet as the coffee machine hissed and gurgled to heat up. Above the cabinet hung a gold-plated mirror. Marcus looked at his three-day stubble, the specks of grey getting more pronounced. He poured himself a large Benriach – it matched the strength of the espresso. The villa was quiet and still. Marcus was on his own. By the espresso machine was an old iPad, which could connect to the Sonos system. Marcus picked a random playlist, and to the sounds of Radiohead's 'Creep' he slumped into one of the leather chairs, briefly mulled over the obsessiveness of the lyrics, finished the coffee in two gulps, rested the whisky tumbler on his knee, closed his eyes, leaned his head back onto the shoulder of the chair, and silently lip-mimed words to the song, drifting away, self-questioning whether he was a weirdo, or a creep, or both, and what on earth he was doing there.

Marcus drank a couple more whiskies in the afternoon. The call with Steve Johnson to persuade him to undertake an Asia compliance audit was smooth enough – the region was due a review and Steve had heard of some of the bullying behaviour through HR.

The one with Pierre was short. He didn't bother to ask how Marcus was or when he planned to get back. In reality, no one in the office was particularly bothered about anyone else's well-being but it was normal practice to at least pretend. Perhaps Pierre was just heavily distracted or just didn't want to appear close to Marcus as their future relationship could get strained. The Epsilon review was going badly, though Pierre didn't elaborate on any new developments. A culture and diversity study that Marcus suggested for Asia was acknowledged as a good idea, but Pierre wanted it to be global. Marcus should present the idea for discussion at the next senior management executive committee 'Exco' call and Pierre would support, so should go ahead. Pierre ended the call by saying that he expected there to be some senior-level changes on the back of the Epsilon report. He didn't have all the findings but wanted to be ahead of the game. Marcus understood that to mean 'let's look for scapegoats before anyone starts to challenge us'. Was that a hint that Marcus would be asked to leave? It wasn't obvious from Pierre's tone. Getting fired might not be the worst option; he could potentially keep his deferred pay if he could get out without evidence of negligence, and he'd possibly be secure from any further investigation into his own role. On the other hand, TDT may fire him, leave him to fight on his own, be the scapegoat and cancel his deferred pay. Maybe he should put his hand up, pretend to fall on his sword to save others, negotiating to keep his stock and exoneration from any future sanction.

There was what should have been a more disturbing call with Rahul. Over the past year there had been a handful of incidents in the female toilets where someone had soiled the walls of the cubicles and the shared wash area with presumably her own faeces during the early evening. There were obviously no cameras in the area, and data from security card entry/exit times had not particularly narrowed down the individual – the damage had been spotted around 6.30pm–7.00pm, when a lot of the staff would still have been at work. All but one of the incidents had been on the trading floor – the exception had been in the toilets next to the plush client meeting rooms on the top floor shared with the senior TDT executives. However, it was not necessarily the case that the culprit was someone who sat either on the trading floor or within the executive suite, though they had tight security access. In fact, it was not even necessarily someone female. The bank, or rather the UK head, had paid the cleaners large cash bonuses to remove all traces and stay quiet, but they had described how the individual had used their nails to scratch into the walls, and even superficially etch the mirrors to embed their waste into the creases like a macabre Polyfilla. Marcus, Rahul, and a small number of senior London management had kept the matter confidential with the facilities team, issuing a general circular for staff and management to keep on top of their and their teams' mental health issues. Although publicly he would speak passionately about staff care, Marcus's view on the matter was that people were paid enough to keep their issues out of the office and should focus on making money for the bank. It wasn't his job to give them a kiss and a cuddle.

When the call came from Rahul, Marcus knew it wouldn't be something he necessarily wanted to hear about.

"Rahul, what's up, bud?"

"Good, Marcus, how are you?"

"Completely swamped with calls." Marcus sighed, though the reality was more that Rahul was disturbing his light post-whisky siesta. "Listen, while I have you, there is going to be compliance audit in Asia, just so you're prepared, and also Pierre wants to do one of those pointless HR exercises, a cultural study – global – but keep that to yourself for now."

"I realise you're busy, Marcus, won't keep you long, but need to get your thoughts on something. You remember this saga with the ladies' toilets?"

"Yeah, you've found the culprit? Just tell me it's no one in my world."

"I may have. I was in Paris last week and out for drinks with a few of the operations team. You know it's a smallish office so nothing stays secret there. Anyway, someone spilt over some wine, screamed '*merde*', and headed to the toilets to wipe it off, at which point another guy cracks something in French and they all started giggling. It turns out that a couple of months back, they had a similar incident to ours in one of their toilets on the trading floor. So, I called around the other offices to see if there was anything anywhere else and, sure enough, last autumn, in Madrid, the same. I thought maybe if it is the same person, it would almost certainly have been someone quite senior and in sales who would be visiting clients in different regions."

"I don't like the sound of where this is heading, Rahul."

"No, you won't. I cross-checked the dates with call reports and narrowed it down to one person who was in all those offices on the relevant dates – Simone de Chassey."

"Simone! No, from Private Banks! Are you sure? I had to push really hard to get her to MD."

"Well, as I say, we can't be 100% sure it's her or even that it is a 'her' or the same person in the different locations. This whole thing would have started before she became managing director. Question is what to do. Don't really want to discuss it with anyone else, would stigmatise and could even lead to legal issues, but not an easy conversation to hold directly. Somewhat embarrassing if we've got it wrong."

"So much for a female role model. I can't get my head round it. We just promoted her, gave her a team to lead, arguably maybe a little ahead of time, and she's relatively well paid. Try to see if there are any issues out of work."

"She is very good and would say definitely a role model for all, male and female. Usually so calm as far as I can tell. That's what makes it so hard to believe. There could be other things going on out of work, Marcus, but I got hold of the photos from facilities; really not pleasant, but basically looks like whoever did this spread their shit all across the wall using their hands and then tried to write something on the mirrors. A couple of times you can make out words like 'F off TDT', 'TDT shit here'. Even in Paris, it was in English!"

"I still can't believe it's her, I need to think about what to do. Can you check her emails and listen to her phone tapes for forty-eight hours before each incident? Let's see if that dumps anything – pardon the pun." Marcus let himself have a wry smile, and then saw another opportunity for his wit. "Not ideal if this hits the fan, ahem. If you need higher approval to get access to the tapes, tell them I have some compliance concerns that I can't discuss at the moment – they should release the recordings. Call me back once you've done that. Is there anything else cooking, Rahul?"

"Only other thing is that when I was talking to the facility guys, they mentioned they'd found a couple of bags of white powder in the client meeting rooms."

"I'm not surprised, frankly, but could be anyone in the building, and what do they mean, white powder? Have they tested it?"

"It's true it could be anyone in the building but when you're back, you'll see this juvenile tittering on the floor when various managers come back after lunch, with whispered comments and backs of hands raised to nostrils, all to jovial laughter."

"OK, Rahul, they're a bunch of arseholes. I've got to go. I'll raise it with Pierre." Marcus switched off the phone. He had, of course, no intention to raise with it Pierre, but he was now wishing he hadn't kick-started the culture review.

Marcus shuffled into the sofa and pondered over the discussion. Virtually everyone they hired came from a highly educated background; the jobs were interesting relative to most, they were extremely well paid, and the pressures were certainly nothing like those of some other professions. But half the floor had some issue, couldn't handle what they had but wanted to be promoted, were paid well above their value but didn't think they were paid enough. Some of them would spend half their day licking his arse, and telling him how great their teams were, but had the loyalties of a turkey farmer doting over his flock of fowls before Christmas. Yes, there would be a lack of job security but any firing decisions were often political; keep your head down, talk the talk and there was plenty of mediocrity that survived any culls. So why did people put that at risk? Did they just attract risk-takers? Did they have such private wealth they didn't care? Was it overbearing competitiveness that everyone wanted to be the wealthiest, have the most attractive partners, take the wildest holidays? Did they earn so much that the only excitement left was in taking drugs or curating self-exhibitions in the bathrooms. *Simone is above all that*, he thought. He really hoped it wasn't her. His contemplation ended on getting a text from Emma – 'Ollie is home'.

He didn't have much to say but had promised to speak to Ollie that evening, and it sounded like Emma was desperate to talk to him too. He heard Urs come back and glanced out of the window to see him talking seriously with Muttu, both with signalling nods.

"Hello, Daddy, how are you? Is your FaceTime not working again?"

"I think it might be. I just don't like to use it so I can concentrate better on what you are saying. How was your day at school?"

"Fine."

"Emma said you had your first hockey match this week. She was saying how much you enjoyed it."

"A bit boring. I only got one touch of the ball."

"Oh, it will come with practice. How was the first golf lesson?"

"Fine. When are you coming home, Daddy?"

"Very soon. I loved your painting, Ollie. Lovely colours. Where did you get the idea from?"

"Don't know. Are you feeling better?"

"Yes, thank you. Maybe the idea came from somewhere we went on holiday. Maybe that trip to Morocco."

"Don't know. Bye, Daddy. I think Emma wants to talk to you."

"Oh OK, bye, Ollie. Love you. Speak soon."

"Hello, Marcus." Emma had taken the phone.

"Hello, Emma." Marcus felt she sounded a bit tight, as much as Ollie had been childlike short earlier.

"Marcus, I'll come straight to it. I need to know how you are, to see you. I've arranged for Ollie to stay the weekend with Jemima in two weeks and am coming over for the weekend."

"Really, Emma, I'm fine. I'll be back soon."

"Well, if you're in London before that weekend, that'll be great, and I'll cancel the flight, but I'm all booked up. Should have done it much earlier to be honest."

"Sure, Emma, OK."

"Listen, I need to get Ollie his dinner – he's starving. Can talk later if you have time but need to go now." Marcus felt the tension in her voice, and his anxiety with the perspiration in his palms. He put the phone in his pocket. He could hear Urs outside.

Urs was getting something out of the car. Behind him, darkish clouds trundled across the sky, magnetically dragging their shadows across the valley slopes.

"Hey, Urs!" Marcus did his best to sound strong and authoritative though the short gulp for air and a faint burp revealed something wasn't quite right. "Emma is coming over for the weekend in two weeks. Her sister is looking after Ollie."

Urs stared at Marcus for a couple of seconds, looked straight into his moistened eyes, then glanced sideways at Muttu who had walked out on the veranda. "Did you catch that, Muttu?"

"Yes." Muttu was looking at Marcus and Marcus noticed a rare occasion when Muttu had momentarily contracted his smile.

"Good." Again a solid, deep, I'm-in-charge, I'm-in-control voice, as Marcus turned and walked quickly back to the library and poured himself another bigger glass of the Benriach.

THIRTEEN

Each day my reason tells me so;
But reason doesn't rule in love, you know.

His knuckles ached after another drunken bout with the punchbag. A tattered blood-tinted A4 picture of Rohan Bhogal, the ex-TDT compliance officer now in charge of the FSA investigation, lay on the gym floor. Marcus had then let out his anger and frustration at a printout of Pierre who, deliberately or not, wasn't providing any clarity on the investigation.

It was a heavily overcast, blustery morning. He brought his coffee up to his room and sat at the little desk by the window and observed the rain splattering against the pane, listening to the ghoulish howls of wind encircling the villa, whipped into a frenzy like orca whales feasting on a shoal of tuna. He found it grim to stay in his room alone, but on days of little light like this one, it was even darker in the library, and it made no sense to be outside.

The call with Emma the previous night had taken the timing out of his control. She had been terse and stubborn as she sometimes could be, but he'd tell her he would come back in three weeks and hopefully she'd cancel her ticket. He had been away too long. He was struggling to see the solutions, but he needed to restore an image of being in charge, of being positive, and of not risking appearing to be the fall-guy for Epsilon. A brief conversation with Urs that morning had firmed up his convictions and injected a little much-needed positivity.

"You know, Marcus, I don't think it's in any way a foregone conclusion that they'll stumble across any of your private emails or anything unrelated to their primary focus."

"I know but I am pretty sure Tani was one of those pushing those products."

"Yes, but your guy in Asia – wasn't he saying there was hardly any risk out there?"

"Andrea, yes, you may be right, Urs. They should only be taking a cursory look."

"You know as well as I do that the regulators and management need to be seen to be doing these things. They'll stop wasting their time when they see there is nothing there."

"Hmm, yep, maybe I'm getting too fatalistic out here in the Swiss cold." Marcus sighed.

"Agreed. I think your imagination is running ahead of you." Urs smiled reassuringly. "Deal with Epsilon and don't let other anxieties clog your mind. You can't see the path in a fog. Then you can handle the other stuff in your own time and place."

"Yeah, fuck, I need to get back. If these guys start sensing I'm weak, they'll kill me, even if I do survive Epsilon. Been dithering so long, I've let the worst-case scenario become the fucking default in my head."

"Exactly. Show them the healthy and fit Marcus is back."

"Yeah. Thanks, Urs. This fucking Emma visit has taken the timing out of my control."

"On the other hand, it's sprung you into action."

Marcus knew Urs was just keen to get him out, but he also felt Urs was being genuinely sympathetic and was grateful for the conversation.

He would start by handling the day-to-day issues head-on, as he would have done in the office. There was a management team 'Exco' call later that week and he needed to prepare himself; be bullish, speak like a man who had no concerns, be familiar with the detail, and play the politics as per normal.

He'd speak with Zhao Kun on some pretext of wanting to hear about his latest algorithm, and then check if all is good. If the topic of culture came up with his peers at the 'Exco', he could take the attack to Handscombe by pretending Zhao had been in touch, say how impressive and important he is to the bank but that he seemed out of sorts, and mention the bullying case in front of Pierre.

He needed to call Emma. She'd be getting back soon from the school run. She actually called him first.

"Hello, darling, listen, I'm so sorry I was so short on the call last night."

"That's OK. I was just about to ring to see if you were OK."

"Sorry, things just came out a bit wrong. It's just that you hadn't been in touch for a few days. I do worry about you, and I need to come and see you. I know you said you'd be home in three to four weeks, but Jemima has the weekend at home on her own and wanted to have Ollie, and I just thought I could see you and also visit where you have been all this time." She spoke quickly, wanted to sound empathetic, and whereas before he had manged to dissuade her from visiting, she definitely wasn't going to give him the option of changing her mind.

"But, darling, as you say, I'll be out of here myself in two to three weeks—"

"Yes," she interrupted him, "but I want to see where you have been all this time and meet Urs and Muttu and see the mountain view. All these things you've been talking about. It will be a nice break before you come back."

"But we can return in the summer for a few days. It would be lovelier and I'm sure I'd be feeling better."

"Oh, but you know you'll be busy at work, and we'd have Ollie. It won't be the same."

"OK, I'll let Urs know. You're right. It'd be great. And don't worry about last night. I know I've been a pain these last few weeks. Do you mind if I go – I need to call some guys in Asia. Can we speak later?"

"Yes, of course, really looking forward to seeing you and holding you."

"Me too. It's been too long, as you say. Love you and speak soon."

"Love you."

Marcus went downstairs and stood under the canopy outside the entrance, stroked the scarring on the knuckles of his right hand, and lit himself a cigarette. He stood in his gown – the escaping heat from the open door behind keeping him sufficiently warm. The rain thrashed itself onto the drive in angry and uncontrolled bursts interspersed with swirling horizontal blasts, like a boxer exploring new unprotected angles of the protagonist.

His mind switched to the monsoon rains in Singapore and how they provided a soothing reprieve in the heat; something to step into, something that had infused their passion into his and Caitanya's dripping wet bodies when they would walk back surreptitiously to his apartment.

* * *

The first time Marcus passed Caitanya Iyer (German Indian, then mid-twenties) was at lunchtime outside one of the cafés in the air-conditioned ground-floor mall adjacent to Marina Boulevard. Or so she had said. He had been engrossed on his Blackberry and had not particularly noticed the young associate who had joined his salesforce after graduating from Insead. She had been getting a sushi takeaway pack when she noticed Marcus walking along past the shops and positioned herself to make eye contact and smile, but the interaction was fleeting, and the next time their paths crossed was late at night in the gym at the Shangri-La hotel in Tokyo.

Marcus thought about how different things could have turned out had his local lover, Satomi Matsui, been well enough to entertain him as she would normally have done when he stayed in Tokyo. He would spend his evenings there for his two-to-three-day business trip with the hotel booking a wasted and expensive front. This time, she texted just before he boarded to say she was down with flu and couldn't see him. His agitation turned to double-strength irritation when the flight was delayed so he didn't arrive at the hotel until well past midnight. Despite having enjoyed the business-class alcohol, he decided he needed a swim to get to sleep. He moved gracefully and alone, gliding the lengths of the dimly lit pool, its floor-to-ceiling glass along three walls staring into the gloom-leaden darkness hanging above the ember glows of the Tokyo canopy, lost in his thoughts, lost in the din of those countless blurred lights from the tower blocks. So lost as to not notice the silhouette of a young slim body with hair tied up, running on the treadmill in the gym, through the darkened windows on the other side.

It took her a few minutes to be certain as to who he was, but then carried on running in the hope he would look up and she could introduce herself. When she had arrived in Singapore, she had made a mental note of all the desk heads and senior executives and was attuned enough into the office gossip to know that Marcus Flint was tipped to be the next Asia sales head, her boss. Well, actually, her boss's boss's boss.

He obviously hadn't seen her, and probably wouldn't even have recognised her. She wondered if it was appropriate to acknowledge him so late at night in a faraway hotel; sweaty, though she didn't feel too odorous, dressed in a short red gym top with black leggings. Maybe he'd be embarrassed being interrupted in the pool. Perhaps it would be better to come down early for breakfast and catch him then; though then again, he might not have breakfast there, he might have a meeting, he might be with others. In any case, what was the harm in saying hello; she was in his division, he was the big boss, nothing for him to be embarrassed about; they were hardly naked in a Finnish sauna! She was in sales, she needed to be bold – imagine if it got out that they had been in the same place, and she had been too timid to introduce herself. No, she would just say hello and goodnight. At least when he next saw her in the office or saw her sales' numbers, he'd know who she was.

She removed her trainers, entered the pool area through the corner door, cleared her throat and waited for him to stop at her side of his length.

"Marcus Flint!"

Her voice came out a little firmer, sharper, and harsher than she had intended, rising in intonation and volume as if she were calling her maid, Chandni, from a neighbouring room.

It completely and visibly startled him. He belched but pretended to clear his throat.

"Sir, my name is Caitanya Iyer. I work at TDT." She realised she'd unsettled him, and her voice tailed off to a whisper. "For you, I mean, sir."

"Yes, yes, I know. How are you?" Marcus wiped the water from his eyes and instinctively held out his wet arm to shake hands.

She realised her own palm was a little clammy but felt obliged to take his. "I'm sorry, I didn't mean to disturb you." She noticed his wide forearms and how his smile skewed slightly to the right. It reminded her of the Popeye cartoons she used to watch as a child. That would become her nickname for him when they started to spend more time alone together.

"No, that's quite alright. I'm just finishing. Look, it's late but I'm going to dry off and go to the bar for a nightcap. Please join me if you can, though I realise it's late."

"No, of course I can, sir."

"Please, call me Marcus. Did you say Tani Iyer?"

"Caitanya, but Tani or Tanya is fine."

Twenty minutes later, they met in the bar. She was surprised by how short he was close-up – not much taller than her in her heels.

Marcus was astonished more by how quickly she had done her make-up and transformed from gym buff into an epitome of refinement in a perfectly ironed black sleeveless cocktail dress with ankle-length boots. She had wrapped a cream pashmina shawl around her shoulders and elegantly seated herself on a bar stool next to his, wrapping her thin smooth calves, and resting her feet on the metallic pedestal. When she leant forward, he could smell her subtle perfume – one he didn't recognise but was warm, gentle, and slightly musky.

He took a double Yamazaki whisky. She asked for a rooibos tea. He wasn't able to tempt her into taking something alcoholic as she had a client meeting in the morning. Although the view was almost identical to the one from the empty pool, the bar was packed. He joked it was full of Europeans who couldn't sleep for the time difference, like in that Scarlett Johansson film.

"*Lost in Translation*, you mean. Yes, I love that film, and it has male stars too." She giggled.

"You know, I can never remember their names."

"I can imagine." She giggled again.

"It's a great view, don't you think, of Tokyo? That's why I always like to take a swim here during the night." Marcus's mood had mellowed significantly in Caitanya's company. He could not help but notice her large light-brown eyes, her mannerisms and accent that were more Continental European than Indian, and that she looked as captivating in that black dress hugging her slim frame as she had done in the gym. He wondered how he had not seen her around the office before.

He asked who she was meeting. She was there to see a couple of family offices and she asked if he was able to join her – it would be a great learning opportunity for her to watch one of TDT's top salesmen in action. He obliged. He was in Tokyo mainly for internal meetings but obviously, clients came first, though in reality the number of clients he'd actually seen that year could have been counted on the fingers of one hand.

The two meetings went very well, and he suggested they should do it again. He opined how they worked so well as a duo. She was able to offer the content in deep detail and he provided the charisma, the gravitas, the feeling for the client to seem important as one of the senior bank executives had deigned to join them, and, naturally, a broader perspective of TDT. She didn't feel any dismay as to his total myopia of his own arrogance seeing it simply a function of his success, seniority, position, and power.

Over the next few months, he joined her in a handful of meetings. She would only invite him when she was planning to attend alone so as not to create any unnecessary envy in the office, or even any suspicion as to their closeness. All the meetings, but one, were in Singapore so they would arrive separately – it was an unspoken tactic that Marcus appreciated. The one overseas trip was in Hong Kong and Marcus thought about arranging an evening junk boat trip across the harbour but decided against it and settled for an early evening dinner alone. He realised he was growing fond of Caitanya but was conscious that she was a junior member of his team, and he would need to keep things in control.

Nevertheless, when she mentioned the mentee programme for junior employees and asked for his recommendation as to who to approach to be her mentor, he couldn't resist suggesting himself, even though that was strictly against the guidelines as he was also hierarchically her line manager. She, obviously, was very appreciative, and in any case, it would have been too awkward for her to say no. This meant that not only did he have a regular weekly meeting with her, but he could also invite her to some internal management discussions or the occasional client event. That was how he once introduced her to Urs Waelchli. When HR questioned why he was a mentor to someone in his team, he passed it off as: having seen Caitanya at a couple of client meetings, he felt that, in the short term, she would best benefit from having some direct senior sales guidance from him.

In actual fact, he was very impressed with her professionalism, drive, and detailed product knowledge. So much so that he sponsored her for her first promotion after just a year in the role. Indeed, she was the only one promoted so early from her MBA cohort. At this stage, no one in the office would have noticed them as anything other than distant colleagues, mentor and mentee. In truth, they were getting to know each other quite well and the staid office interactions had moved onto some gentle flirtation.

She would tease him that he strutted around the office like the peacocks in her garden back in India.

"Bet you'd like to see me unfurl those feathers," he mocked.

"Yes, Marcus, go on, do a dance. I love peacocks dancing

and I've never seen you dance." She chuckled, stroking her long hair behind her, exposing her slender neck, and instinctively but subconsciously, innocently, and fleetingly licked her upper lip with the tip of her tongue. It was innocent and natural, but she knew it was seductive.

Marcus couldn't help but notice the flick of her dark tongue brush her lips. Despite his evident self-confidence, it took him a split second to recompose. "Me, dance! Come on, Tani, that'll just kill me with embarrassment."

"Oh no, I don't want you to die. A dead peacock – it's only useful as a feather duster." Their eyes caught each other. She blushed, making them both wonder what she meant. She looked at her watch. "Oh, I've got to go," she blurted before quickly getting up and walking off.

Marcus got to know that Caitanya had grown up in Germany. Her father worked for an Indian IT consultancy and had come to Europe reluctantly, and initially only for a few months, to assist with an outsourcing project back to India. Although stylistically very Indian, his clients appreciated his hard-working mantra, his integrity, and his plain-speaking. So much so that he was asked to move permanently and became key to the growth of the business, learnt German and French, and after a year brought his family to settle in Eschborn just outside Frankfurt.

Venkat Iyer's European earnings allowed him to support not only his parents and in-laws back in Kerala, but also the education of his three younger siblings, allowing them also, ultimately, to emigrate to Australia and Canada. He constructed a large house near Alleppey, along the coast, that had the potential one day, he hoped, to be run as a hotel. But he was never truly comfortable in Germany. Even though they went back to India every summer holiday, he desperately missed his family and his home in Kerala. The family were culturally very conservative. Even amongst their Indian friends, none unfortunately from Kerala, the Iyers were considered very traditional – they didn't smoke or drink, indeed, were repulsed at the idea, and never touched meat. Generally, they, therefore, kept themselves to themselves, smiling at, but never really engaging with, their German or Turkish neighbours. It was the earnings and the support it provided the wider family that kept them there.

They would do anything for their daughters, but the Iyer parents found it difficult to watch Caitanya and her younger sister, Lavanya, growing up as young German teens – the clothes they wore, the way they spoke to their elders, and the carefree mingling with boys. Caitanya and Lavanya also struggled living a double life – one at home and the other outside. They were so grateful for everything their parents did for them but felt so constrained, and this made them even more rebellious in pushing the boundaries of what the parents allowed. It felt like they were even more restrictive than their family and friends back in Kerala. They had started to secretly go to parties, pretending to go to friends' houses for homework, and changing into more revealing outfits that they kept in their friends' cupboards.

The arguments around their behaviours got louder and longer. Things were set for a tense explosion and explode they did.

Venkat Iyer had been away on a business trip but got an earlier-than-planned flight back so he could arrive just in time for the girls' school day to finish. As always after his trips, he was laden with gifts for his wife and the girls and was looking forward to seeing them and enjoy the delight of them unwrapping their presents. He decided he could make it back in time and pick up the girls just after school, surprising them on their way home. Caitanya was walking back in a short skirt, an off-the-shoulder top, her school bag draped over one shoulder, playfully laughing with a group of boys. As her father drove closer, he could make out a white stub and a red glow in her right hand. She took it to her mouth and puffed out the smoke just as his car pulled up.

That was the final straw, and despite the break in their education, the next summer the two girls were taken out of the local school and sent to India to live with their grandmother and attend the St Mary's Convent boarding school near Cochin.

Marcus sensed no bitterness or anger in this story within Caitanya, but just a respect and affection for her parents, and a feeling that she had let them down. It was obvious that she enjoyed her time in India – the sisters had spent a lot of their childhood there on holidays and she adored her grandmother. They were mocked for their accents but at least didn't get any of the casual racist abuse that sometimes surfaced back in Germany.

By the time she had graduated from the Indian Institute of Technology Madras, she felt she had become the complete image of what her parents expected her to be, but she craved to work before they chose, or ideally she chose with their blessing, who she should marry, and so they agreed for her to move to Mumbai where she worked in the strategy department of a German multinational.

After four years, she was selected for sponsorship for an MBA, and she won a place at Insead. Her parents were suitably proud but those months in Fontainebleau reawakened her love of Europe, the West, and the perceived freedoms that included a regrettable drunken night in a hotel in Paris with a fellow German student. Her parents expected her to return to Mumbai, but she applied for a job at TDT in Singapore, thinking this would allow her some space, yet still be close to them now that they had returned to Kerala, and so they would be less worried about her returning to the days of her youth. And the fact she had doubled her compensation in joining TDT helped to persuade them that TDT Singapore was indeed a great choice. Despite her protestations that she was still so young, her mother and grandmother started to entertain potential marriage proposals ideally with a suitably successful local Keralite that would bring the Singapore sojourn to an automatic end.

Marcus's longest relationship had lasted under three months and that was when he was in London. His upbringing had shown him no value in commitments. His life was a series of short flings that occasionally included colleagues from other departments and even clients, but after a couple of incidents with interns as a young managing director that could easily have ended his career, he had a clear and firm look-but-don't-touch policy to underlings.

Despite his aversion to relationships, he would still look on enviously at other loving couples, grudgingly but heartily congratulate their engagements, attend the marriage ceremonies, coo convincingly when they started families, and then smile inwardly if they then separated and divorced. He recognised it as something he didn't have but couldn't synthesise what he truly missed – the companionship, the love, the image that he perhaps needed to progress his career, or just the experience, but he definitely missed something, and that feeling had been getting progressively stronger.

His feelings for Caitanya had also grown stronger and confusing. He had started thinking about her in between their weekly catch-ups and would look for other opportunities to see her, but he had no idea what she thought, and in any case, there could be no future. He had promoted her; she was his mentee and worked in his team; if anything happened between them and became public, his time at TDT and possibly his career in banking would be over. He'd learnt his lessons, but the tension had become so strong that he decided he had to do something to create some distance between them. He would start by transferring her mentorship to somebody else.

Caitanya had also noted the time she was spending with Marcus beyond the mentor/mentee meetings. No one had said anything, but she was conscious that her peers may start noticing and commenting. She also wondered what he must be thinking. He had been so good to her, and she loved his company, but he was the boss; how could she suggest that perhaps she had a different mentor? But surely if the issue was important, that was something that he should be worrying about as well. Equally, maybe even more, it was her growing fondness of him that was also bothering her. There was absolutely no future there – *he'd never pass as a Keralite*, she reflected amusingly, and Marcus had never said or done anything to suggest he had any feelings, in any case. However, she needed to be cooler, respectful, of course, perhaps not invite him to her client meetings unless he asked but move the relationship to something similar to the ones she had with the other management.

It was, therefore, with some nervousness that she watched Marcus approach her at the end of a leaver's drinks party one evening, in front of the whole division. He smiled but spoke firmly, formally, and perhaps, loudly enough for any nearby eavesdroppers to hear.

"Caitanya, I was wondering if you could pop by my office tomorrow. I've been thinking and now that we've done a number of client meetings together, perhaps we should transfer my mentor role to another of the senior executives in a different part of the bank. It's more in line with the firm's policy and you'd get to meet others to build your network."

He had anticipated that she might look a bit upset but she looked blank, unsure as to what was happening.

"If you pop by, we can take a look at who else could be most appropriate, and if we agree I'll drop them a note. Most people would be very happy to take on the role. Would that work for you?"

"Yes, of course. What time shall I see you?"

"Towards the end of the day, I should be free. We won't need that long."

After she left, Marcus called Andrea saying he fancied a drink. The two stayed out until the early hours. Marcus didn't say anything, but Andrea could sense Marcus was upset about something. Caitanya went back to her apartment and cried. Even though she had got what she had wanted, she felt a feeling of rejection and loss. Both had a sense of relief that something dangerous had been averted. Unfortunately, that feeling lasted less than twenty-four hours.

After their chat the next day, during which they selected a managing director from the finance function to take over as Caitanya's mentor, Marcus tried to sugar-coat the conversation with comments like his door was, needless to say, always open to her, and that he was available for any client discussions if she wanted him there, but sensing the need to finish things on a happier and more positive note, he suggested they have a quick drink nearby. The one drink became dinner followed by more drinks at a beach-side bar.

The next morning, she awoke naked wrapped under his Popeye-like forearms, her long dark hair with its soft highlights spread across the white pillows and bedsheet. She opened her eyes to see him sleeping underneath her. At that moment, she felt both sad and happy, annoyed and calm, excited and regretful, clear but confused. Her eyes moistened as she thought of her father, of the cigarette incident, and of the night in Paris when she swore she would never repeat that again until her wedding night. They lay still. Marcus was actually awake but kept his eyes shut. He took in and loved the sensation of her soft cool skin in that Singapore heat; her light exotic scent of spices, temples, and the gardens of India; the gentle, sensual, arousing weight of her thighs on his; and the caressing forearm lying across his chest. But he needed to make sure that this didn't get out. He hoped that this could just be a one-off and forgotten about. They both knew that wouldn't be the case. A line had been crossed and the passion had been too great to hold back.

FOURTEEN

Love is of all passions the strongest,
For it attacks simultaneously the head, the heart and the
senses.

The call with Marcus had gone better than she had hoped, with little pushback to her visit. For the first time in a long time, he sounded positive, ready to come back. It felt like a corner had been turned. She mustn't let the situation revert though, no matter what his stresses at work. She felt a sense of guilt that she hadn't taken a more active role and been closer when he had needed her. Yet she continued to have an uncomfortable, lingering anxiety about what had overcome him, but she wouldn't let that conversation get in the way of making the coming weekend perfect – he could tell her in his own time.

She would get her hair cut, short, like when they first started seeing each other, and get some new clothes. The call with Marcus the previous night had been brief and stressful. This morning, she felt a true positive energy. Perhaps she could persuade him to give up work – they certainly didn't need any more money, and they could spend more time with each other and Ollie. But Marcus was so ambitious and absorbed in his work; it would take a real effort to get him to walk away from

TDT. But now could be the time. It would need some thinking and planning. She would have to think of a new direction, develop other interests in him. It would be the best way to 'repay' him, though that wasn't the right word, for all those months and years when he stood like a rock with her, when the world around her had eviscerated.

He had to be able to lean on her at this, his time of need. They would resolve everything together. She wasn't going to make the same mistakes as she had with Sanju.

* * *

Emma didn't see Sanju for about three years after the pool incident. He had not come on their annual French holidays with his parents and was now at university. She knew that he'd seen Jemima at a couple of parties and met her for drinks in Blackheath Village. As Jemima hadn't said anything, it was safe to assume that he hadn't shared the 'pool kiss story' with her, for which she was relieved. The Kapoors lived in Maze Hill, the other side of Greenwich Park from them in Blackheath, just far enough away for her to feel relatively safe that she wouldn't accidentally bump into him. He did, however, turn up to her eighteenth birthday party.

She had not been keen on having a party, but her parents had insisted on a black-tie function like the one they had had for Jemima. Obviously, the Kapoors would be invited and as her birthday was in July, there was a strong possibility that Sanju would be at home. The whole prospect of seeing him on her special day had made her even more antagonistic to the party. She didn't want him there but couldn't disinvite him without raising the reasons. The embarrassment from three years ago had turned to a humiliated and scorned anger. She didn't wish to see the hubris in his eyes. She didn't want to feel the inferiority again. Hopefully, he'd be diplomatic enough not to show up, or at least to keep away from her.

Emma placed herself in the dining room and kitchen area where the drinks and food had been laid out. That way, she could see or hear who was arriving and being met by her parents or sister. The guests would then come through to get their drinks where she would welcome and talk to them. Just after 8.00pm, the Kapoors arrived. The house was already quite full, and it would be easy to avoid someone if she wanted to. She could hear Jemima welcome them and ask why Sanju wasn't there.

"Oh, he's coming. He just drove us up the hill. He'll be here once he's parked the car." The exchange sent a chill through Emma's spine and made her even more annoyed as to why she was so concerned about his presence. It was her birthday, after all. She calmed a little as Mrs Kapoor came into the kitchen, gave her a warm hug, told her how beautiful she looked, and reminded her again how Emma used to love the rotis she cooked when Emma was two.

A few minutes later, Sanju arrived. She could see him out of the corner of her eyes. He was taller and fuller now. The hair was the same, but the persona was all south London swagger.

"Good evening, Mrs Roberts." He kissed Emma's mother and said something to send her into a gentle fit of laughter. Emma couldn't make out the conversation, but every syllable uttered by Sanju seemed to be getting her mum screeching ever more loudly. Her father joined them, and the two men chortled over something else before her dad started slapping Sanju heartily on the back. Mrs Kapoor left the kitchen to greet her son.

"*Aré* Sanju, why don't you go and say hello to Emma, it's her birthday. *Kitchen mein hain. Ja na.*"

"Sure, Ma, I can see her."

Emma turned away to get a drink. She poured a vodka with some orange juice, which she unintentionally finished in one gulp, so she still had her back to him, refilling, when she heard his voice over her shoulder.

"Hello, Em. Happy Birthday."

Emma turned. "Oh, hello, Sanju, I didn't realise you were here," she spoke with the indifferent tone of a soporific court clerk reading the day's timetable, then jerked to grab a hand on her left. "This is Rhys, my boyfriend."

Sanju sensed the cold abruptness in her voice and perhaps he had expected it, but for a split second, as she stared at him blankly, he experienced something he certainly hadn't expected. He froze like a man who had just found a previously unnoticed map to the treasures of El Dorado lying at the bottom of his sock drawer. He hadn't seen Emma for a few years. The braces had gone. The long thick wavy blonde hair was now a bob that shaped her small face like an art frame displaying two beautiful emerald-like eyes sitting above those high cheekbones. She was wearing natural pink lipstick with long pearl-drop earrings and a silver necklace. Her sleeveless shiny silver-grey dress hugged her lithe body. Sanju would be astonished even years later about how much he remembered in detail of how she looked at that moment.

He turned to Rhys. His mouth was dry. The swagger had hit a momentary blip. "Hello, Rhys, very nice to meet you. Emma and I are old friends."

"Family friends," she blurted sharply.

"Hi, what was the name? Was it Sanju? Don't think Emma has mentioned you previously."

"No, hasn't crossed my mind." Emma was now looking round the room with an expression of intense boredom. Rhys detected the obvious tension but chose the wrong tack to try to diffuse it.

"Was it not Sanju in some of your old holiday photos?"

Sanju and Emma could not engage themselves fast enough to change the subject. Both mumbled something incoherent over each other before Emma uttered disinterestedly, "Sanju is studying physics at Oxford, as you do, la-di-dah!" and shrugged her shoulders as she semi-rolled her eyes.

"Yes, that's right. Have you decided what you'll do now – I think you were planning on law last time we spoke?" Sanju realised straight away what he'd just said, but too late. A flash of anger blitzed across her face. Sanju was captivated again. She looked stunning.

"That's right. At Bristol. Anyway, enjoy the party, Sanju. Must mingle. Come on, Rhys." They walked away as Sanju walked across to the table to get a drink.

"Hiya, Sanju, what have you and Em been gossiping about?" It was Jemima.

Sanju kissed her on the cheek. "Oh, just mulling over the past and future. Your sister has really changed. Last time I saw her she was wearing braces."

"Oh yes, she's definitely popular with the boys now. Talking of the future, what are you planning after the summer?"

"Going into banking. I've got an offer from TDT."

* * *

The Wills Memorial Building sits at the top of Park Street – its gothic-inspired grandeur hosting the University of Bristol School of Law. A navelike structure encloses the double-storey library, with wide columns of books partitioning the monastic silence, and concealing students along long wooden tables, scribbling notes from volumes of legal cases.

It was here that Emma had spent the best part of her daytime over the last three years, taking breaks only for lectures, tutorials, exams, and for lunch at the bakery across Queen Street. She had sat at the same seat almost every day for the whole of that period, diligently absorbed in her work, with the only distraction to the subdued humming of studying being the occasional scraping of chairs, the shuffling of papers, the low thumping thuds of books being taken off or being put back on shelves, and the isolated rushed whispers of student talk. Indeed, the only noise of note she remembered during her time was a scream in Year Two when someone had hidden a large plastic spider under a female fresher's folder.

Like a holy place of meditation, nothing to raise the heartbeat was anticipated, or, indeed, welcomed. It was another ordinary afternoon. Emma, now back with long blonde hair that fell over and across her books, was in her regular trance-like state, scribbling some minutiae of contract law. She hadn't expected her name to be called from behind to break the silence. She certainly hadn't anticipated the voice that called it.

"Emma Roberts?"

Like at the drinks' table on her eighteenth birthday, she turned with, "Oh, hello, Sanju," but this time the voice shook, surprised and startled, and her face blushed to a bright crimson.

"I'm sorry, Em, I didn't mean to scare you."

"That's OK. How are you?" she whispered. "Listen, we'll get into trouble talking here." She put down her pen and walked him out of the library into the entrance hallway. "What are you doing here?"

"I'm here for a graduate recruitment event for TDT. It was a bit last minute, otherwise I would have got a message to you that I was coming, but anyway, I challenged myself to see if I could find you. Do you have time for a coffee?"

"Oh, that's sweet but I have a tutorial in five minutes."

"That's OK. No problem. I know I just turned up unannounced. But if you're free this evening, perhaps we can have dinner or a drink. Maybe you can show me a bit of Bristol. I don't know it at all."

"I'm sorry, Sanju. I've got something on tonight."

"Ah OK, that's fine, Em. Maybe another time. I know you were rushing to something. I'll let you get back."

They looked at each other. Emma had been completely caught off guard. She was in her final year, she had so much on her mind, and Sanju's arrival felt like some sort of distant dream. He was in a suit – she had never seen him so formal.

Sanju had hoped to clear the air from those years ago. He didn't just want to turn up at her flat and had shied away from calling first. He realised his approach hadn't worked but at least he tried. He gave a faint smile and lightly said, "Bye then," before turning towards the exit.

She responded with her own, "Bye," and walked back towards the library.

He walked into the afternoon sunlight and paused for a few moments to admire the dominating Wills Tower jutting above the building.

"God, she's pretty." He sighed and decided he needed to have a coffee across the road to calm himself and get over the disappointment. The Clifton traffic kept him at the pavement side just long enough and was just quiet enough for him to hear her voice behind.

"Sanju, yes, OK. What time?"

He turned round. She was a little out of breath and had obviously run down the stairs. He couldn't really collect himself to say anything other than, "Seven thirty – does that work? I'll pick you up at your place," and continued to cross the road.

Emma rushed back to her tutorial briefly contemplating how he knew her address.

He was still in his suit when he arrived at the flat, not far from the Downs, that she shared with four other girls.

They looked at her knowingly as she left. 'Family friend', she mimed.

Sanju asked what she fancied eating and they went for a pizza. Emma noted that he enquired about Rhys. It was in a passing tone like someone asking which day the bins get emptied, but he was clearly interested to know. She told him they'd split but didn't mention her current boyfriend. Sanju spoke a lot about work, what he did out of work, holidays, but didn't mention his partner either. They both avoided any discussion about Provence. He asked if she fancied going for another drink before his train back to London, but she had an early start and really needed to get home. He walked her back to the flat.

"And where was the graduate recruitment fair today, Sanju? Bet TDT pull out the stops."

"We hired a room by the university. There was a presentation followed by drinks."

"Drinks? During the day? What time was it?"

"It was actually this evening. It started at seven thirty." Sanju looked across at Emma; they had just arrived outside her flat. "I forgot to attend."

Emma smiled. She thought about giving him a peck on the cheek to thank him for dinner but stopped herself. "Bye then." She turned and went inside.

* * *

The next time they would meet would be nearly two years later. Emma was training as a solicitor with law firm Evershed Shapley and had moved in with a couple of friends in a flat in Putney. Although Sanju wasn't far away in Wimbledon, they actually met at a New Year's Eve party at Jemima's. It was through Jemima that they had heard a little of each other and, in particular, that Emma was going out with a brash, loud (Jemima's words) South African, Scott, from university, and that Sanju was in a long-term relationship with a Swedish girl, Karin, who had effectively moved in with him and whom Jemima didn't like much either.

Emma had arrived in the afternoon and had been helping with the preparations. She still felt mild flutters at the thought of meeting Sanju, but any anger had dissipated after the dinner in Bristol. She had never met Karin and wasn't particularly keen on the idea of seeing her either. She also wondered what Sanju would make of Scott – Jemima would certainly have given Scott a bad press, but Scott hadn't planned to arrive until late, as he was having drinks with some work friends before.

Sanju arrived around 9.00pm. Emma looked round to see that Karin hadn't come. Apparently, she had gone back to Stockholm for the holidays. She grabbed a couple of glasses of prosecco and went straight across to meet him as he was getting rid of his coat by the stair cupboard. He still had some curls of hair cascading down his forehead and partly across one eye, not as unkempt as in his teens, but still pretty enticing.

They spoke almost continuously for the next two hours, talking about films; he teased her about whether she was old enough to go and see adult films like *Pulp Fiction* – only with grown-up geriatrics, she had replied. They discussed music, Bristol vs Oxford, Massive Attack vs Radiohead. It wasn't really her area of expertise, but she let him entertain her and giggled at his jokes. Every so often, she'd throw in some archaic legal English words and enjoy studying his face to see if he'd pretend to know what she meant or drop his ego to ask. He mentioned that he'd just bought an Alfa Romeo Spider; she shocked him by saying she only liked the Series Three, a line she had already prepared after Jemima had told her about the car – she'd never previously heard of Alfa Romeo, let alone the Spider.

The conversation ended abruptly when Scott arrived, slightly inebriated, talking loudly and, on seeing Emma speaking with Sanju, putting his arm firmly round her.

Sanju tried to have a conversation with both of them but got a little irritated with Scott's juvenile possessive put-downs, so left to join Jemima in the kitchen.

"You two have been talking a long time," she noted. "You probably haven't seen her since her eighteenth, have you?"

So, Jemima doesn't know about the Bristol dinner, he thought.

At midnight, they put on the television to listen to the chimes of Big Ben, the party linked hands to sing 'Auld Lang Syne' and then walked around pecking one another on the cheek to wish each other a Happy New Year. Emma and Sanju met in front of the stair cupboard. He leant down and she moved forward to kiss on the side of their cheeks.

Each felt that the contact had lasted longer than a peck. Each felt the side of their lips lingering touch. Each felt the enjoyment of the moment. Each wondered whether the proximity and duration were deliberate or by chance. Each would think about it for weeks to come.

They started to call each other towards the end of the day once Sanju finished trading when the markets closed. This turned into meeting for after-work drinks as their offices were so near each other in the City, which turned into occasional dinners and trips to cinemas, all hidden from the gaze of others, until, by the summer, they were seeing each other two or three times a week. It was then that Sanju asked if she would join him for his division's annual dinner. She waited a second and saw a slight twitchiness in his eyes that she would get to know whenever he felt a little nervous or vulnerable.

"It's at the Hurlingham Club, just across the river from you," he blurted out, as if stressing that the primary reason for the invitation was the proximity and convenience of the location to her.

She also responded indifferently. "Yes, why not, it will be fun." As if she had nothing particularly pressing that night, but her heart was racing. She was over the moon to go and spent the next three weekends looking for a black dress, new shoes, and matching jewellery.

He arrived in his red Spider to pick her up. "It's a Mark Three, as you can see."

"Absolutely. I wouldn't be getting in it otherwise." She smiled and wondered what would happen to her hair that she had just spent the last hour fixing into place. "Nice evening to have the roof down."

"Is that OK, Em?"

"Sure, the car wouldn't look so good with the roof up, right?" She did actually think they'd look quite cool together in the open top, but her tone and facial expression were enough to relay her concerns, and she noted that he drove deliberately slowly across Putney Bridge. By the time they arrived, she nevertheless looked like a model in an '80s New Romantics pop video.

"Is my hair looking OK, Sanju?"

"You're looking gorgeous, Em." He looked a little sheepish as soon as he said it. She wondered if his choice of 'gorgeous' was just him overcompensating for her messed-up hair, but his shy recoil did seem like the reaction of someone letting something hidden slip out.

They had champagne and canapes on arrival, and by the time they had finished dinner, with a round of port, the effect of the alcohol had started to take hold. There was an auction, ostensibly for charity, but Emma could sense it was an opportunity for the slightly drunken alpha bulls of TDT to compete with their wealth, outbidding each other to stay in each other's second villas in Tuscany and Provence, paying well above face value for tickets to Lords, Wimbledon and the Champions League, pitching for boxing, golf and tennis lessons, and offering extortionate sums for dinners with celebrities and politicians. They then moved into the next room, where a casino had been laid out and they were handed some play tokens. Here, too, a group of senior-looking executives had sat round a table for a serious game of 'proper' poker.

Emma wanted to go outside for some air. "Do you enjoy your job and the people you work with, Sanju?"

"Yes, mostly. All jobs have their positives and negatives. Ours is not so difficult and it pays very well – allows you to live your dreams outside work – nice holidays, nice cars. We take risks with other people's money and when we win, we make a cut. I try to stay connected so I know what's going on and manage the risk, so any potential losses are capped. As long as you win regularly enough, everyone stays happy. If you lose, well, you could probably get a similar job somewhere else. I've learnt not to get too emotionally involved, and anyway, I'm too far in to do anything else, and senior enough to walk away if it gets too ropey. And some of the new products are more interesting and demanding.

"As for the people, well, you got a flavour for it tonight. Fair to say, it goes to some of their heads. Stay friendly in the office, I say, and limit the social stuff to what's necessary when you walk out that building. Look, I know you're probably thinking they are a bunch of arses but there are a lot of nice people too."

"Can we walk up to the river?"

As they moved along the gravel path, she rocked unsteadily in her heels, like a boat in choppy waters, and their hands glanced each other's momentarily. The second time, though, she grabbed his hand and held on. He felt the soft skin of her palm and squeezed it lightly. From the riverbank, they looked across to the other side. The fluorescent London lights illuminated the dusky city sky as a line of flashing planes queued into Heathrow and the orange sunset beyond. She asked the question she'd been holding back for weeks. "Is Karin away?"

It was the first time she had mentioned her name. "We split up last year, just before Christmas. I haven't really told anyone." There was a pause. "I hope Scott doesn't mind you being here with me."

"Oh, not at all." She looked at the river – there was a strong tidal flow – it looked cold and muddy. "We finished a couple of weeks ago. I thought this might happen."

"What might happen, Em?"

"This." She released her palm, put her arms around him a few inches above her and kissed him on the lips. This time, there was no reason to jump in the water. He wrapped himself around her, brought her as close as he could and kissed, and kissed again. They found a bench and sat there by the side of the Thames, all the chains unlocked, their famine-starved desires gorging at a feast, until the club lights went out and he walked her home, thinking how dreams can come true.

It took three months before they decided to tell their families, which they timed together. Emma thought to tell Jemima first before her parents. She wasn't sure how Jemima would react, but she was totally thrilled and spoke with a 'what took so long?' tone. By the time she called her mother a few minutes later, her mum was in shrieks of excitement. Mrs Kapoor had already rung her and was driving up the hill with a bottle of champagne, notwithstanding that she hardly drank.

"I think she's coming to discuss marriage plans."

"Very early days, *Maman*."

By the end of the year, Emma had moved into Sanju's place in Wimbledon.

FIFTEEN

The first symptom of true love in a young man is timidity,
In a young woman, it is boldness.

Emma looked back on it as the start of the happiest period of her life. After just a few weeks, she had decided she wanted to spend the rest of her days with Sanju. She only wished he worked a little less and prayed that some of his colleagues' personalities wouldn't rub off on him. They both worked long hours, but Sanju would be up at 5.00am and would spend weekends and holidays reading research reports on the financial markets. He never seemed to have a break. She just wanted to spend more time with him.

She found many of his colleagues dull, with little interest other than in making money, showing off about their girlfriends, their second homes, and how well they were managing their portfolios. Always outwardly over-confident, but often fragile underneath. Indeed, the first time she met Marcus was at Marcus's leaving do to go to Singapore, and despite supposedly being a good friend of Sanju's, he had come across to her drunk and leery, suggesting she should dump Sanju and come to Singapore with him as he was better at sex, and then carrying on to say Sanju was too nice to be truly successful, and you know, his face probably wouldn't fit at the highest level. She had never told Sanju or indeed mentioned to Marcus that story, hoping he was too drunk to remember.

Their careers were progressing well, and she was on track to qualify as a solicitor. Sanju was now in charge of his trading desk (something to do with interest rate derivatives that she didn't really understand) and was keen to get promoted to managing director. The promotion opportunity came but not quite how Sanju had wanted it. He hardly spoke for a few days before he came around to telling Emma that he had been asked to take on a global role, but one that meant he would need to go to Singapore for a couple of years to build the Asian desk for TDT.

She knew he really wanted the promotion and was excited for him, and as much as she knew she would hate to be away from him, she rationalised that if one day they were going to live their lives together, they should be able to spend time apart. If anything, Sanju struggled more with the decision and, in the end, Emma had to convince him that he would regret not taking the opportunity, and who knows if and when such a chance would come again. After a couple of weeks, an agreement with TDT that he would be able to come back for a few days on business every few weeks, and a couple of drunken and tearful nights with Emma, he accepted the Singapore offer. She would stay in his place in Wimbledon and spend her holidays with him and they would be able to see a lot of Southeast Asia and enjoy the Singaporean weather. He didn't quite say it, but intimated that when he came back, he'd be asking her to spend the rest of her life with him.

Sanju packed his stuff and had it shifted to Singapore. Emma felt the house bare even before he had gone. Sanju was even more upset when, due to a staffing issue, he had to go to Paris on his way to Singapore, so effectively leaving a couple of days earlier than planned. There were tears in Wimbledon, more tears at the airport and for Sanju, plenty of despondency at his first night alone in his Parisian hotel. He called the next morning to ask if she would come over on Friday, and he'd delay his flight by a day so they could just spend another twenty-four hours together – he just wasn't in the right place to leave without seeing her again.

She got an early Eurostar, dumped her bag at the hotel – TDT's corporate hotel was the Ritz in Place Vendome – not Emma's sort of place, *but hey, everyone needs to rough it occasionally*, she thought – and then wandered out into the drizzly autumnal Parisian rain. She wore a long dark raincoat, knee-length boots, and a dark vermillion beret – a mix of London panache and French chic – self-evidently enjoying the stereotypical look. An English girl (who was actually half French), being French. She loved Paris and wanted to make the most of the time before Sanju finished work. She zig-zagged her way to the Marais, tootling through some of her favourite boutiques, grabbed a coffee as the rain got heavier, and then spent a couple of hours under the arches of the Place des Vosges, warmed and partially dried by the café heater, watching and musing on life, and thinking about how she would cope with her upcoming time in London alone.

In the end, she ran out of time to get back to the hotel to change for dinner – Sanju was able to get away from La Defense earlier than he had feared. They met at a bar near Rue Vieille du Temple, both slightly damp from the endless spray of fine rain, but both cheered to see each other. Sanju had booked a restaurant – Campagne et Provence – just on the edge of the 4th. It was the first time they had touched on anything Provençal since the infamous pool incident, but she was relaxed, loving the home cooking, sitting in a dining area the size of a living room, with the host husband offering on-the-house peach aperitifs and a thyme-based liquor, and talking to the wife, the cook, in a local Provençal dialect. Sanju also seemed just happy to be there and to have her there for another evening. They even spoke about some of the funnier holiday incidents from when they were children.

The drizzle was relenting as they left the restaurant, and so they decided to walk back along the Seine, but a heavy mist was starting to descend, and by the time they reached the south side of Ile St Louis, they could barely see beyond a couple of metres, and that only as the thick grey fog shifted slowly like a giant ghostly perforated blanket, revealing one patch of empty street then another, with the street lamps struggling to offer a diffused orange glow to the silent necropolis of commuting spirits.

As they passed Pont St Louis, the mist broke above for a brief moment, revealing a handful of scarcely visible stars and a faint moon.

"I don't think we're alone," she said.

"I agree. You see they've now got a telescope pointed at a piece of totally empty space about a tenth of the size of that moon. To the naked eye, you can see nothing in that place. It's dark, but that telescope can see thousands of galaxies, each one with about 100 million stars, with their own system of planets, with some potentially like our Earth. Multiply that across the whole sky, and we couldn't possibly be alone. It fascinates me, Em. If I wasn't a banker, I'd…"

"I meant there is someone on the other side of the bridge."

A tall man, in a large overcoat and trilby, stood in the middle of the bridge on the other side. He would appear and disappear as the mist moved, alternating with Sanju and Emma in being visible then shrouded. He had placed a music player on the floor and was holding a silver saxophone. He acknowledged the phantom silhouettes of his audience staring in his direction with a short, unthreatening nod, and switched on the player before taking the saxophone to his lips.

Emma cuddled up to Sanju. "This is wonderful, Sanju. What a lovely evening. Thanks for inviting me. What song is this, do you know?"

"I think it's the sax solo on 'One More Night' by Phil Collins, quite appropriate."

"Indeed." She looked up at him. His eyes were moist. "What's the matter?"

He looked nervous with that vulnerable twitch and his voice became a bit shaky. "I've been thinking about it for a while and should have asked in London, but would you consider coming with me to Singapore? I realise, you know, with your career, and it'll be boring and…"

She reached up and kissed him, and they kissed until the music tapered off as the mist swirled around them. She recognised the next song. "'Smooth Operator', how appropriate," she whispered in his ear.

The dampness had started to make her shiver. "Come on, Sanju. I'm feeling cold now. Let's get back to the hotel."

Sanju glanced across at the evanescent saxophonist as they left. She realised she hadn't answered his question, and that he would have noted she also hadn't said no, but he didn't bring it up again.

By the time they got to the hotel, the rain had started again. Sanju loved the Bar Hemingway and they decided they needed a little warming nightcap. It was nearly midnight, and the small bar room was empty but for a group of four or five young men, who appeared to be just visiting the bar rather than attending as hotel guests. The wood-panelled room, with framed photos crowding each wall, the dim lighting, the upholstered leather chairs and the barman in a crisp white jacket gave the place the ambience of an intimate gentlemen's club, and everyone turned to look at Emma as she walked in and sat down on the side sofa. Sanju started to talk to the bartender – he had undoubtedly been there the night before and perhaps more often than that – they spoke like regulars, as Sanju asked for recommendations for a couple of warming cocktails.

Emma asked for a pile of drink mats.

"Oh, come on, Em, seriously! Not here, not at the Ritz!"

"Yes, yes, you're just scared I'll beat you again."

"Fine. Jerome, can you give me some bar mats? She's got this game she likes to play and has had a bit too much to drink tonight. I'm just going to the loo. You can have a practice." Jerome passed some across knowingly.

By the time Sanju got back, Emma had taken off her coat and was sitting in her floral black-and-white dress, loosely exposing both knees, with one of the young men stroking his beard sitting opposite her as she piled up the beer mats, placed them on the edge of the table, flicked them with the back of her hand and caught them after one spin in a stack. "That's twelve!"

"I don't think we've met." Sanju spoke directly to the Bearded Stranger as he sat down with them.

"No, we've not been introduced." The Bearded Stranger was English and spoke with a confident tone that recognised that he was concurrently trespassing, entertaining his friends and enjoying the company of the one female in the room. "That's twelve for me too."

Emma piled up fifteen bar mats. She was quite tipsy and enjoying the attention of being the only female. She also realised the situation was irritating Sanju but was enjoying the game – he'd have to be less possessive – and she also knew, as long as she didn't push it too far, he was a better lover when wound up. The Bearded Stranger matched her at fifteen and then caught eighteen bar mats with a little fumble.

Sanju could see that as the Bearded Stranger looked down

to focus on his turn, he would spend an uncomfortable amount of time staring across the table at the top of Emma's uncovered knees.

"One attempt only," he insisted as Emma piled up the mats.

She caught eighteen and screeched at Sanju, "Haha, that's beaten your record!"

Sanju could not have felt any glummer.

At twenty mats, Emma dropped them on the floor but so did the Bearded Stranger. "I'd say that was a draw. Let us start at twelve again."

Sanju was keen to bring matters to a close but didn't want to let the Bearded Stranger presume it was his presence causing the rush. He was sure the Englishman wouldn't understand any French. He could also see the effect the whiskey cocktail was having on Emma as her eyes started to glaze. He wanted to get her up to the bedroom.

"*On y va?*"

"*Attends.*"

"*Vraiment je suis fatigué.*"

"*Arrête*, Sanju, *deux minutes, j'arrive.*"

Sanju rolled his eyes and knocked back his drink. He could feel the Bearded Stranger's friends staring at him. This time both Emma and the Stranger finished at fifteen.

"Let's do one more game then. I see you've finished your drinks. Perhaps I can get a round." The Bearded Stranger was clearly enjoying getting familiar. "And get to know you a bit better?"

Emma looked at Sanju. He was close to his red line.

"Wait." Sanju picked up Emma's fifteen mats and took the pile off the Bearded Stranger and didn't bother to count the total. "About thirty plus, I'd say," he spoke directly to the Bearded Stranger.

Sanju piled the mats on the edge of the table, flicked them up and caught the whole deck before stretching to hand them over in one swift move to the Bearded Stranger. He sat back and breathed out a whistle of air from the edge of his mouth that lifted his curls before they settled across his forehead, taking the opportunity in the brief moment when his hair was off his face to look across at the Stranger's friends. It was his best Clint Eastwood spaghetti western impression. The south London swagger was on full throttle.

It had the desired effect on Emma. She looked across at him intently, eyes wide and determined, bit her lower lip gently and grabbed her coat and beret.

"*OK, allons-y.*"

By the time the lift had reached their fourth floor, she had taken off her boots, earrings, watch, undone her bra, and removed her underwear. She hadn't taken her eyes off him. "I've come two hundred miles for this, Sanju, no pressure!"

He loved these transformations of her from sweet innocent solicitor to sex-powered nymphette, was aching to be with her with every cell, and had realised that he'd got the upper hand with his bar-mat trick and wasn't going to give that up without one last word.

"Let me know when you need to break to breathe."

Sanju woke just before ten. He was exhausted. His first exultant thoughts of the evening and night turned to a sadness as he reflected that this would the last time they'd be together for a few weeks. He rolled sideways to see Emma wasn't there. Her coat was still on the floor. She must have gone down to get some air and was probably hungover, as he himself felt a little heavy-headed. He'd have a shower before going to look for her.

He heard the door slam as he was washing his hair. He shouted out to make sure it wasn't the cleaners. Emma walked in. He was amazed how quickly she could remove her clothes.

He felt her naked body, cool from being outside, as she walked up and put her arms around him.

"Are you feeling OK? Bit hungover, I guess?"

"A little, but not too bad. I needed to make a couple of calls and didn't want to wake you up."

"What on a Saturday morning? For work?"

"Well, one was to Charlie."

"Is all OK? Is it because you took the day off yesterday?"

"I'm taking two weeks off. I've cancelled the Eurostar and booked myself on your flight this evening. Charlie and I have been talking about it in case you asked, and he is also going to confirm if I can have a two-year sabbatical, and whether they can keep my job open. He thinks it should be OK as I'm one of their stars," she finished off with a wink.

He looked into her eyes and lifted her up as she wrapped herself around him like a young vine on a tree, as he was inside her again.

"Em, you're amazing. I love you."

"I love you too, Sanju."

SIXTEEN

Things are not what they appear to be;
Nor are they otherwise.

The heavy rain of the last two days had eased to a laden dampness. From his window, Marcus could see a police car parked behind Gilbert's yellow Volkswagen. It had been the third time during his stay that the same two policemen had made a visit up to the villa. They were in deep conversation with Urs, with Gilbert listening silently. It looked like a routine 'hope everything is alright' conversation, but Marcus felt something a little more sinister. Muttu was not around, and maybe it was just a coincidence, but Marcus recalled that he had not been there during the previous two police visits either. He decided he'd go for a walk, taking the opportunity to pass the quartet and see if he could get a better sense of what they were discussing, but as he stepped outside, they simply tailed off their conversation and his German was too elementary to follow anything from what he had overheard.

Over the weeks, Marcus had often wandered down the hill from the villa, sometimes taking his laptop to work elsewhere for a change of scene. The descent from the villa was a single-road track that zigged and zagged past various large farmhouses with their steep roofs, separated by bare grassy fields sometimes dotted with the local Braunvieh cows, their alpine bells breaking his silent thoughts, and dormant storage barns that no one ever seemed to visit. As he got lower, clusters of spruce and firs would make way to isolated maples and oaks. The trail would merge with other similar tracks shooting up and along the hills. Any opportunities on the stroll to take in the view and contemplate the challenges of life would dissipate suddenly with the need to negotiate long stretches of black ice, particularly after a fresh frozen gleam from earlier rain. There were various passing places for cars, where the ice had formed into mini glaciers, and whereas Marcus needed to move at an appropriately glacial pace, he would admire the elderly local ladies and gentlemen skipping with ease up and down the hill. As the track approached the Teiflaubach, the houses became more congested and the roads wider and clearer, with the main thoroughfare heading along the river in both directions

Marcus had got to know some of the café and restaurant owners along the Meiringensee and in the village of Weisenberg. Being generous with his tips, he had struck a sort of friendship with the otherwise-reserved owners. Once they opened up though, he was privy to a whole trove of village rumours and gossip and even a couple of interesting snippets about the villa.

This was how he first discovered how the first owner, Josef Traxler, had died after falling off a ladder, though many believed he had been killed by his wife after she discovered he was having an affair, and that his body was buried in the woods nearby. There were also rumours about the disappearance of a family member of one of the other owners, the Aljawahiris, who supposedly left suddenly, but there was no trace of his current whereabouts.

It seemed that whereas Urs kept himself comparatively private, Muttu was a regular and popular visitor to Weisenberg and the lakeside bars and cafés, popular in particular with the younger ladies, and would sometimes make Indian meals for the locals. Although as soon as Marcus tried to learn more about them, the locals would become unforthcoming and quiet, and deliberately change the subject.

Marcus stopped off for a coffee in the nearest café-cum-bar. It was a small dark place with a few stools near the counter and a couple of round metal tables outside by the road and overlooking the lively frothing river. Marcus lit a cigarette outside, asked for a black coffee, and started to scroll through his emails. He didn't have so much time, as the fortnightly 'Exco' call of his divisional peers was at 1.00pm and he wanted to be prepared both on the content and on his approach before heading back.

* * *

"Hey, who's that on the line?"

"This is Glenn, how's life, Hankie?" the Australian greeted his fellow regional head, with the outward enthusiasm of someone meeting a long-lost brother, perfectly disguising any trace of the intense rivalry and animosity he felt for the American.

"Fucking snowed under, though we've been killing it, Handy. Reckon this could be our best fucking quarter yet. Who else is on? Is Pierre there?"

Just hearing Shoulderchip's voice made Marcus's skin curl and cringe. Every quarter he'd be 'killing it'. Every quarter, until the actual revenue numbers came out, would be the 'best fucking quarter yet'. Every call was an opportunity for upmanship. Every discussion a reminder to all that the Americas was the biggest profit-generating region. Every meeting an occasion to impress upon anyone bold or stupid enough to challenge him that he, Shoulderchip, would be the rightful heir to the global head position should their boss, Pierre, ever move on.

"Not yet. In London, we have Dave, Joachim and myself." It was Pierre's COO, Jordan Styles (American mid-forties). He spoke with his usual quiet humdrum voice.

Dave Ross (British, early forties) was head of foreign exchange and Joachim Kowalski (German, late thirties) ran the smaller commodities business – they both headed their global businesses from London and although technically the products and regions overlapped in a matrix, they were less controlled by the regional fiefdoms of Asia with Glenn Handscombe, and the Americas with Hank Sharp II. Provided they were left alone to run their areas, Marcus found them less confrontational, but he wouldn't count on their support one iota if the regional guys started to gang up on him. Jordan's job was to ensure that the business controls were effective; he would speak of his role as the first line of defence against misdemeanours as if some Spartan warrior but would roll over at the first hint of conflict.

"Still no sign of Marcus. Fuck, man! When is he coming back? Sales guys here are just totally out of control." Marcus was expecting a cheap shot about his absence even though he had only missed one Exco. "Anyone heard anything about Epsilon?" Handscombe continued.

"I'm expecting some update from Pierre today."

Marcus waited for Jordan to finish his line before entering the call in a slow, deliberate voice. "I'm pleased to hear you're missing me, Glenn."

"Hey, Flintee! You're still alive. How is the holiday going? Getting any skiing in?" This time, it was Shoulderchip chortling in, to team up with his fellow trading head against Marcus – the guy just running sales considered at least a couple of rungs below them in the pyramid of humanity.

Marcus needed to stay calm with the teasing, but plainly irritating, niggles. However, before he could answer, he heard the rustling of someone new joining the call.

"This is Pierre. Who do we have on the line?" Pierre de Montalembert (French American, late forties) must have been taking the call from his office away from the others in London.

"Full house, Pierre."

"Good, we have a lot to get through. What's on the agenda, Jordan? Wait, let's start with the actions from the previous Exco." Pierre's voice was detectably more rushed and tense than normal. It had been the same as on his last call with Marcus, exposing stress-induced scratches under the usual smooth veneer of his mix of comforting Californian drawl and philosophically intellectual French self-confidence.

"First, we have from six weeks ago, 'Hank to deliver update on Brazil and Mexico'." Jordan would have struggled to make the business sound any duller.

"You have that right, Jordie? I sent it through last Friday." Shoulderchip spoke with the haughtiness of someone who felt that he had been given a task several grades below his talents.

"Great, but how come I haven't seen it, Jordan?" Normally, Pierre would have just accepted the answer and followed up later, even if the issue was something evidently more important.

Jordan spoke hesitantly and even more quietly. He didn't like challenges. "Well, I think I could probably work with Hank to add a little more detail and context."

"You mean the report isn't worth the shit it's written on!" Pierre spoke with a measured but obviously irked tone.

"Listen, Pierre, I don't have much to say. I need three to four good hires in the region. That should turn it around." Shoulderchip would have done better to take the quiet hesitancy steer from Jordan, but his dismissiveness of Pierre's update request clearly lit a fuse.

"Six fucking weeks, Hank, for a report, and your answer to two significant loss-making desks is to ask me for more fucking headcount. I want you to get your arse on a plane next week to Sao Paulo; do some research and get me a report, not a fucking headcount invoice, by next Friday." A small pause. "Please!"

Marcus leaned back in his chair. He had heard about Pierre losing his rag occasionally but never experienced him this testy. The meeting could get interesting. He'd have to choose his words carefully. Pierre's outburst left total silence on the call as every region muted their phones.

Jordan ran through the other actions. No one volunteered any updates and Marcus was pleased there were none allocated to him. Pierre listened silently to the list and then launched into another rant. He was undoubtedly in a foul mood, which had the effect of enhancing the French in the Franco-American diatribe.

"Guys, this is not serious. We don't have these Excos to sit here and play with each other's dicks. Not a single action completed. Forgive me if I haven't noticed but are we in a period of mourning because someone has died? *Oui, non?* Fuck, *merde, putain*! By next Exco, guys, I want a proper update on these actions. Is that clear? Jordan, you will take a progress report next week and update me. Right, what's next?" By now, he was as good as shouting into the phone.

"Asia audit. I'll just bring Steve Johnson into the call to tell us the details."

Johnson came on to take them through the purpose of the internal audit, to indicate that the region was due one as it had already been three years since the last, to summarise the content and timetable, and to outline that it would look at adherence to policies, potential operational risks, and be primarily focused on the sales and trading front office functions.

Handscombe unmuted himself. It was clear he hadn't been informed prior to the call that the audit was coming to his region. "Look, I think it's an excellent idea, Pierre. I'm just wondering if the timing makes sense with everything else that's going on." His mixed words belied a complete repulsion to the idea.

"It's not my idea, but something we do regularly. With everything that's going on, it seems the timing is perfect. I want to see Asia get a clean bill of health. Can I rely on that, Glenn?"

"Yes, of course, Pierre."

Marcus felt now was the moment to strike back at Handscombe, and his supercilious and despised sidekick, Starc, had provided the perfect target at which to take aim. "Steve, will you be looking at HR issues? The reason I ask is that I had a call with Zhao Kun last week. You know he still doesn't seem happy after that bullying saga, and it would be good to hear that everything has now calmed down and…"

"Bullying saga… what's that?" Marcus's hunch was right – Pierre didn't know.

"Oh, I don't know any details, Pierre. We were just talking about developments around the algo. I thought…" Marcus would let Handscombe explain for maximum impact and, as hoped, Handscombe interrupted him on cue.

"It was just a bit of office banter, Pierre – maybe got a little out of hand. I didn't think it was worthy of troubling you."

"Office banter or bullying? Did HR get involved? Who was he accusing?"

"Yes, and Starc. They gave him a caution." Handscombe volume had noticeably dipped.

"Wait, a senior trader gets reprimanded, and not for the first time, and you don't think it was worth troubling me, Glenn?"

"My apologies, Pierre. I should, of course, have updated

you." He went on mute and Marcus felt a glowing satisfaction of a small victory. He knew Handscombe would think he had been stitched up.

"OK, Steve, lets add an HR element to the audit. Glenn, please call me after this to provide me with more colour and that's a useful segue way into the culture review, Marcus."

Marcus talked about a new approach to the culture and diversity review. They had had one before and generally found it to be a waste of time as everyone gamed it to score people highly in their teams, as well as their friends and political allies. This time, Marcus said he would like some in-person interviews on top of the questionnaire, to get some proper insight. He would have anticipated a lot of resistance and pushback, but after Pierre's earlier outburst, everyone accepted, and as far as Marcus was concerned, this review, together with the Asia audit, should be the final death knell for Starc and knock Handscombe down a few notches.

"Listen, guys, I think Marcus's idea is an important one," Pierre chimed in with his support, although with him in this mood no one was going to challenge it anyway. "We need to be close to our people. I'm hearing stories of drug abuse here in Europe, in America, mental breakdowns, now bullying. I'll come onto it in a minute, but our division is under watch, and I really don't want surprises."

They heard Handscombe unmute. Marcus wondered what he was up to. "Listen, another great idea. Pierre, look, we have drug issues here also, mainly, I suspect, with the expats though. It's not just in Europe and America." It was an attempt at empathy across the regions, but Marcus knew what he was getting at – there had been a long-running joke about Andreas' ex-girlfriend being Columbian. There was no basis to linking that with drug-taking, but Handscombe was undeniably sowing a seed. Marcus stayed quiet and Pierre ignored the remark.

They all wanted to get to the last agenda item.

"I have an update on Epsilon. This is obviously highly confidential. We are actively supporting the regulators in their investigations, but senior management are feeling that the regulators believe that breaches have occurred across EMEA and in the US, and possibly Asia, and are therefore reserving for a potential fine. We don't know how big the fine would be; the activities that are being assessed were common across the Street as you know, but we are first on the hit list. The hope is that the more we can work with the regulators – show that we've got our house in order – the lower the fine. Worryingly, some clients are also seeking direct redress and their legal teams are sending letters through. I don't have much more than that, but with the penalty reserves, I don't have to tell you that this year's bonus round will see a lot of doughnuts so, without mentioning Epsilon, you may want to start managing expectations.

"We need to be ahead of the game. Clearly, most of the client contact happens with sales and, as I say, we need to show we are starting to put our house in order."

Marcus dived in. "You mean sales management will take the hit and yet we haven't even seen the report and had the chance to respond. What about the responsibilities of legal and compliance? This all happened years ago and was mostly standard practice at the time, as you say."

"The regulators have requested interviews with a number of guys – sales and trading – including you, and I need to discuss that offline. There will be a headcount hit across the board, Marcus, and yes, the client-facing teams will likely take the brunt of that."

Someone had unmuted their line. It was Shoulderchip. "Look, Pierre, as you know from the numbers I sent a few days back, we've had some great client results in the States, but you know with Maley gone, we are missing the sort of leadership we need here in New York. Some of the guys are so out of their depth, they'd drown in a puddle, especially, as you know, with Marcus away."

Marcus was seething. It was another needling attack. "I don't agree with the you, Hank. Maley was, as you know, doing just the sort of things that Pierre mentioned he was concerned about earlier. Colvin is head of sales in the region, and, as you say, look at the results, and anyway I'm back shortly."

"Things are also messy out here in Asia with Marcus away. There is no one to take decisions. You know Andrea was running a desk in EMEA when all this Epsilon shit was going on."

Marcus sighed. These guys had got their chance, and they were not wasting time sticking their knives into his local sales heads.

"Listen, Glenn, I talk to Andrea and the other guys regularly and if there is an issue, I'm here on the phone. Just call when I'm needed, and in any case, I'll be back shortly."

"Guys, I don't want this bickering. We need to work through this as a management team – collaborate, challenge, but let's be constructive. Marcus, you and I need to have another chat. Get the thoughts of the other guys, Dave and Joachim as well, and let's talk in a couple of days." Pierre's tone had calmed once he had got the Epsilon update out but the 'let's talk in a couple of days' sounded ominous. "Let's wrap up now unless there is something else pressing, Jordan."

* * *

Marcus spent the afternoon mulling over the 'you and I need to have another chat' line from Pierre. Clearly, there was more to be said but it felt like Pierre wanted to wait a little longer.

Marcus had been asked to go through the motions of getting 'the thoughts of the other guys' but knew that would be a complete waste of time. It sounded like he would need to fire some of his team but had no indication of how many, and at what level. Not for the first time, he wondered whether he himself would be on that list, whether that could actually be something good for him, but there would be the interviews with the regulators first. Again, he had the uncomfortable feeling of the situation being out of his control.

He could feel the stress getting to him. He asked Urs to join him for dinner as a distraction from work. The decided to eat inside in the 'dining room', sitting in the corner facing out onto the valley lights. The emptiness of the place made it feel cold, made worse by the distance from the kitchen, which Muttu had to cross through the vacant tables and chairs with their food and drinks.

Everyone could sense the sombre mood.

"Put some music on, Muttu, will you? It feels a little desolate in here." Urs was impeccably dressed as always in a blue gingham wool jacket and cravat but noted that tonight Marcus had also made an effort with an ironed shirt, a russet-coloured merino V-neck and chinos with leather slip-ons. "How was your day, Marcus?"

"This parsnip soup should warm you up. I've sprinkled on a little extra paprika." Muttu laid out the bowls and walked across to switch on the soothing tones of Debussy's 'Suite Bergamasque'.

Marcus didn't want to start with work. "I wandered down into Weisenberg this morning. That path is lethal, you know. How do you guys walk down there without breaking something?"

"We don't. We drive." Urs smiled. He poured Marcus a glass of Châteauneuf-du-Pape , who took it one gulp.

"That's nice. Just what I needed, Urs." Marcus leaned across with his glass for a refill. "Muttu, I keep hearing what a big hit you are with the local ladies. They like a bit of exotica around here, I suspect. Perhaps it's your familiarity with the *Karma Sutra*," he finished off with a little chuckle.

"Not at all, sir. I believe the Teiflaubach water makes them sapiosexual." Muttu had his normal smile and nodded his head in the left-right-up-down 'yes-no', 'maybe-probably not', 'absolutely right – you haven't got a clue' South Asian fashion.

"Sapiosexual, what in fuck's name is that?"

"It means they're attracted to intelligence."

The comment made Marcus laugh out loudly and splutter out some soup into his napkin. It completely eased his mood. "Yeah right, Muttu."

Urs was also smiling, and a relaxing vibe started to ease away the earlier miasma of despondency. Marcus went through his afternoon call with Urs. Urs listened intently without offering any input. Marcus wasn't expecting anything, but it was something shared with someone who could understand the office dynamics.

Muttu cleared the plates and brought through their main course – a crisped duck confit with white asparagus and fondant potatoes.

"What brings the police here from time to time, if I can ask?" Marcus had waited for Muttu to be around before raising the question.

"They like to drive around the hills and villages checking if everything is OK. There really isn't much for them to do around here, Marcus. They have to pass the time somehow." Urs spoke in a matter-of-fact way.

Muttu simply continued to pour the wine, nonchalantly, as if he hadn't heard the question or the answer.

Marcus continued, "In town the guys were talking again

about how the fella who built this villa was killed by his wife, an otherwise super hostess and great cook, after she discovered he was having an affair." He looked directly across at Muttu. "It seems the body is buried in the woods."

"Hmm, you've mentioned it before. It would have been a very long time ago, but I find it hard to believe." Muttu spoke like a scientist dissecting a peer's theory. "You see, a decaying human body would release substantial nitrogen compounds such as ammonia, which would fertilise the area perceptibly enough to affect the coloration of the nearby leaves, in my opinion, thereby making the hidden corpse eminently discoverable. Now, particularly if the individual was a smoker, which he would likely have been at that time, that would add cadmium into the mix, which I believe would also affect the chlorophyll in the leaves.

"Naturally, you must be thinking that must be the case with any wild animal such as a wild boar, though they don't typically smoke, but you see these wild animals get ripped apart by scavengers such as foxes and magpies, etc. The only way to achieve that with a human body would be chop it up into small pieces – a messy business with lots of traces unless one is careful. So, she may not have given him a ceremonial burial, but I don't think that the body is buried in the nearby woods."

Marcus listened intently, seriously, and silently without taking his gaze of Muttu. It took a couple of seconds before he spoke. "I think I might have had too much of that Teiflaubach water also."

Urs broke the ensuing smiles. "You may also have heard the story about one of the younger Aljawahiris disappearing. He has not been heard from since he left here. But total village, how you say in English, tittle-tattle. There is nothing to the story. I saw him off myself and they are a very private family. But come on, Marcus, you've had a tough day, let's enjoy the wine. Muttu, this bottle is finished. Please find us another Châteauneuf or, you know, how about that nice neighbouring Vacqueyras; let us see which one Marcus prefers."

The evening finished with Urs confirming that Emma was still arriving the weekend after next and retiring to his room. Muttu hadn't joined them for dinner and must have eaten whilst clearing up, and then returned to his lodgings behind the stairs. Marcus relaxed in the library with a couple of cognacs. The whole place was now empty and quiet.

Marcus wandered down to the gym for his nightly rendezvous with the punchbag and laid into A4 printouts of each of the Exco members in turn, with particular violent force directed towards Handscombe and Shoulderchip. He rested for a few moments on the bench to ease his breathing before climbing back up the stairs to the ground floor. All the lights were off now. It wasn't particularly late but there was no life in the villa or, indeed, in the hills and the mountains outside. He switched on his phone torch to turn upstairs to his room, but noticed that Urs' office door, typically locked, was open.

Unable to resist his inquisitiveness and with the brazen-inducing effect of the brandy still fresh, Marcus used the torch light to quietly ease the door of the office open. The place was tidy, with no paperwork or files on the desk, but he could see some labelled client files through a couple of locked glass cabinets. He opened the desk drawers and had a quick peer inside. He realised that Urs wouldn't be so careless as to leave anything interesting lying around but his curiosity around Urs and Muttu had reached uncheckable heights. He was about to see if any of the glass cabinets could be prised open when he heard a noise outside. He scrambled to switch off the phone torch and prayed the light hadn't been seen before he hid behind the long mahogany desk.

Through the gap in the open door, he could see Muttu walk up to the front entrance. He must have heard something as he peered outside through the windowpane. Muttu then looked into Urs' office, but Marcus was well hidden behind the desk unless Muttu chose to walk in. Marcus thought quickly as to what he would say if he was discovered, but his attention was suddenly jolted as Muttu turned back towards the front door and Marcus saw a glinting object in his hands pointing upwards at head level. It was some sort of handgun and Muttu clearly looked very comfortable holding it. Marcus could feel his heartbeat rising like an accelerating propellor. His hands started to feel clammy. He thought about saying something and standing up to get Muttu's attention calmly, but the completely unexpected shock of seeing Muttu there with a weapon kept him quiet.

Through the legs of the desk, he saw Muttu come again towards Urs' office, and his body shape indicated he was peering inside. The glinting object was now hanging by his side and was clearly visible as a gun even in the faint light. Muttu stood there for a few moments before shutting the door. Marcus feared he would now hear the sound of a locking key, but Muttu mustn't have had the key on him as all he heard were Muttu's steps walking away. He wondered whether Muttu would come back to lock up or wake up Urs. He thought about whether he should try to get out while he was temporarily away, but he decided he didn't want to accidentally startle Muttu, so stayed put.

Muttu didn't come back. Marcus waited for another few minutes to be sure that everything was quiet again. By now, he was stone-cold sober. He came out from behind the desk – the office door was unlocked thankfully – and looked down the hallway as best as he could in the darkness. Muttu must have gone back to his room, so he felt his way towards the stairs and walked as quietly as he could up to the bedroom, exhausted but relieved, gulping for breath, and releasing a very audible stress-induced burp that had been building up.

What he didn't see was Muttu sitting silently by the side at the bottom of the stairs, the gun now hidden way. He waited for Marcus to leave and go up to his room, before coming out himself and locking the door to Urs' office.

SEVENTEEN

By plucking her petals,
You do not gather the beauty of the flower.

Like travellers venturing onto an unknown place, when the sense of excitement overcomes their anxieties, and the joys of new discoveries surpasses the fears of obvious dangers, Marcus and Caitanya embarked on their secret journey. Marcus recalled how, after that night, he had planned once again to speak with her the next day to say how much he cared for her, but an office relationship would simply not be possible. However, when they met for dinner two days later, he couldn't help leaning across to hold her hand, bewitched by those large, almost iridescent eyes, and unable to erase the memory of her sensual caress from his mind. He was captivated as he had never been with anyone else before. He wondered if this is what love should feel like, a love he had never previously experienced.

She realised she had tiptoed slowly, but consciously, to the edge of a cliff and stumbled, or maybe even jumped, and now the only thing holding her were those firm Popeye arms, far from the distant coconut trees and waterways of Kerala. She had gone to the office with trepidation the morning after that night, wondering what now, now that the lust and the alcohol had worn off – he was the boss, he had wanted to create distance between them hours earlier by transferring her to a new mentor; he was in total control, and yet, better if he said it was a mistake. She would deal with it, she would throw herself into her job and she would go back to the marriage proposals that her grandmother kept sending her. What she didn't want was the impenetrability, the ambiguity of silence, of feeling she didn't have the self-esteem to go and talk to him should he choose to ignore her. There was no communication the first day and their paths didn't cross in the office. The second day, they saw each other as Marcus had come on to the floor to talk to one of the traders. Soon after, he sent her an email asking if she was free to meet for dinner.

She could have taken the taxi back on her own to her condominium near Orchard Road, but he offered to escort her home, and she didn't stop him. They couldn't restrain themselves from kissing in the taxi and for the second time that week he stayed in her small one-bedroom apartment.

"You know, going forward," he spoke gently as they lay there, "we should come back to my place in Sentosa. It's quieter there."

She took the sentence in. There was a lot to reflect. 'Going forward' – so there will be a 'forward'. 'Come back to my place' – she hadn't thought to ask but it didn't sound like there was anyone else, and 'it's quieter there' – she understood that he needed to keep things discreet. *That is better for me too*, she thought, away from any office gossip, and away from any tiny risk of leakage to her family.

The next time they met was at his penthouse, with its floor-to-ceiling windows and wrap-round balconies overlooking the Singapore Strait. She wore a thin-strap cream dress that fitted tightly all the way to just above her knees, and she could sense his protracted gaze when she arrived. They watched the sunset as she sipped champagne, feeling not only high above the ground but elevated to a different world.

He had his arm around her, but he seemed agitated, bothered by some internal strife, but before she could ask, he suddenly veered away and blurted it out, releasing the torment, not so much sharing, but loading without any care or concern as to how it might land.

"Look, Tani, the bank doesn't take easily to office relationships. We need to keep this very private."

For a moment, she felt like a secret mistress, not fully belonging there, someone passing through his life without commitment, something bought at the market to be replaced when it had served its purpose, something to be hidden out of view, and he must have seen the fleeting confusion and disappointment in her face before uttering, "Please don't take it badly, it's just the way it is."

"I understand," she said whilst wondering how that would work 'going forward', and if it would always be 'quieter there'.

They would arrange their meetings by email and try to avoid each other in the office, but over the next two months, she had started spending most of her weekends at his place and increasingly during the week. She had moved some of her clothes there, but they would take separate taxis into the office. They would only rarely be seen out together, such as at the Swiss Club where Marcus was a member, or occasionally they would go to one of the restaurants on Sentosa, but he would always seem slightly on edge in case they were spotted. That meant that she mostly cooked at his place, or they got a takeaway and they stayed at home. It felt confined but she was happy in his company.

Her friends, nearly all of whom were colleagues at the office, started to comment that she was rarely able to join them for weekend meals. She was particularly close to another

MBA graduate, Ayla Finn from New Zealand, who worked in corporate finance and had shared a flat with Caitanya when they had first started working at TDT. Their paths crossed one lunchtime when Caitanya saw Ayla too late to avoid her.

"Hey, Tani, haven't soon you for ages."

"Yeah, sorry, Ayla, I got your messages. Been meaning to call but been really busy with work."

"Yeah. It has been a little while. I was thinking I'd done something to upset you." Ayla let out a false giggle.

"No, don't be silly. Of course not." Caitanya reached out to touch Ayla's elbow apologetically.

"Have you been working weekends too?"

"No, not that much. Just relaxing."

"Oh, it's just that I popped by a couple of times."

"Really! You should have left a note. I'd probably just gone out food shopping or something." The idea that Ayla could have popped round had caught Caitanya completely off guard.

"Why don't we do something weekend coming? Can do a lunch rather than have a late night." Ayla didn't dawdle on her previous visits any further and just seemed interested to reconnect.

"Erm, maybe not this weekend, am just finishing off on a new product launch."

"OK, what about weekend after, when it's all over?"

"Actually, I thought about going away for a few days. I have a client meeting in Hong Kong and thought I'd stick around and, you know, see a few tourist sites."

"On your own?"

"Yeah." Caitanya could sense Ayla's mix of curiosity, concern, and consternation.

"I could join you for a couple of days."

"Oh no, Ayla. I could do with a couple of days on my own. But we'll definitely go out when I get back. For sure."

What, of course, Caitanya omitted to say was that Marcus also had meetings in Hong Kong and would be taking some concurrent time off too.

TDT's Hong Kong presence in investment banking was quite small, and the chances of bumping into anyone who would recognise them were minimal. On this trip, Marcus did reserve the corporate junk boat, and the two of them sailed, sipping cocktails, across the bay to Lantau Island, disembarking via a sampan, and eating by the beach at the Frog and Toad as the sun set across the sea. By the time they left, the stars and moon glistened across the South China Sea, skirted by the distant flickering Hong Kong office blocks on one side and the vast dark ocean emptiness on the other. She lay protected in his arms, thinking how free it felt that they didn't have to worry about who may be watching, or about to turn up. He smelt her hair and squeezed her tighter, before leaning across to the ice bucket and expertly grabbing the champagne bottle with one hand to fill up their glasses.

"Popeye, stop. I won't be able to make it off the boat if I have any more."

"Don't worry. Wouldn't it be wonderful just to sleep here on this rocking boat."

She giggled. "Maybe, but not with that pilot watching." She looked at their interlinked hands – the intertwined cliché of dark brown and white piano keys. "You know, I'm very envious of your colour – all my life I've always wanted to be fairer. I was thinking if we ever have a child, he or she would have such beautiful skin. If it's a girl, we should call her Olive."

"Have you got something to tell me, Tani?" Marcus put on a mock-surprised voice as he leant forward, raising his eyebrows and smiling in a teasing way.

She giggled again. "No, of course not."

"Wasn't Olive Popeye's girlfriend? Slightly weird for his daughter's name!"

"Maybe, but Sweet Pea Flint doesn't really work."

They laughed again and clinked their glasses together, unhindered by the forces that would soon start to pull them apart.

They returned on separate flights. She went back to her flat. There were several messages from her sister, Lavanya. She had told her family that she was in Hong Kong for business, but not that she would stay over for the weekend. Normally they would not ring that often, but her grandmother had been a little unwell. The messages, the reminder of home and family, the perfect memories of the last few days, all collided to expose the complicated reality of the situation, leaving her with a heavily pressured feeling of insuperable melancholy.

She so wanted to tell Lavanya about Marcus and her weekend away. She had never kept anything from her sister and knew that Lavanya would have sensed that she was hiding something but telling her would put her in the difficult situation of having to lie to her parents on her behalf. Her parents would not tolerate such an informal relationship. The pressure would be on for her to introduce Marcus to them and then to get married as soon as possible to him, or if not possible, to the next suitor in Kerala. As much as she desperately wanted to talk to Lavanya, she also wanted to talk to Marcus. But what would he think? They had only been together a few months and he wanted the whole thing hidden. She also wanted to talk to Ayla, to another friend, to anyone. She just wanted to share the things on her mind, to explore ways to find a way forward.

Marcus found Caitanya's discretion yet another quality that had increased his fondness for her. It had started off as an irresistible attraction, evolving into something fun between consenting adults that, in his eyes, they must both have recognised as something temporary, but over time and particularly after the weekend in Hong Kong, he had started to feel a deeper, and somewhat unfamiliar, stronger bond towards her. He wondered again if this was how love felt. The longer things continued, the more permanent they would feel, and the more difficult it would be to manage or resolve the issue of keeping things hidden.

The circumstances became more complex when, after another few weeks, Marcus was informed that should things continue along the current career path, he was on the 'very' short list of candidates to become global sales head and transfer back to London. He would join the global Exco for markets. The timing wasn't specific, but it would be within the next twelve to eighteen months.

Although the Singapore transfer had been presented to Marcus as an opportunity, he had never seen it as anything other than a demotion, and it was that inner anger and rancour that had driven him much harder to eventually become head of Asia distribution. He was very conscious though that being based in the smallest region wasn't ideal for global visibility and any further progression. He had started to accept that the next likely step, if it came, would be local and, ultimately, limited. However, the London conversation had relit his broader aspirations and the dormant fires of ambition started blazing stronger than he could ever have anticipated. The opportunity, for him, would be a suitable, deserved, and arguably overdue progression for his career; a natural reordering of things, and potentially a launch pad into the higher echelons of TDT, and nothing should be allowed to detract from it. That also meant that his relationship with a junior – whom he had mentored, promoted, and for whom he had signed off large bonuses – becoming public had now become an even more significant risk.

That, then, was his prompt and timescale to resolve the Caitanya situation, and the simplest solution it seemed to him would be for her to resign, and he would help to find her a role with another bank or potentially a client. They could then pretend their relationship started sometime after, and, sure, it would be a little awkward at first, but the situation would resort to normal over time. The only question was he didn't know how she would take to it, and it would be a difficult topic to broach.

It was also around this time that Sanju, and then Emma, arrived in Singapore. He viewed them as the perfectly polished couple, and Emma, beautiful and intelligent, the ideal professional partner, with their relationship, unlike his, open for everyone to see. At various events, it was obvious that they would attract the attention of the senior executives and their partners and, he had no doubt, were being invited as a couple to other couples' socials and the more select client functions. Of course, it shouldn't matter – it was the twenty-first century – but he wondered if he could lose out in those marginal distinctions that influenced promotion decisions, like missing out on the proverbial shooting party. He resented the need to keep Caitanya, beautiful, intelligent, and professional herself, hidden from view, without really knowing at whom or what to direct that indignation.

Renu, who was the wife of Deepak Prasad, overall head of the Asia region, seemed particularly enamoured with Emma. Marcus was on reasonably good terms with Sanju and would introduce him as friend, even though he was a trader and Marcus found him too straight and, frankly, a bit dull. He tried a few times to speak with Emma also – she was polite but clearly not particularly interested in spending more than a few moments with him. Although he couldn't remember exactly what he had said, he did remember that at his London leaving do, he had made some sort of drunken pass at her, but that thankfully she seemed to have no memory of it.

Marcus and Caitanya struggled to find an opportunity to say what they both wanted to about their relationship – both thinking that maybe the best time would be on another relaxing weekend away. The trigger, however, came unexpectedly one Sunday morning as they were walking along the beach on Sentosa and bumped into Andrea.

Caitanya realised that Andrea must have seen them holding hands, but Marcus seemed very relaxed. She knew them to be very close, and possibly the only person she would describe for Marcus as a friend.

"Andrea, you know Tani, right?"

"Yes, of course, how are you?"

They spoke for a few moments before Andrea left.

"Poppie, are you not concerned that he saw us?" Caitanya asked, wondering if a page had been turned and they could perhaps be more open, but she was to be disappointed.

"Don't be concerned about him. He won't say anything."

"But you trust him, yet you don't want me to talk about us to any of my closest friends, or even my sister?"

Marcus could sense the tension rising but he didn't want to talk about his plans right now. "Listen, Tani, let's not argue about this. The guy comes across very smooth now, but he was in a mess a while back – needed to leave Europe – I sorted him out. If he fucks with me, he's out of work and he's out of Singapore with nowhere to go. That's why I've got nothing to worry about with Andrea. Though, sure, there is a risk of bumping into someone else or letting something slip." Marcus raised his eyebrows with arms outstretched in a questioning disdainful 'you get it, right?' look.

Caitanya looked stunned – her eyes wide open.

"Oh, come on, Tani, don't give me that stare." Marcus's voice had raised. She stayed totally silent for a few moments longer before saying, "I think I'm going to go back to my place, Marcus."

"Fine," he clipped before muttering, "fuck it," under his breath.

* * *

A couple of days later, Marcus called to apologise and said he'd be going to Tokyo in three weeks, and why didn't she join him, and they'd have a chance to talk and plan the way forward. He meant persuading her to start looking for work elsewhere, before starting their relationship afresh.

She took it as the chance to decide the timing for her to introduce him to her family, hopefully over the next few weeks.

After that call, Caitanya started to anticipate that matters would soon resolve. She just had to stay patient and discreet as Marcus had said. Yet the sustained hidden deceit and the ongoing blatant lying to her family and friends continued to be intolerably stressful. She could feel herself drifting away from them and knew that they knew she wasn't being honest. She began to avoid people in the office and would spend as little time as possible outside in case she met someone – the whole place, even the trips to Sentosa, had started to feel insufferably claustrophobic.

Inevitably, this led to increasingly tense calls with her sister.

"Tani, I feel something is not quite right. You seem so quiet. There is something you're not telling me. I've spoken to Papa, and I'm planning to come and see you in a couple of weeks, just for the weekend."

"I'll be away then, Lavi. I've got a business trip to Tokyo."

"Over the weekend?"

"Well, yes, and also to look around."

"On your own?"

"Nothing wrong with that. Anyway, everything is fine. Sure, come over, but come for longer, for a proper holiday. I'd love it, but I can't do that weekend."

There was a moment's pause. "Is it a guy?"

"You think I wouldn't tell you if there was?"

"Maybe not, maybe not if it's a *gora*."

"Oh, *gora*, that's below you. What difference does that make – you weren't exactly impartial to the boys in Germany?"

"It makes a difference to Papa, Mummy and Dadi – they're spending a lot of time looking at proposals, and they've got their hopes set on a nice, settled professional from Kerala."

"Why don't you take one of them then?"

"I'm coming to Singapore."

"You can, but I won't be here, Lavi – final!" Both put their phones down in a fuse of anger and tears.

Matters started to spiral further out of Caitanya's control, and two days later she called her sister. In an emotionally distressed, compunctious, and whimpering call, she couldn't resist but reveal everything. She then took a taxi round to Marcus.

"I really needed to talk to you. I've told Lavi about us."

She had anticipated some annoyance but not the strength of his rage, nor what he had to say. He told her about his pending promotion, asked how she could take such risks and be so selfish, suggested she shouldn't have got into this relationship if she didn't understand the consequences before divulging that he had planned to discuss their future in Tokyo, but may as well do it now: she needed to leave TDT, their relationship couldn't continue as is, he would help her find a new role in Singapore and then they would start from fresh as if nothing had happened and everything could be done 'above board'.

She listened without interruption, memorising each point made.

"So, there is no point in my coming to Tokyo now, Marcus. Lavi wanted to come and stay this weekend anyway.

I better go and clean the flat out." Her words were spoken slowly. She had more to say but her voice was shaking with fury, and she needed to get out of his apartment.

In fact, she didn't go home but went to Ayla's, where a lot of tears were shed and some, too much, wine was drunk before they both called in sick the next day.

Marcus continued with his trip to Tokyo, thinking that being on their own would not only help him to reflect, but also a chance for Caitanya to coolly think through and ideally agree his idea as a way forward. He couldn't resist but spend his two nights with Satomi at her place, and his only real deliberation was whether things weren't, in reality, better before Caitanya; when he lived his life free from concerns about what someone else may say, do, or decide. He spent time on the return flight thinking about his last conversation with Caitanya. He shouldn't have lost his temper, but he had dreaded her talking about their relationship with anyone, and really did need to draw a solid red line that this was something she couldn't discuss – what if she next blurted something out to a colleague. He needed to deal with it calmly but firmly. Yes, he probably loved Caitanya. He didn't want to lose her, but the opportunity to get onto Exco, indeed reboot his career, after all these years, could not be jeopardised, and if she didn't accept his proposal, he would need a Plan B.

He took a taxi back from the airport straight to his apartment. There was a note in his mailbox.

Hello Marcus,
Last week when I came, I said I had some news, but the conversation moved in a different direction. I'm pregnant. I guess things are now already 'above board'.
Tani

EIGHTEEN

Si tu pouvais lire dans mon coeur,
Tu verrais la place où je t'ai mise.

She had never been outside of Europe and was a little tentative as to what to expect, but she recalled how, at times, she was like a young child at a theme park, almost effervescing with excitement during that first fortnight. She loved the heat far away from the drizzles in London and Paris. She had always been drawn to the new and the different. She was enthralled by the sights and smells of the hawker food markets, a smorgasbord of Malay, Chinese, Indian, and even European, with the unique local fusion of styles. She was fascinated by the different neighbourhoods: Chinatown, Joo Chiat and Katong, Kampong Gelam, and Little India, with their temples, mosques, heritage shops and traditional facades. She relished being able to swim in the outdoor pool at the Mandarin each evening before dinner, as she had done on holidays in Provence. After all the trauma of Sanju deliberating over whether to come to Singapore on his own, he now seemed totally elated to have her there, and even more elated when she told him that Evershed Shapley had approved a one-year sabbatical to stay with him.

TDT had arranged a number of apartment viewings, but after the first Tuesday, Sanju became too busy at the office and left it to her to select something.

"I'm thinking we'll go for something central or with a sea view."

"Sure, you'll know the place better than me!"

"Yep, I think I've just about seen everything in these two weeks."

"Hey, I hope you're not getting bored, Em."

"Well, it would be nice to see more of you, Sanju. You're hardly out of that office during the week and you're still tapping away on your keyboard half the weekend." She smiled with her gentle dig at him.

"I'm sorry, Em. It's always busy at the start, you know."

"It's OK. It's kinda what I expected. I like the place, love the different cultures, and I guess I'll get to know some more people. Might just take a little getting used to not working but the year will go quickly." Emma was excited to be with Sanju, but having observed the hours Sanju was working, she was in some ways also happy that it was only a one-year sabbatical rather than the eighteen months or two years that she had originally requested. She was also secretly keen to have some time on her own in the Wimbledon house to clear out all trace of the ex's, Karin's, earlier presence.

"Talking of people, we've been invited to Deepak and Renu's in a couple of weeks, you know the regional head and his wife. Apparently, she was very impressed with your five words in Hindi!"

"Oh yeah, I was talking to her about your mum's parathas."

"She would have loved that. Look, we don't need to go if you just want to spend time together."

"No, it's OK. The office crowd here are nicer than in London."

"Well, yeah, I guess it's a smaller place and we're the new couple in town."

"Hmm, exactly. And your glamorous girlfriend isn't doing your networking any harm." She giggled and leant over to kiss him.

"Nah, it's a meritocracy at TDT, as you know," he retorted as they both burst into laughter.

* * *

Emma remembered seeing Marcus at a couple of client events, though recalling his lewd comments at his leaving do in London, she chose to try to ignore him. Sanju would refer to him as his friend, though privately would describe him as arrogant, entitled and someone he couldn't trust. She also remembered Caitanya: beautiful, glamourous, and confident, and though they were only introduced once, Caitanya had definitely left an impression. She also recollected seeing Caitanya talking to Marcus at the end of an evening once, and thinking they appeared quite familiar with each other with a certain chemistry, so wasn't surprised to learn that there were some rumours about their relationship. Marcus later told her how envious he was about her free and visible relationship with Sanju for all to see, and that his was so hidden. He had actually thought it was very well hidden and wouldn't believe her when she mentioned there had been some office gossip about them.

Emma made friends with some expat wives – Americans and Australians mainly – and they would meet for a regular weekly lunch. Sanju's Singaporean PA, Jenny Yip, didn't work on Fridays, so, once a month, she and Jenny would meet so she could go around the city 'like a local'. The cleaner would come once a week. On Monday mornings, she would run through her work emails though they were mostly administrative.

Emma was amazed that after making time for calling friends and family, dealing with house chores and any admin, Sanju's work events, and the other occasional lunches or coffees, how the weeks passed so quickly. She had hoped to read more, play her guitar, maybe do a course in cooking or something artistic, but the whole year passed like for an ornithologist waiting in anticipation to spot some rare migrating birds, locating them expectantly on the horizon, watching them pass fleetingly and unexceptionally in full flow, and then seeing them gone, leaving a memory of something that happened too quickly, and now seemed a long time ago.

The break from the routine and comfort, and a greater semblance of adventure, came on their few trips away. They got to visit Hong Kong and Tokyo when Sanju had to go there for work meetings, and he was able to tag on a weekend. Most of the time she'd be on her own and even on Saturdays, Sanju would spend part of the day working, and although she wandered around the cities, and could enjoy the luxury hotels with their spas, what she enjoyed far more were their occasional weekends in Malaysia.

The first time they went, they had planned to stay on Tioman Island, but en route they came across a family hotel near Cherating on the east coast and were attracted to its small number of private homely beach huts interspersed amongst the palm trees, and it became their go-to Malaysian destination. Inside each hut was a simple bed, and the only air conditioning came from the gentle sea breeze wafting through the open door. By the side, enclosed in a rectangle of wooden poles, was the outdoor shower, which was tight for two, but Emma wouldn't use on her own in case she encountered an unfamiliar insect. In front was a small veranda with a hammock, which merged into the beach. A couple of times they slept together on the hammock, under a thin sheet to ward off the mosquitos, and woke up with the taste of salt across their faces from the sea haze. She sometimes wondered nostalgically if that hammock could have supported both their weights now.

The other huts were never fully occupied – most of the backpackers stayed in cheaper places elsewhere along the coast, and it was too rustic for anyone looking for comfort. The food was cooked by the landlady and was exceptional. Over the year, they went about half a dozen times and got to know the extended family, including both sets of grandparents, as well as the grandchildren and some of the in-laws and local friends. They would ask in advance to request the hut at the end of the beach with the greatest privacy, so could sleep with the door open with no fear of anyone walking by and seeing their perspiring bodies inside.

During the day, Sanju learnt to windsurf. Emma spent her time experimenting with Batik art with one of the grandmothers who spoke little English, so the designs sometimes looked more Jackson Pollock than traditional Javanese, doing watercolour paintings, learning to cook a couple of dishes with the landlady, and taking photos – all the things she rarely got to do in Singapore, but most of all she loved the fact that there was no Wi-Fi, and they needed to walk up the wooded hill behind the huts to get any telephone reception. This meant that, seemingly much to his irritation, Sanju was limited in what he could do workwise and effectively forced into a complete break over the weekends.

She often reminisced how despite having stayed in the best hotels and villas since, nothing quite matched those days and nights in that beach hut, and how perfect she felt at the time. She also knew that even if Ollie hadn't been with them, she would never have done a holiday like that with Marcus. It just wouldn't be his thing.

She would hark back to their last night there when she lay

in the hammock, and Sanju sat on the veranda outside the hut with a small incense candle and a dim light coming through from the bedside lamp, and suddenly bursting into tears.

"What is it, Em?"

"Nothing, Sanju, I was just thinking how perfect this is – you and me – you know, and that things just don't stay perfect for ever."

Sanju stood up, held her hand and used his other hand to wipe away the tears. "This place certainly sets the bar high, but we have a long time to live to start thinking about things going downhill."

And their next break, the last one before Emma returned to London, did, in many ways, set the bar even higher. Sanju could only take a couple of days off, and although Emma suggested maybe they just stay in Singapore and do a longer holiday later, he was very keen to have one final trip before she left. Until they arrived at the airport, she didn't actually know where they were going. They flew into Hanoi – bustling, crowded, and chaotic – a perfect antithesis to their disciplined established days in Singapore. Emma wanted to stay in Hanoi longer, but Sanju had already reserved a taxi the next morning to Halong Bay. He had seemed quite tetchy, just like when he had left for Paris, which Emma didn't understand as this time his time in Singapore was coming to an end, and he would be back in London in three months.

The taxi took them straight to the dock where they boarded a small private junk boat with two large russet-red crimped sails. There was a small cabin just large enough to take a bed, a covered area with a white cloth-draped dining table all laid out, and on the deck were two loungers. They were welcomed with two cocktails by a husband and wife; the alcohol seemed to relax Sanju a little. Shortly after, they set sail into the clear turquoise water interspersed with stunning clusters of towering limestone rocks and islands, topped with thick vegetation. Soon, the many tourist boats dispersed, and they were on their own in the still and tranquil calm, drifting gently towards an Elysian world. The husband would occasionally point to some geological feature, a cave or a strange sculpture, and places where some member of his family had sighted a bizarre creature called Tarasque, all of which they were struggling to understand until Emma discovered that the couple spoke French. The wife was cooking and although they couldn't see her, the beautiful smell of fresh herbs wafted over the sun canopy. They passed fishermen and floating villages and Emma got into various conversations about their lives with the husband and wife, though she noticed how distracted Sanju was, engrossed in the natural beauty of the bay, hardly saying a word. She also noted that he had not checked his phone once since they arrived or taken the excuse of an idle moment to peruse a TDT research note.

As the sun set and its rays elbowed their way through the islets, the wife served some Vietnamese spring rolls with peanut sauce, and a couple of bottles of beer. They then ate dinner at the table: grilled fish with rice followed by fruit, and by the time they finished the sun had set, the moon was out sending shimmering streaks between the silhouetted rocks, and the boat had docked near a small village.

"Wow, you have really raised the bar with this trip, Sanju."

He pondered as if about to say something before uttering, "Yes, it's lovely."

"And we'll be together again in a few weeks in London."

"Yes, I hope so."

She went to bed wondering what was on his mind. It was an odd sentence. Had he been asked to stay longer? Could he be getting bored with her? But the gently rocking boat and a warm hug from him lying next to her soon dissipated those thoughts, and she fell asleep.

They woke with the wife bringing them two mugs of coffee. It was a cool and cloudy morning, and Emma wrapped a shawl around her shoulders and went to sit on one of the loungers. A thick haze lay across the placid water with the nearby islets now just tall, dark, ominous shapes, with nothing to distinguish their rock from their foliage. The vibrant colours under the sun from the day before had gone, to be replaced by monochrome shades of grey moving slowly with the mist and the opaque sun, amalgamating their ghostly palette across the sea, sky, and land. The husband untied the boat to drift slowly into the bay, alone in the eerie emptiness.

Sanju was standing behind Emma.

"I didn't realise there were so many variations of grey, and that they could be so beautiful." Emma looked round at Sanju, still a bit withdrawn and looking a little tense.

"Is everything alright, Sanju? You've been very quiet."

Sanju stayed speechless for a few seconds and cleared his throat. "Well, I did want to tell you something last night but then thought it could get a bit awkward on a small boat." He spoke slowly and nervously with that noticeably visible twitch.

"Awkward. Why? What's happened?"

"I, er, ahem called your father from Hanoi, you know to make sure, you know, any objections, and obviously depending on you, of course."

"Objections. I'm confused. What are you talking about? Are you OK?"

"Yes, no, I know. Let me get to the point. Spit it out." He took a deep breath and jutted out his lower lip to blow his hair. "I'm very happy, and hope you are too." There was another pause. Emma stood, baffled, trying to make sense of his rambling words. He took another breath. "Right, it didn't go like in the rehearsal but, Emma, will you marry me?"

"Hold on. Wait." She looked down, taking it all in like a

forensic lawyer. "You rang my dad, so my parents know and probably Jem?"

"Er, yes, and my parents. I told them before too."

"So, the whole of Greenwich and Blackheath knows about this?"

"Quite possibly." Sanju had started to recover his composure now he'd got the question out.

"So that's why you've switched your phone off, so they're not texting to check the answer every two minutes."

"Look, perhaps I've got the process wrong but I, for one, in case you haven't noticed, am getting a bit anxious and eager to know the answer myself." The voice was back to normal.

Emma got up, smiled, looked into his eyes, wrapped her arms around him and pulled back her head to be staring straight into his face. She smiled again, lowered her eyes, and whispered, "Yes, more than anything else."

She held him tightly and could feel him bursting into tears. Behind them, she saw the husband and wife, smiling broadly with a bottle of champagne that Sanju must have bought on board for this high-bar moment.

NINETEEN

The dancing of the peacock and the singing of the cuckoo bird is a sign that rainfall is certain.

When Sanju arrived in London two months later, plans for the wedding were well under way, though perhaps it was more accurate to say that conversations around ideas for the wedding were well under way. Emma's mother had anticipated a small intimate wedding at their local village church in Provence, followed by a reception dinner at a nearby farmhouse restaurant run by family friends, with its exceptional *terroir* food and wine, outdoor seating, and an unmatched view across the hills towards the Mediterranean. The ceremony would be a rerun of her own, and her mother's wedding there, and something she had been dreaming about from the day the daughters were born.

Mrs Kapoor had envisioned something much bigger – a pseudo-traditional Hindu ceremony followed by a large reception of several hundred people, ideally at a plush hotel in central London. She had already started discussing dates to fit around the Indian school holidays, so that her siblings, nephews, nieces, school friends, etc. could come across, not to mention members of her husband's wider Kapoor diaspora in the States, Canada, and Australia.

Emma felt that the nature of the wedding should be decided by Sanju and herself. She didn't mind if it was a Catholic or a Hindu ceremony or both but wanted something small in London just for close family and friends. She didn't want to get into a row with Sanju's mother while he was still in Singapore, so waited until he was back. Sanju explained it would be difficult to persuade his parents to cut back the numbers to the sort of level Emma had in mind – that would be considered an affront to them, and to those not invited – but he did like the idea of doing something in France, perhaps a Hindu wedding in a chateau to bring both cultures together, an idea to which Emma gave short shrift by suggesting that if that was what he wanted, he'd have to find time in his busy work schedule to organise it himself.

The mothers would meet with Sanju and Emma each weekend, but everyone's positions were ensconced, with the conversations getting slightly more heated by the week, and only Sanju sitting there with little input into the process, other than commenting how excited he was that they were going to be one large family, and not wishing to take sides between his mother, his mother-in-law to be, and his future wife, and two months after his arrival no agreement had been reached.

Emma made a special effort for the following Friday, cooking an Indian butter chicken to try to find favour with Sanju's mum, and a tarte tatin, which was her mother's favourite desert. She tidied the flat extensively and lit a full selection of perfumed candles. But the evening was another one for passive-aggressive interaction between the mothers, with Sanju quiet, and Emma continuing to get frustrated, staring at her untouched glass of wine.

After they left, Sanju topped up his glass.

"Not drinking, Em?"

"Sanju, you're going to have to get involved and say

something to your mother. I can deal with mine but don't want to row with yours. It's our wedding." She spoke with a simultaneously pleading yet uncompromising tone, placing stress on the word 'our'.

"Don't worry, Em. It will sort itself out. Give it time. It's important for them too, and I'm an only child."

"Time! We've been talking for months. Anyway, we don't have time."

"What do you mean?"

"I'm pregnant."

There was a second's silence, but it was a long, lingering second – one of those seconds that feels longer than a few minutes.

Sanju stared at Emma with a combined look of confusion, fear, and exhilaration, like turning up to a friendly five-a-side tournament and seeing Ronaldo warming up for the opposition.

"What, how?"

"How? Hmm, allow me to explain."

"But we're always so careful."

"Perhaps you shouldn't have been quite so cock-a-hoop that night when you learnt of your MD promotion."

"Cock-a-hoop," he mumbled contemplatively, then smiled as Emma's words started to sink through. "Oh my God, Em, I'm going to be a dad." He walked over and gave her a big hug. "Are you feeling OK? My God, you'll be a mother. You should sit down. Let me take the wine and don't stress about the wedding, I'll deal with it. I'm so happy. Are you?"

"Yes, Sanju." She looked up at him. "But I don't want to be showing in my wedding dress."

"No, of course not. It'll be tricky explaining it to Ma. She's not noted for her liberal views. Hasn't even told anyone that we're living together, not even when in Singapore, but it'll be OK." He sighed.

"Won't be straightforward with *Maman* either – they don't call her Mother Térese for nothing." They both burst into laughter – the carefree, blissful sound of lovers that couldn't be any happier together.

They were married two months later at Our Lady Star of the Sea church in Greenwich, with the reception at the Admirals' House, so Emma got her wish of a small London wedding, but not before promising to have a ceremony and large reception for the family in India, a follow-up reception sometime in the future for Sanju's parents' friends in London, and Jemima committing to their mother to a Provençal wedding when her time came.

"You seriously owe me a big one," she sniped at Emma.

News of the pregnancy united the two mothers. First in dismay, but then shortly after in jubilation, like local competing traditional artisans who had been squabbling over customers, coalescing around their combined distaste at the arrival of cheap copy-cat factory goods, before rejoicing in the recognition of the beauty and quality of their unique hand-made merchandise.

Things got strained again as the shortened guest lists started to be drafted, and Sanju was forced to give both families a quota, as if allocating risk thresholds to his trading desks, recognising that if he didn't give his parents a larger pool of invites, their relationships would go into complete meltdown, but which still wasn't anywhere near large enough for them, yet was perceived as highly unfair by Emma's mother, leaving neither side happy. This, the short notice, and the agreement to an Indian follow-up meant that only two of Mrs Kapoor's sisters were able to come from India. This resulted in her taking every opportunity when Emma and Sanju were within earshot to call one of the uninvited guests or relatives to apologise profusely, making sure to speak in English so that everyone understood who was responsible.

"You know children nowadays… yes, they don't respect their traditions… *aré* forget it, no, they don't listen to their elders. Can you imagine us behaving like that? Look, it's just the Western way. We're living here… We have to accept."

All the negotiating on the numbers meant that Sanju and Emma were only able to invite a few of their closest friends, one of whom was Jenny Yip from Singapore. It was a chance to catch up on some gossip, and that was when Emma first learnt that rumours about Marcus and Caitanya had become rife, and that Caitanya had suddenly resigned from TDT and returned to India.

They scrapped their plans for their honeymoon in Antigua when Emma's morning sickness became too pronounced, but, after all the heat of the wedding preparations, took a week's break in the cool, fresh greenery of the Isle of Skye. A few months later, and late by three weeks, Anshu arrived in their lives with thick, dark hair and bright-blue eyes. Both parents and both sets of grandparents as well as Aunt Jemima were ecstatic. The grandmothers entered a new and open rivalry of gifts and cuddles. Sanju started to get home noticeably early from work, and the confident strutting trader transformed into a risk-averse iron-coated protective blanket for his son, as Emma's life for the next six months became a mix of sleepless nights and doting motherhood.

* * *

Emma remembered her first moments at Indira Gandhi International Airport as a totally intoxicating assault on the senses – the blast of heat and humidity upon leaving the plane onto the boarding bridge turning into Arctic-esque air conditioning in the terminal, the strong distinctive smell of the cleaning agents walking to passport control, the silhouettes through the glass panes of rhesus macaque monkeys scuttling on the roof, the calm silence of the airport building with its modern décor where they were met by someone to be taken through the VIP lane, and then exiting into the bright blinding sunlight outside.

They were met by their mid-twenties driver, Ashok, who guided their luggage trolley as they followed quickly behind, holding hands, with Sanju keeping a tight grip around Anshu, through the thick throng of people and the constant din of honking horns to the parking lot.

She had seen poverty and homelessness in England and across Asia, often in the wealthiest areas like the rough sleepers of Mayfair, but she was still shocked by the contrasts of wealth and poverty so openly on display on that first chaotic drive. They drove alongside Mercedes and BMWs speeding on the four-lane highway to arrive in Agra, where barefoot children would beg through their windows at junctions. But as with many visitors to India before her, the shock melted into an instant and ultimately turbulent love affair with the people and the sights, all the culture and spirituality, the hospitality and food, the mystique, and the vivid contrasts and diversity in every direction.

Their 'wedding reception' was planned in Mehrangarh Fort in Jodhpur, where Sanju's maternal family hailed from, towards the end of their three-week holiday. The guest list ran to over four hundred, with aunts, uncles, cousins, second cousins, aunts and uncles that had become designated aunts and uncles by virtue of being close family friends, and other aunties and uncles who were just aunties and uncles as they happened to be about the right auntie and uncle age. In short, more people than Emma thought she actually knew. The itinerary for the trip itself had been subject to intense negotiation between Sanju and his mother.

"*Beta*, I have told your *Mama* in Lucknow that you'll stay with them first, before going to *Chacha* in Gwalior."

"But, Ma, you have to talk to me first. Emma doesn't know anybody. We can't just turn up everywhere for a couple of days."

"She would have known them if they had been invited to your wedding here, Sanju!"

"Let's not go through that again, Ma. They'll both be at the reception. It's her first time in India. It's so different in Lucknow. They're very conservative. It'll be harder for her. We'll visit them next time."

"Well, they'll be very upset if you don't visit them and they're so excited to see Anshu."

"And that's another point – all this travel in the heat – it could make Anshu ill. Really, I think we should just see *Mossi* in Agra – Emma really likes her – and then come to the reception."

"*Aré haan* – let us not risk his health, but what will I say to them now?"

"They'll understand. Just say we're looking forward to meeting at the reception."

"OK, but you must go to visit Jaipur Aunty. You'll have a few days to…"

"Ma, I'd like to get to Delhi for a couple of days, take a break and recharge…"

"What? Why you want to go to Delhi? Such a rude place. You know Jaipur Aunty is my closest friend. Our grandfathers grew up in the same village…"

In the end, they were able to agree a stay just in Agra, with a short break in a nice hotel in Delhi and a stopover in Jaipur. Emma was also happy she'd get to see some sites rather just than shifting from one family to another.

They stayed for three nights in Agra with Sanju's aunt –

who was one of his mother's sisters at their wedding – and her two sons – Sanju's cousins – and their families, who lived altogether in the same large house in Idgah Colony. The family and the young children made Emma feel immediately welcome, but the star of their attention was Anshu, as his various second cousins couldn't do enough to keep him occupied and would squeal with delight if Anshu deigned them with a faint smile.

Even the adults couldn't resist holding him, and he would be passed from person to person as they admired his blueish eyes that had started to darken. They would purr over a small birthmark on his cheek which Sanju's mother would always refer to as the 'beauty spot' and stroke his long, wavy hair tied into a ponytail – they had been asked not to cut for a year in respect of a tradition that Sanju said he didn't understand but hadn't questioned. With his not-unsubstantial baby fat, inherited plump lips and pout from his mother, and a scarf tied round his head like a bandana to protect him from the sun, he looked every bit like a cute miniature Sicilian gangster. The family offered to keep Anshu at home while they visited the tourist spots, to protect him from the heat, but Sanju insisted on having him with them at all times.

"Be careful," Sanju's cousin advised. "These touristy places can get very crowded and there are a lot of pickpockets and aggressive hasslers wanting to be guides."

"Yes, I know. I've been many times."

"Not on your own," his cousin continued before turning to Emma, "and keep a solid hold of that beautiful boy. We're a friendly place but in a billion people even a small percentage of bad eggs can make a stinkingly foul omelette."

"Honestly, we'll be fine." She smiled, not totally following the metaphor. "And we have our driver, of course."

"I can put on a kurta pyjama. Emma can borrow a salwar kameez. We'll look more local," Sanju tried to reassure.

"Hmm, doubt it, there aren't many Indian ladies with blonde hair. You know what, I'll take a couple of days off and show you around. That'd be better," the cousin continued, which soon evolved into a longer and wider family discussion and ended with both cousins and their families crowding into two cars to tour with them around Agra. Emma loved the company and hearing the local stories from the guides and the two cousins' wives, getting particular joy in smiling and pointing out she was half-French each time the guide at the Taj or Red Fort talked about how the Britishers had taken or destroyed this or that. Anshu was just excited to have their children running around after him, playing peek-a-boo or finding some new toy for him to play with. Sanju and Emma were also happy to have relatives share the weight of carrying Anshu in the heat – they realised that it was pointless to have a buggy with all the crowds – and the baby backpack was just too hot. Plus, the cousins and the cousins' wives and the aunt were only too happy to have a hold.

During the trip to Fatehpur Sikri, Emma had stopped to sit in the shade for a few moments with Anshu and was immediately surrounded by some local ladies fawning over him, which quickly grew into a small crowd. It all seemed harmless, but she was comforted that she was with relatives who could usher them away. By the end of the four days, she had gotten quite close to the whole family, and was pleased they'd all be coming to the party in Jodhpur. Nevertheless she was really looking forward to their hotel stay, just the three of them, in Delhi – she had hardly spent a moment on her own with Sanju, or with Anshu. It had also become a little frustrating that she couldn't understand much of the conversation when it inevitably drifted into Hindi, which Sanju could understand even if he could hardly speak it.

With Anshu getting so much family attention, Sanju had

started to revert to taking time to catch up on work reading that he had reduced with Anshu's birth, but at any moment they were alone, Sanju would be totally engrossed in everything Anshu did. He had become extraordinarily protective, a side to Sanju that Emma had not seen before fatherhood, cleaning everything before Anshu touched it, buying Western baby food jars and not letting him eat anything local, keeping a tight grip in crowds, and only allowing family members to get close. On a couple of occasions, he even told Ashok, their driver, to take his time and go slower – no need to overtake on blind bends against oncoming traffic. For that, even Emma was relieved.

They stayed for three nights in Delhi, where Ashok took them around the main tourist spots. They were able to do things in Delhi at their own pace and will, and get Anshu to bed at the right time, and to have some holiday time with each other for the first time since they became parents. It was on that second night when they were coming back from dinner that Sanju spotted Marcus in the Leela hotel bar with some clients. The clients seemed very keen to solidify their relationship with TDT and, owning some boutique hotels, offered them a stay in one of their newly refurbished heritage palace acquisitions.

Sanju wasn't keen, as he wanted to get to Jodhpur. It had been hard enough for him to persuade his mother to have the short break in Delhi, but Emma was totally enthralled by the idea of having a couple of nights living like a princess from *One Thousand and One Nights*. It seemed like the place was on their way, and as they had planned to break the journey in Jaipur in any case, it would only add one extra day. In the end, she was able to persuade Sanju and they were not to be disappointed.

The drive from Delhi took a few hours through dusty, desert-border villages, past hills with each seemingly having its own decaying fort guarding past glories, green fields dabbed with ladies in bright saris, and passing virtually every assortment of transport possible – bicycles, motorbikes, trucks, horse-drawn carriages, donkeys, bullock carts, camels and even an elephant. As they veered further from Delhi, the landscape became sparser, with scattered villages all blessed with grand old havelis, funded by fortunes made on ancestral trade routes, or modern glass-fronted villas of younger businessmen, passing proud men with large handlebar moustaches with heavy colourful turbans and rough heat-dried warrior skin, who would reluctantly step aside to let their car go through. This was truly the remote Rajasthan that Emma had seen in television programmes and dreamt about visiting.

They arrived at the hotel, which once served as the fort and residence of a small local Shekhawati clan – the main building encircled by a solid double layer of majestic high-stone vertical walls only interrupted by a large iron-gated doorway, through which the narrow driveway took them up to a three-storey inner palace, all clean cream, with stately round domes resting on exotic arches, and towers, turrets, and spires jutting against the bright-blue cloudless sky. Whereas the desert outside was largely sand and shrub, the irrigated gardens had luxuriant lawns and tall trees overlooking an inviting swimming pool. They were met by the concierge who took them into a large, vaulted, double-storey reception, which must have been where the Rajput head held court. The mezzanine floor looked onto two red-cushioned throne seats facing large Dijon-coloured upholstered wooden sofas that lined three sides of the room, each in front of arched doorways, all decorated with intricate bridal henna-like designs on a pale tangerine background in a mix of paint, coloured glass, and embedded stones. Huge chandeliers hung between several large ceiling fans. All the walls boasted pictures of presumably previous residents, mostly in battle-ready regalia. Emma and Sanju stared at each other and wondered that if this was the palace for a lowlife princeling, how must the big boys and girls have lived. They were met by the manager.

"I'm afraid we are officially only opening in three weeks, so currently we only have three other young families here sort of testing the place out, though that means you'll have a lot more space to yourself, but we are ready to have you. We have arranged the Royal Suite – it used to be called the Badal Mahal, Palace in the Clouds – for your stay. Everything is complimentary. All we ask is that you let us know if something is not to your liking so we can correct for our future guests."

There was absolutely nothing not to their liking. The Palace in the Clouds was on the top floor, opening onto a large roof terrace that seemed to cover a fifth of the hotel building and overlooked the inner courtyard, as well as having views across the fort walls to the desert and hills beyond. A small, covered section, with an elongated dome at the far side of the terrace had a comfy sofa where they were offered welcome cocktails. The bedroom was large enough to incorporate a sitting area and a study desk with an elegant black-leather office chair, though the Wi-Fi wasn't yet functioning and the telephone reception was poor, for which the hotel apologised profusely, but which for Emma was again very much to her liking. A large cot was placed next to the bed – they joked Prince Anshu may not adapt too well after that to the discomforts of low-life Wimbledon.

In one corner of the bedroom was a passageway into a private corridor painted in deep blue, with a sequence of arched windows that were probably once used by the queens to observe the comings and goings into the fort, but now had had their carved trellis removed and replaced with a bright assortment of multicoloured stained glass. It led to another room with walls and ceilings also painted in deep blue but covered with swirling patterns in gold and lit by what seemed like hundreds of lanterns. This was the dining area to the Royal Suite with a large table and dining chairs and yet another seating area. It was the most opulently beautiful room Sanju and Emma had ever seen.

Two burly turbaned men were at their beck and call as butlers, even though, from their looks, they were probably more suited to working as VIP security guards. They had just returned from hospitality training in Mumbai and, diligently and delicately, set the dining table and served the food and drinks, being visibly most excited with the simplest task of warming up Anshu's Heinz baby-food pot.

"How did we land here, Sanju?"

"I did ask Marcus. The hotel owners have been working with the bank to renew a loan facility; wanted to be 'friendly', I guess, and they also wanted feedback on the hotel from some Western guests. But honestly, I wasn't expecting anything this exclusive. We are plainly in breach of our gifts policy, but here we are, in the middle of a desert, so can't do much about that now. May as well enjoy."

Ashok had a small room in the drivers' area, originally the stables, and had planned to drive them around the local area but, after just a couple of hours, Sanju and Emma decided that they would just stay and enjoy the hotel for the two days. They had also grown fond of Ashok since being picked up at the airport. He was even more cautious about bad hygiene and where they ate than Sanju. During the long drives, he had given Emma a full introduction into Bollywood stars on the roadside posters, the playback musicians on the radio, Indian politics after the news bulletins, and who should and shouldn't be in the Indian cricket team, with particular passion reserved for the last topic. Wherever they stopped, he would brusquely tell anyone who came to beg for money, offer to be a guide, and particularly if anyone took an interest in Anshu, in what seemed like some colourful language, to firmly push off. Before they had changed plans to go to the palace hotel, they learnt that Ashok had planned to visit his sister in Jaipur on their original route, so they gave him the time off to go and see her in spite of his insistence that he stayed with them in case they needed him.

They spent the day exploring the hotel, sitting by the pool, having exclusive use of the games room with its old billiard table, enjoying coffee in the dungeon that had been converted into a bar with a small dance floor, and lunching in a huge ballroom, which was now the main dining room.

In the evening, as the temperature started to cool, they took a stroll around the adjacent village with its large, mostly empty havelis spread across the handful of narrow roads, a couple of small *kirana* shops, a temple, and a mosque. At each junction, there would be a small gathering of typically elderly men with the wildest moustaches, chatting and smoking, who would smile enthusiastically at Anshu, displaying remnants of jagged teeth, touching his hair and squeezing the baby fat on his cheeks, asking his name and where were they from in broken English, as Sanju held on and avoided engaging too much in any conversation despite their welcoming demeanour. A few times, a small group of ladies, sometimes with younger children in tow, walked past dressed in brightly patterned saris with their dupattas falling across their foreheads, and stopped to smile at Anshu. But only if Emma, another female in this conservative world, was holding him, making friendly warm gestures at Emma, as she admired their jewellery and the colours of their clothes.

At night, they ate on the roof terrace under the starlit sky, having the most gorgeous biryani, as Anshu slept in his cot with the bedroom doors open, providing a light cooling draught of wind.

"This is so perfect, Sanju. Everybody is so friendly. I wish we could stay a little longer."

"I know but we need to leave early. I got some phone signal on our walk. There is a rumour that the Fed is going to announce some forward guidance on interest rates. There is going to be a lot of volatility in the markets tomorrow and I need to talk to the team." Her frown must have been obvious to Sanju. "Don't worry, the fort at Jodhpur is far bigger, and equally impressive and friendly."

Emma sighed internally, thinking it will also have a few hundred guests she didn't know. "I know, but here it's just the three of us."

"You're forgetting Muhammad Ali and George Foreman. Look, here they come with the wine."

Emma chuckled, and then looked down, slightly melancholic.

"What's the matter, Em?"

"Oh, I just want to freeze this moment."

Sanju leaned across and held her hand. "Why? Our journey with Anshu has only just started. There is so much to look forward to."

The next morning, despite the drive from Jaipur, Ashok was at the hotel by six.

"Good morning, Ashok. Listen, can we pull over for half an hour when we get a decent phone signal. I need to make a couple of calls."

"Of course, sir. There is a service station just after we hit the national highway. You should get a good signal there. It does great coffee too and there is a shop. I know Miss Emma wanted to buy some local things."

It was mid-morning by the time they got to the national highway, and Sanju was getting visibly more anxious as the odd hint of telephone signal would release a string of emails exposing intense market volatility upon Asia opening. He was desperate to talk to his desk in London before the markets opened there and go through their risk positions. Everyone could feel the tension as they drove without talking until, finally, they pulled up at the roadside service station.

A couple of tourist coaches were parked to the side of a large dirty-white, one-storey building, with a handful of cars spread across the rest of the parking area. The building was split into a restaurant and a shop selling local souvenirs. A couple of steps descended onto a plush lawn bordered with shrubs and laid out with a handful of deckchairs where the coach tourists sat, chatting loudly, sipping masala tea, and taking fingerfuls of Bombay mix and other snacks from various plastic bags. At the edge of the lawn and to the side of the road were a small number of wheeled stalls selling trinkets, tablecloths and other local items, all run by ladies, again with vibrant patterned saris with their heads covered.

On both sides of the road were cornfields with tall green stalks, through which you could just about make out the farmers tilling away in white kurtas, and in the distance, low caramel hills with the inevitable indistinct ruins of a fort perched on top.

"Sir, the reception would be best in the restaurant."

Sanju rushed out of the car and headed into the building.

"Ashok, I think it's obvious I need to change Anshu's nappy. Let's open the doors and let some air in." Emma smiled at Ashok knowingly.

"Please let me get rid of that smelly sack, Miss Emma." By the time Ashok came back, Anshu was fast asleep again in the car seat – his forehead and black-and-white striped top covered in sweat.

"Shall I put the AC on, Madam?"

"No, let's get some fresh air in, Ashok. I won't strap him in until we leave."

"If you'd like, please take a look at the shop. I'm here with him."

"No, I won't, but I'll just go and browse at that stall, just there with the lady in that red and yellow sari. Those bracelets look lovely."

"Yes please, Miss Emma, I'm here only. Let me know if you want any advice on the right price." He said the last part loud enough for the stall lady to hear.

Emma walked across. The stall lady pulled back her sari a little over her overhead, comfortable to show her face in the company of another lady and smiled, beckoning Emma forward. "Please, look, but I no speak English."

"That's OK. I don't speak Hindi." Emma picked up a golden bracelet with yellow sapphire stones. "May I try?" It was a little tight, but the stall lady took Emma's hand, gently stretched out the fingers, and slid the bracelet on. "It's beautiful. How much is it?" The stall lady had such a lovely smile and mannerism that Emma had already decided she was not going to haggle the price.

They were interrupted by a sequence of cracking sounds coming from the restaurant and looked round to see some customers streaming out.

Emma shouted across to Ashok, "What was that?"

"I will take a look, Miss Emma."

"No, you stay there. Sanju will be too absorbed in his call to listen to you. I'll go." She tried to get the bracelet off to give back, but the stall lady ushered her on. "No, OK, please go."

Emma walked quickly across the lawn towards the building. The restaurant was emptying, and some smoke was coming through the door. She called out for Sanju and finally he came, one of the last to leave the building, coughing.

"What happened?"

"Some idiots let off a couple of fireworks. No idea why. The place is full of smoke."

People had gathered on the lawn, taking sips of water, as the manager opened all the windows, shouting at his staff to smother the small fire. They were all distracted by a loud thud, followed by the screeching of an accelerating motorbike, and a woman's scream.

As they looked across, they saw the stall lady lying in the middle of the road up from the restaurant, clearly having been dragged along the tarmac. A motorbike was speeding away into the distance. A moment's eerie silence was punctuated by a loud scream as the stall lady looked back towards the restaurant, screamed again, waving her arms, and shouted, "Baby, baby, *bacha*."

Sanju and Emma glanced across at the car. They could see Ashok picking himself up over the bonnet, and then the blood running down his face.

"Mr Sanju, come!" he screamed. "Anshu's gone! Taken. Get in the car. We'll get them!"

TWENTY

One must be a sea,
To receive a polluted stream without becoming impure.

The night had brought a coverage of snow thick enough to obscure the edges of the driveway and the borders of the paths around the villa. Intermittent flurries continued to intermingle with the loose ground cover being whipped up by gusts of wind, leaving the individual snowflakes searching for direction and their final landing place in a crowded chaos.

Marcus stared out of the window, his mind searching for its own direction, straining to see the outline of any paths. The swirls outside seemed free, euphoric, and random, but, ultimately, they were yielding to the natural forces of gravity and the whims of air currents.

He had struggled to get to sleep after the Muttu incident. Although he didn't feel any danger during the night, thinking that he hadn't been seen, he felt vulnerable and shaken that a slight noise could have caused Muttu to pull that trigger, and fundamentally shocked that someone in whose company he felt so comfortable had seemed that at ease carrying a gun in the dark, ready to shoot. He had felt nervous enough, though at the same time somewhat silly, to place a chair behind the door before getting into bed. He hoped he wouldn't bump into

Muttu until later, when his uneasiness would have started to dim, and his own mannerism and expressions wouldn't reveal anything noticeably different. He had been downstairs to make himself a coffee in the library before anyone was awake and had placed the 'do not disturb' sign on his door until he was ready to grab something to eat.

He had started to piece together Muttu's position at the villa, thinking through the police visits, the dinner conversations, the taciturn villagers, the gun incident, and the curiosity and desire to confirm his beliefs had grown exponentially. But he needed to focus on and prepare for his upcoming conversation with Pierre. Perhaps unsurprisingly, the episode with Muttu had created an additional sense of urgency to move on.

"Hey, Rahul, you in the office yet?"

"Hi, Marcus, just walking in. What can I do?"

"Listen, there is going to be another cull. Big one, I think. Not public yet. Can you send me who survived from the list last time, the country numbers, performance appraisals of my directs and one below them, soon as you can?"

"Oh, it's senior guys?"

"Yep, going to be a bloodbath. Can you also tell me their service duration? At least I can work out how much it will cost to exit the London guys and summarise for me any HR issues around exiting anyone from the other offices."

"Any risk to my COO team, Marcus?"

"Don't think so, unless they were signing off on dodgy trades around fifteen years ago." Marcus released a mildly sarcastic chuckle.

"So, it's about Epsilon?"

"It's about who we can pin for Epsilon." Marcus scoffed sardonically. "Is Pierre around the office much?"

"Yes, quite a lot. He seems in a grumpy mood, sitting in his office with his door shut."

"So much for open-door policy," Marcus muttered to himself. "Did you get a chance to listen to Simone's tapes?"

"Yes, well, the only work-related thing bothering her big time is that the country sales guys have been talking with her private banking clients, and having the usual arguments that they know the dealing desk better, or that the clients aren't really private banks. I guess she's worrying about losing production and it seems she's getting it in the neck from her team."

"Has she raised this with Ashleigh?" Marcus felt he spent half his life arbitrating to decide which salesperson or sales team could service which clients, and which clients fitted whose mandates. The firm talked about collaboration but rewarded people for maximising their own revenues rather than the firm's. His direct reports, themselves rewarded and driven by crediting maximum production to their tribe, were totally apathetic, or just unable to resolve such things in a mature, unbiased fashion.

"So it would seem. Obviously, I can only hear what's on the tapes, but she's also been talking directly with the country heads."

"And what are they doing to help her?"

"Oh, nothing, I think. General sense I get round the office is that she's been over-promoted."

"Doesn't sound like she's getting much fucking support from her boss. Which countries are the biggest issues?"

"From the tapes, it's not possible to tell what Ashleigh has been saying, but Simone seems to be getting into arguments all round. There was quite a rowdy exchange with Guenter over the summer. I suppose that's why she also went to France and Madrid."

"Guenter, hmm, for all his qualities, he's not exactly a team player."

"Yeah, he was round my desk last week complaining about the middle office again."

"What? He was in London?"

"Yes, been here three or four times last month. Been seeing Pierre, I think."

"Really! I didn't know that. Interesting. Any of the other continental guys been around?"

"I've only seen Eric – once last week – also spent best part of the afternoon with Pierre."

"What about Mark and Ashleigh – they been summoned to his office?"

"Ashleigh – have never seen them together. Saw Mark talking to Pierre outside a few days back when I was getting lunch, but it sounded like they were discussing football rather than work."

"Interesting. Listen, I need to run, Rahul. Get me that data will you and we'll talk again."

"Fuck me," Marcus blurted out as he got off the phone. Neither Guenter or Eric had mentioned being in London or speaking with Pierre and he'd only spoken to them a few days ago. Nor had it come up in any of the countless emails and texts he received telling him how wonderful they were relative to their peers, while pointing out issues in other teams.

What was Pierre up to? Maybe he just wanted some detail on the business. No, that was naïve. Guenter had been over three to four times, and surely Pierre should have spoken with him, Marcus, first. Pierre was plotting who would take over if he left or was pushed. That felt like paranoia but he, for sure, didn't trust Guenter, and he needed to get to the bottom of it.

Dr Guenter Meier (German, early forties) had joined TDT about five years ago as head of Germany. A hard-working and hard-driving rates salesman, he had increased TDT's share across all products over that time in a difficult, competitive, market. He was also unashamedly ambitious, and his direct style and self-promotion, whenever possible, had made him unpopular with most of his peers and many of his direct reports. Nevertheless, he was considered a bit of star by the traders, hence Pierre. Marcus had taken the approach of adding more responsibility to his mandate, first by adding Switzerland and Austria, and then more recently Scandinavia and the Netherlands, whilst offering him professional coaching on his management style. Pierre had been suggesting that Marcus had a regional EMEA head to cover Europe and the Middle East, with a nod towards Guenter for that position. But Marcus had resisted, as almost certainly that would have meant departures amongst his other senior guys, and also make his own position politically less secure.

"Hello, Marcus, so nice to hear from you. How are you?"

"Feeling better, Guenter. How are things in Frankfurt?"

"*Ya* super. Everyone is working their butts off. Great revenue. I've been spending more of my time with the Scandis and the Dutchies – as you know, we don't have the best crew there, but really with my direction I think we're starting to turn a corner."

"Good to hear." Marcus reflected on the totally contradictory picture he would get from the team in Amsterdam and Stockholm. They utterly detested his style and the damage being done to their franchise and team morale. "Listen, Guenter, a couple of things – we may have to cut some costs. I don't know how many but at the senior end, so could you dust off your list."

"*Ya, ya*, look, we have the best team in Germany and Switzerland now after three years, but I see it absolutely as an opportunity to give some youngsters a chance in the other regions." Marcus could sense Guenter chomping at the bit to fire anyone senior left who he still perceived as a threat.

"Sure. Secondly, I'll be back in the office in two weeks. Why don't you come over to London? We can talk more, and I don't think you've been over for a while." Marcus waited for the response.

"Oh, Marcus, so good to hear you're back and that would be super to meet. Why don't we have a nice dinner and wine? And *ya*, I need to come to London."

"Brilliant. When were you last over?" Marcus couldn't help pushing him to tell the truth or lie openly.

"Oh, it's been a while. Actually a few weeks back – had a client meeting but very short trip – hardly spent any time in the office. But I meant to tell you – met global CIO of Delphi Managers. The TDT relationship has been poor but now I think we are sorted in Germany. The real mess is in France. I dropped Eric a note, but you know Eric; don't think he's going to do anything."

Well, that confirmed Guenter was hiding something about his discussion with Pierre. And the backstabbing of his senior peer, Eric, though not out of character, seemed telling.

"I didn't see the call report of the meeting. Why don't you forward it and I'll speak with Eric? You know we should set an example of following processes within our team, around travel notifications and call reports and all that. I know it's a bit bureaucratic, but it sets a standard and also keeps everyone in the loop." He knew that no record of the meeting discussion would have been made, let alone circulated. Despite all his exhortations for everyone to follow processes, even the senior guys rarely shared details of their client discussions – perhaps they were just reluctant to expose the true strength of their relationships, or perhaps they were just hiding that they had too few, or indeed too many – why risk being challenged or encouraged to pass on some to a junior and lose that revenue against your name?

"*Ya*, of course. I should have told you, Marcus, when I came."

"How are things in Switzerland? Is everything working smoothly with Ashleigh's team?"

There was a second's silence that Guenter took to reflect on his response, or at least to create the impression he was giving the matter some mature consideration. "Well with Ashleigh, *ya*, but I have to tell you, I'm afraid that Simone is proving very difficult. I get it. She's been promoted, wants to do well, be tall in front of her team, ticked the diversity box, but fuck, really?"

"What's up? I haven't heard anything."

"I'll give you one example but there are plenty in Switzerland, and I'm sure Eric has some more. We're making one hundred Swissie with Gaumet. At my old shop, we did over five hundred each year with a weaker platform. My guys know the PMs and they want to work with us, get the numbers up, but she just gets in the way – you know who Gaumet are, right?"

"Yes, I have some old connections there." Marcus reflected on Urs, the ex-global head of Gaumet, being downstairs. It would be easy for him to check how much each bank was earning with Gaumet and test Guenter's bragging and relationships, but he let it go. "Look, she's new to the role and maybe needs a little hand-holding."

"Ah, come on, Marcus. This is an IB. We're not shrinking violets here. She's like dealing with a fucking squirrel with vertigo – has she been moaning?"

"No, not at all. Just that I know you have aspirations for a bigger role. I was suggesting experimenting with a different management approach."

"Oh absolutely, absolutely, Marcus, you're so right. Listen, if I can be so bold as to make a suggestion on your headcount question. Undeniably, the other areas that are underperforming in EMEA are Eastern Europe and the Middle East. As I've said previously, a lot of the Polish and Czech clients speak German. I feel in a good position to help turn that around. You've already seen what I'm doing in Scandi."

"Yes, thank you, Guenter. Let me bear that in mind."

Marcus maintained his calm despite Guenter manifestly not telling him the extent and nature of his trips to London to see Pierre. His bullying contemptuous nature towards his juniors and backstabbing of his peers was in stark contrast to his charming arse-licking sycophantism towards his bosses and traders, but he wondered if the HR review would tease some of that out and take him down a peg. For now, he had to keep him on side – it would help uncover what was going on and what he'd be saying directly to Pierre and, in any case, he couldn't get rid of him, as Guenter had fired any potential replacements who he had perceived a threat.

Eric Chevalier (French, late thirties) had been with TDT since he graduated and had evolved from selling vanilla to more esoteric structured credit products. He had developed a significant network internally, was popular with senior management and with the French client base, making him effectively indispensable commercially or politically. In any case, French employment law would make any process of trying to release him both time-consuming and prohibitively expensive. Although his promotion to head of France had been delayed until the previous incumbent had moved on, Marcus had been subsequently quick to promote him to head of Southern Europe, giving him responsibility for Italy, Iberia, and Greece. This was as much to balance Guenter's growing mandate, as well as ensuring Eric's personal continuing loyalty. Eric tended to leave his guys to their own devices and this, as well as his fierce protectiveness towards them, made him popular with his teams. The downside was he was slow to root out pure performers or drive his team to better results.

"*Salut*, Marcus, how are you? I heard you'll be back soon."

"Yes, hopefully in a couple of weeks, Eric. You should arrange to come over and we can do a fuller catch-up."

"Actually, I was there last week. As you know, Pierre had asked for a meeting."

"I didn't know but that's great. Was it a good discussion?"

"Well, yes, sort of – he said the two of you had been talking about creating a head of Europe role."

Marcus felt relieved that at least Eric was being open unlike some others, though the last time Pierre had discussed head of Europe with him was at least six months ago.

"Yes, that's right. What do you think?"

"Well, I can tell you that if that German fuckwit is my boss, I'm out of here faster than a TGV and am taking my whole team with me. Have you spoken to Mads or Ruud recently? We'll be fucking lucky if we have anyone left in Stockholm or Amsterdam soon."

"Did you share your reservations with Pierre, Eric?"

"*Oui*, sure, but not in those words exactly, but he knew. He suggests a co-head model where we complement each other, but within six months I think I'll kill him unless he gets me first. What's wrong with the current model? You're back in two weeks, as you say." Marcus could feel a growing confidence – this feedback would give him some protection with Pierre.

"Let me speak with Pierre about it. The reason for my call is that we'll need to pare back some costs, don't know how many, but—"

"Pare back some costs! Marcus, we're working to the bone. Everyone I have is the best on the Street. Sure, maybe I can trim a couple of graduates, and everyone can work an hour longer, but soon we won't bother going home."

"I know. It will need to be at senior levels, MDs to directors."

"Oh, fuck, Marcus, *merde*, how many?"

"I don't know – will come back to you, but significant. Hey, look on the positive side, at least it's you and not Guenter deciding." Marcus released a humming smile, but his humour wasn't shared by Eric.

"Are we done?"

"Just one more thing, Eric – Guenter mentioned Simone."

"Ah, you have an MD candidate right there for your list, though, I have to say, Guenter's style leaves a little. They deserve each other. For my part, she was here a few months ago and demanded us to hand over all our private banking clients in Monaco and Luxembourg, ones we've been covering for decades, and where she has zero relationships. We tried to discuss it but then she just lost it, right in the middle of the trading floor, as if someone had peed in her handbag."

"Did you tell Ashleigh?"

"Ashleigh, yes, but man, Marcus, Ashleigh has just totally checked out; but you need to get Simone back in a box. I offered to let my guys have a dotted line to her even though you know some of them are far more experienced and senior. Anyway, she wasn't interested in that at all."

"OK, Eric, I'll let you go."

Ashleigh Hudson (American, mid-thirties) ran the private banks, sovereign wealth funds and central banks team. She had transferred to London from New York about five years ago and had been considered a star, potentially on a career path to become a future head of markets and even go beyond. She had requested the move after going through a messy divorce, and although based in London, her mandate was global. Marcus was delighted to have her in Europe, where he had felt a need to boost his management bench strength, but things suddenly changed three to four years back when there was a noticeable dip in motivation. One evening after client drinks, she let out that she had been having an affair with Pierre, which he had ended and wanted to keep totally confidential to protect his marriage. She had respected his decision and, despite the fact that she could have created havoc for TDT, she had maintained total discretion at least until then, but she had hated the threatening style with which he had spoken to her.

Pierre had never mentioned this to him and had always been very flattering about Ashleigh professionally, being the only one of Marcus's team where he didn't question the generosity of any bonus proposal. The whole thing had signalled that even if Ashleigh's motivation had slackened off, she would seem untouchable as far as redundancies were concerned, but Marcus had also been convinced she would be leaving voluntarily and had been surprised that no offer had been forthcoming and tempted her away – perhaps she was looking to concoct a situation for some sort of settlement after all.

The conversation with Ashleigh was short. As soon as Marcus mentioned headcount reduction, Ashleigh nominated Simone. When Marcus suggested that Simone may need some guidance as she had only just been promoted, he got a sharp retort.

"Marcus, I don't think we're in a candy store. You want headcount out, and in my team she's the obvious candidate," the brutal message was delivered in a soft and relaxed Texan vernacular, as if discussing plans for a children's birthday party.

"I just get the impression that maybe the other guys are ganging up on her, and she needs time and more support. Her team's production is good, right?"

"Support? This lady takes up 50% of my management time. Maybe they are frustrated at her style. You know I wasn't the keenest to give her that role. Yeah, her production is OK but it's nothing stellar. Yeah, she's 10% up on the guy before but that was such a low bar, a lame hedgehog could have cleared it." Marcus couldn't understand the indignation. He wasn't in a position to share just yet that Simone was having a breakdown, but he also felt that it wouldn't make any difference to his management team's views. Perhaps they were right – maybe best for everyone if they counselled her out. Simone plainly lacked support whatever the reason. One less problem for him if she left. He'd speak to HR.

As for Ashleigh, he'd speak to Pierre. Maybe they could agree to transfer her to another part of the bank, which would count as a reduction against his headcount, but he would need to choose his words carefully.

Nicolas Winters (British, early thirties) had been a hedge fund salesman before rising to lead the UK team. He was most in Marcus's mould amongst his directs, easiest to deal with managerially and socially, and they often met outside the office for golf or at the shoot. Marcus had envisioned him as his future successor and despite already running the largest country, had stretched his mandate recently to include the Middle East and Eastern Europe. It was evident, however, that Nick was most comfortable in London and hadn't even visited Dubai. Despite his talents and their friendship, if Pierre insisted that he had to lose one of his directs in London, then Nick would have to be that individual. There was just no reason to justify saving him. No doubt it would come as totally out of the blue for Nick, but this was business; Marcus couldn't let emotions get into it – it was about what was best for the shareholders. And in any case, Nick was young and would undoubtedly find something else. Marcus called him to let him know a cull was coming at senior levels – at least that would put the idea of cutbacks on Nick's radar. But it was clear from Nick's tone that he couldn't possibly conceive that he may be personally impacted.

Marcus had low expectations for any additional insight from his conversations with Dave Ross and Joachim Kowalski, as requested by Pierre, and those expectations were met. The specialist product sales guys selling foreign exchange or commodities had a closer attachment and loyalty to their trading heads like Ross and Kowalski, than to the regional or country sales management such as Andrea, Colvin or Guenter, even though they reported along both axes. Each time the standard narrative would come up that the product sales heads were getting limited opportunity to progress along the country hierarchy, that they needed to be promoted, and that perhaps a joint leadership structure be put in place – none of which Marcus agreed with. Unsurprisingly, no nominations were made as to who in their worlds may be suitable for the cull list, which left open the certainty of a big rumpus when Marcus finally put forward his suggestions.

Marcus decided he had to go downstairs. He needed a cigarette and something to eat and would have to face Muttu sooner or later. His mind was now distracted by the office discussions. He contemplated momentarily how none of the people he would be looking to let go had absolutely anything to do with Epsilon.

There was no sun visible through the sombre and dreary mid-morning sky. The temperature had dropped dramatically from the days before. Marcus wished he had brought down his coat, but the cigarette was already perched between his lips, and once he'd overcome the initial blast of cold, he welcomed the freshness to clear his mind. He saw that a couple of vehicle tracks, undaunted by the lack of visible road edge, had disturbed the snow up the hill to the villa – the daily routines of their drivers so conveniently repetitive that they did not require any skirting guidance to their day-to-day lives.

"Good morning, sir." Muttu had come up from behind him, making him jump and belch.

"Oh, hello, Muttu, you surprised me again." Marcus couldn't contain a startled tone and regretted uttering the word 'again' the second it left his mouth.

"Again? I haven't seen you today. You must be hungry, sir." Muttu continued gleaming with that immaculate smile.

"Yes, don't know why I said that, was daydreaming. Yes, I am hungry. Could you do a bacon bap?" Marcus couldn't believe how comfortably Muttu had transferred to this persona after the version of the night before.

"Right away, sir."

"You know, Muttu, with those good looks of yours and that smile, have you ever thought about a career in Bollywood?"

"Oh no, I'd be awful on stage – petrified. No, I much prefer to be behind the scenes, like here in the hotel, in the dark." The comment, delivered jocularly, made Marcus momentarily flinch – surely Muttu hadn't seen him last night. No, he wouldn't have the brazen audacity to mock him. "But you, sir, you are a global salesperson and senior executive; that must require you to put on a show?"

Muttu, as always, was standing at a respectful distance. Marcus shuffled towards him as he spoke. They were about the same height and build, but Muttu, with his younger, more athletic body, topped with thick black hair, clearly felt more physically confident and stayed on his spot as Marcus trudged closer.

"Depends. First, you need to know who we're dealing with, and here I feel we all know everything about me, but I know fuck all about you." Marcus was approaching the conversation like a tentative skier attempting a new difficult run, not quite sure what rocks lay exposed in the *couloir*, but unable to resist his inquisitiveness.

"Sir, you're our client, so, naturally, we need to know you, and I may say we're learning that your story is certainly deep and complex as we come to the end of your stay. I'm just a humble chef and hotel manager."

"Hmm, what makes me think there is more to you than that?"

There was a moment's silence and a faint hint of a sigh from Muttu before the smile returned. "Sir, you know at different times we all play different roles on different stages – sometimes seeing a small preview can create an unnecessary mystique where there is no twist, and any energy searching for more depth is wasted, just leading to bland disappointment. Perhaps you're sensing more excitement than is really there."

Marcus stared straight into Muttu's eyes. "Perhaps, but perhaps not. Hopefully I'll get some more insight into the plot, a longer preview, before I leave."

"Yes, of course, sir, whatever you'd like to know, but don't the English have some expression about curiosity killing a cat." Muttu smiled cheekily, as he often did when delivering a new, recently learnt, unfamiliar idiom. "I'll get the bacon bap."

TWENTY-ONE

How far away the stars seem, and how far
Is our first kiss, and ah, how old my heart!

For Emma, the moments that followed Anshu's abduction were a dense, disorientating daze, punctuated by instances of intense clarity.

Suddenly, there was pandemonium. Sanju ran to the car. Ashok, blood-soaked, had already pulled into the road and they headed off after a motorbike. Two other cars roared off after them. The station manager came running out holding a long bamboo lathi, his bushy grey moustache shaking with anger, his clingy shirt stained with sweat. He looked across at Emma.

"Don't worry, Madam, we'll find the motherfuckers and they won't stay alive." He got on another motorbike that had pulled up and sped off in the same direction.

She sank to the floor, blank, confused, heart beating quickly, unable to grasp what had just happened, and screamed, a loud wild wail, reverberating across the Rajasthani hills. A sound familiar in those battle-hardened lands to those of the Rajput sati widows of the past.

She could feel a crowd gathering around her, making out the 'what happened?' in the chatter of Hindi. The stall lady burst through the crowd, shouting at everyone to move away.

"*Yahan koi circus nahi hora.*" This isn't a circus show. Her sari was ripped; her hands, forearms and elbows covered in blood. She put her arms around Emma, and both burst into tears.

A young man came across with a bottle of water. "I've called the police. They'll be here shortly. Don't worry, Madam – as soon as they see it's a foreigner's child, they'll panic, and you'll have him back soon."

More cars and motorbikes with bearded turbaned men carrying long lathis, cricket bats, or hockey sticks, shot off down the highway, telling Emma, 'We'll find them.' Some ladies were crying. The crowd could be heard talking despondently about the number of child kidnappings in India, mostly in English, as if not wishing to keep Emma out of the loop – 'over ten thousand per year *yaar*', 'but not round here in Rajasthan', 'we are honest proud people', 'they will be skinned alive'. A couple of ladies came to sit with Emma and the stall lady. 'Don't worry, Madam, they will not dare hurt him once they see it is a white child.'

The police arrived and started to take statements. In her confused state, Emma couldn't focus on anything and struggled with their accents. As she asked for them to wait until Sanju returned, she wondered for the first time where he had gone and what he would do if he caught up with the kidnappers. She was distracted by the stall lady giving her statement, which one of the coach tourists translated in summary.

"As everyone was leaving the restaurant after the bangs, a motorbike pulled up, the back-seat passenger hit Ashok over the head with a cricket bat and snatched Anshu. The stall lady tried to stop them getting away by grabbing the driver of the bike and was dragged along the road."

It happened in seconds. Emma clutched the stall lady's hands as she spoke.

The police didn't want to wait any longer until Sanju's return. The translator helped with the questions.

"Why were the car doors open?"

"Too hot," she replied.

"Why was Anshu not strapped in the seat?"

"Because she had just changed him."

"What was her husband doing?"

"I don't know." She burst into tears.

"Where had they hired the driver, Ashok? Did he seem trustworthy?"

After what seemed like an eternity, Sanju and Ashok came back. Sanju, in tears, wrapped himself around Emma. Ashok's face was a mess of blood and sweat and anger. The police's attention was immediately focused suspiciously on Ashok until Sanju, with his basic Hindi, intervened. The station manager also returned on his bike shaking his head, and also headed straight for Ashok, choosing to speak in English for everyone's benefit.

"A Rajput would have given his life for that child and you, nipple-sucker, are just standing there with barely a scratch. Have you got no shame?"

"Why don't you come closer and talk to me?" Ashok was shaking with an anger that Emma could not have imagined just hours earlier. "Don't you all marry your sisters in these villages? Surely the ones that took him are your relatives."

The station manager let off some swear words before rushing at Ashok, both exchanging punches and landing on the floor before the police could tear them apart, and Sanju shouted at them to stop.

The station manager stepped back with a cut lip still staring at Ashok, who was being held by a policeman but calmer. He looked towards Sanju. "I'm sorry, sir, nothing like that has happened to my guests, or in this district for that matter. They were outsiders and apart from taking a child, they have desecrated our honour. By this evening, we will have been to every village in this area and, if they are hiding your boy anywhere here, you will have him, and I promise you if we catch the bastards, you will have them too, but not alive."

"You should do the search, but they are not from around here. We drove up to Fatehpur. A couple of shopkeepers saw the motorbike, but you know the place is like a warren – no one saw in which direction they went – could have been towards Jaipur, Jodhpur or Bikaner, but they're not local," Ashok added.

"In that case, let's get you cleaned up and go back to Fatehpur. We'll also look for the drain rats there." The station manager picked up his bamboo stick and ushered at one of the waiters to take Ashok inside to stitch up the wounds. He then seemed to usher one of the policemen aside to speak to him quietly.

Emma went through the stall lady's story with Sanju and realised she was still wearing the bracelet – the stall lady signalled for her to keep it. Another police jeep arrived, this time with the district inspector. He made his way straight to Sanju and Emma.

"I'm sorry to hear what has happened. Rest assured; we will find them. You will have the full support of my men. I have asked the station at Fatehpur and all the towns up to Jaipur, Bikaner and Jodhpur to comb the area and alerted my seniors in Haryana. There are roadblocks being put up on all the highways. Nothing more you can do here, and I suggest we take you to Jaipur and find a hotel for you there, and we can talk in the car. Please collect your stuff. I need to ask a few questions, but we can leave shortly." He spoke clearly, slowly, authoritatively, giving a small sense of hope and reassurance to the confused couple.

He turned to the station manager in the local dialect. "This is a senior police matter now. I don't want to hear about any local Rajput justice – the child's life could be at risk. Am I clear?"

* * *

They spent the next week in Jaipur. Sanju's parents and aunt from Jodhpur arrived the next morning, screaming in grief and pleading with the police to do more. They moved in with Sanju's Jaipur Aunty and wanted Sanju and Emma to join them there, but Emma insisted that they stayed at the hotel, just wishing to be alone with Sanju, next to him in that darkness, until Anshu came back.

They would struggle to sleep, lying there holding each other, sensing the other's fears and tears, before drifting off into a happier place and then waking back to the nightmare of reality. She would spend most of the day cold, trembling, empty, feeling alone, despite Sanju and all the relatives and friends and hotel staff trying to talk to them, trying to be comforting, but being nothing more than background voices, noises in her vacuum and solitude. Sanju would flit between quiet, calm hope, as another relative or police officer would reassure them repeatedly about little risk to a foreign child, to a fiery frenzy of anger against the world and himself, to distraught guilt and despair, as hours passed with no news.

They became convinced they were targeted rather than just randomly hit. Perhaps they found that more soothing than thinking it was bad luck, or that they had somehow neglected Anshu in those moments. Flashbacks of those days played endlessly on their minds as they searched for faces in their memories in the crowds, in their passing interactions, scouring clues for who may have followed them and taken their child. The police interviewed them again and again, sometimes sympathetically, sometimes accusingly. They went through the whole episode repeatedly asking about where they had been, the driver, the stall lady, the station manager, their families, friends, any enemies, what Anshu was wearing – the black-and-white striped top, the navy shorts over his nappy, the white dummy that had fallen from his mouth that they had found further down the road. They would ask about any distinguishing features, look at photos, note the black mark on his cheek, the blue eyes that had started to turn green, the pale skin that had started to tan.

They learnt from Ashok's sister who came to their hotel that Ashok had been kept overnight in a cell as the police questioned him aggressively, and then given him a beating, leading Sanju into a shouting match at the local police station that they should focus on catching the proper culprits. They spoke to the British High Commission, who could offer nothing more than saying that they should cooperate with the police.

By the second day, some local media had gathered outside the hotel. The police advised that they shouldn't speak to anybody as that may panic the kidnappers into disposing of the child. That didn't stop Sanju's mother getting into a blazing row first with a couple of journalists, asking if they had nothing better to do, and why they weren't going round the towns asking about the child's whereabouts, and then secondly with the hotel manager on why his security couldn't keep the vagabonds off his site. An official from the tourist board also came to try to reassure them, whilst taking the opportunity again to advise them not to discuss anything with the media as, he was sure they understood, so many livelihoods were dependent on tourism locally.

By the third morning, there was still no news. They had expected the ransom demand by now, and the lack of news could perhaps be a consequence of the kidnappers getting too worried to make contact. Sanju decided he could no longer just sit and wait – he had to go back to the scene. Despite her pleas, he wouldn't take Emma, saying he would be wandering around the villages, that she would be safer in Jaipur, and the police needed to be able to contact them in case something happened. He drove off with a cousin and a family friend, visiting towns and villages near the service station, showing passers-by pictures of Anshu, offering money and guaranteeing not to discuss anything with the police if any news, and they did that every day with increasing frustration for the rest of the week. Still no ransom call came, and the police uncovered nothing new. By now, Anshu could have been anywhere in India and yet they continued to be told not to go to the media.

Emma stayed in the hotel room each day, wanting to be alone, but joined by her in-laws and their friends who would sit around in the room talking to each other in a mixture of Hindi and English, with Emma being too polite and confused to ask them to leave. She would rise in hope when the police came, twice a day, then sink despondently with the same news that they had nothing. Sanju's mother would then mouth something about how useless the police were in India, particularly in Jaipur; how they were corrupt and never solved anything. The conversation would then move onto the number of child kidnappings in India; how Westerners didn't realise how unsafe the country was. 'Can you believe 60,000 people die here of snake bites', '*haan*, *aré* five hundred are eaten by tigers', 'people even get their throats slit from glass-coated kite strings – you just don't get those things in Richmond Park'. And then, by the fifth day, reflections on how they shouldn't have left the car door open, they should really have strapped him in, not left the child with the driver, you know, ultimately a stranger. A local person would have realised the firework could be a distraction – it's such a common tactic. Emma's from a lovely family but had always been a bit naïve. Emma listened silently to it all in the mix of Hindi and English but after two more days she couldn't keep quiet any longer.

"Maybe if it was so unsafe, we should not have come to India when he was so young."

"No, darling, don't be upset; you were not to know. We are just saying you need to be cautious, especially when you are on your own, with Sanju working so hard and on the call."

"Perhaps Sanju should work less!"

There was silence in the hotel room. After a few moments, Emma continued, "I'm really sorry, Ma, it's nice of you to come here and keep me company, but please could I be on my own?"

Sanju's father broke the ensuing silence. "Yes, of course, you need some space." But Sanju's mother stood up in a huff and left without saying anything as Emma shut the door, lay on the bed, and burst into tears. A cry without hope, filled with guilt, anxiety, anger, and when she stopped, she was left again with that unbearable feeling of light-headed nothingness, numb and detached, waiting for Sanju to get back.

When Sanju got home, Emma tried to tell him about the conversation with his mother. He already seemed to know.

"A child can be kidnapped in any country, Em."

"I know; all I meant was that, you know, I'm hearing it's a bit more prevalent here, Sanju."

"That's why all Ma was saying is that we need to be more conscious of the risk."

"Right, so the implication is that it was my fault, right, Sanju?"

"I've never said that, but during all this holiday I have left you alone only for about ten minutes because of work due to extreme volatility, and we would have avoided the disaster if I hadn't made that call. Is that what you were saying to my Ma?" Sanju's voice was raised, though he was clearly trying to suppress his anger. "Maybe you'd, yourself, feel safer back in London."

"Sanju, stop! That's not what I meant. You weren't there. They were making out it was my fault for walking off."

"But that's what you said!"

Emma looked at him silently. Her red eyes flooding with tears again. "I'm going to sleep, Sanju."

But neither of them slept. She lay in the bed. He had stayed on the sofa in the gloom until dawn and was sitting waiting for her when she got up.

"I'm really sorry, Em. I shouldn't have said that. I can't stay here in the hotel doing nothing and it's unfair for you too. Can't be easy with Ma. Why don't you come with us today?"

"Sanju, I can't add anything. I don't speak Hindi and don't really understand what is going on. I'm just in the way. You're right. I'll go back to London. *Maman* and Jemima are in a mess, and I could do with spending time with them. You stay here and I can come back if need be."

Like leaving Anshu unstrapped with the car doors open, leaving Sanju, there, then, in that condition, was the second decision that would come to haunt Emma for the rest of her life.

She arrived in London looking for support, but had to contend with her mother and sister, both too anxious and emotional to provide much comfort to her, unable to visualise and absorb what had happened, to see any sense as to why they couldn't talk to the media, or why the British Embassy couldn't put more pressure on to the local police. And then the comments started – 'probably should have waited until he was a little older before they went', 'why was there such a rush to go?', 'why did the Kapoors not warn us about so many child kidnappings there?', 'did the driver seem trustworthy?', 'maybe the stall lady was somehow connected in providing a distraction?', 'couldn't Sanju have made his call from outside?'. The tears inevitably flowed, as Emma would frantically defend how wonderful and friendly everyone had been until then, and that it was her fault for leaving him.

At first, Sanju would call every day, but the only new news was that, with each day of no ransom demand coming, the risk of the kidnappers being too panicked to contact them increased, leaving them unable to voice in words what that could potentially mean. It was also obvious the police efforts had started to wane.

Every day he would go to some small towns and villages asking for information, standing in the middle of a square offering money for any clues, or hinting at substantially larger sums to get Anshu back, no questions asked, in his broken Hindi. Until, eventually, he was getting so loud in his exhortations that people would start to ignore and walk round him as the madman; the foreigner who hadn't been taking care of his child, whose mother wasn't even there helping the search, mumbling to each other 'but that's what Westerners are like', 'she had probably already found someone else!'.

Over time, the calls became less frequent. His voice was hoarse and he had nothing new to say. She just wanted some connection with him if only for a minute. When she called, he wouldn't always answer – he would just tell her later that it had been too painful for him to talk. She asked him to come back for a bit, to hold him, or offered to visit him, but he told her to wait until he had covered the whole region and visited each police station. The relationship with Sanju's parents had also faded since the conversation in the hotel room, so even though they had also stayed on in India, she could get no news from her in-laws. She had been trying to go to work for some distraction but was totally unable to focus and was eventually signed off for deep depression.

After several weeks, he returned to London. She had worried about what state he would be in, but despite expecting the worst, she was shocked by what had happened to him. He had grown his hair long, was unshaven, had become darker from the sun and had visibly lost weight, looking gaunt and haggard. He was also withdrawn, lost in that angry, guilty, helpless amalgam of emotion. When she tried to hold him, hug him, it was like cuddling a human rock. When she tried to talk to him, she would just get monosyllabic grunts. He would talk for half an hour to his parents or cousins about any news from the police but when she asked for any updates, he would simply say no change.

"I need to know what's going on, Sanju. He was my son too."

"Was. What do you mean *was*? Is!" he snapped. "Do you think I wouldn't tell you if anything changes."

Sometimes as she sat there alone and sombre, or tearful, holding a cuddly toy or a piece of Anshu's clothing, he would come across to embrace her, apologise that he couldn't control his sadness and anger, and wasn't more communicative. But their touch was cold, the marriage had become without expression and occasional poorly worded comments easily became provocations, preludes to arguments, or worse, glacial silence. Both were traumatised by their own guilt and an inability to shake off a paranoia that the other attached some unspoken blame on them for what had happened.

She could feel herself losing him, him losing himself, but just did not have the fortitude, the energy to lift them both. Despite her own inability to work, she encouraged him to return to the office as a distraction, to try to create a feeling of some normality and get a break from being in the house. After two weeks of working, he came home to say he had resigned and that he was going back to India.

"But, Sanju, shouldn't we discuss these things before you make the decisions?"

"I can't stay here when we have no news."

"Why don't we go together?"

He looked at her reticently, but they both knew at that instance that unless news of Anshu's well-being came soon, their relationship was on the precipice of entering that despairing gravitational spiral of irrecoverable disintegration.

"Sanju, I don't want to lose you. You're so far away and you're going further away."

"I'm sorry, Em. I know. I'm totally consumed by this. I can't think or do anything else. I have to be out there looking even if there is no chance. I promise I will call every day and yes, come over in a few weeks, but I think it's easier if I go now on my own."

Again, at first, he called each day, sometimes more than once, but the desperation in his voice was getting heavier, then the calls started to get less frequent. He would say he was sleeping in some village and had no reception. He had spoken to some local journalists, but the story had now become about 'why they hadn't raised the alarm earlier'.

She became fearful for him, for his safety. She started to become scared for herself. She was resigning herself to never seeing Anshu again. She would have panic attacks, shaking uncontrollably, sweating, feeling dizzy and light-headed, unable to shake off the feeling of impending disaster. She stopped seeing any friends or family, became lost in her own company, sometimes forgetting to eat, trying not to drink any alcohol before evening but inevitably starting just after getting up, only waiting from morning to night for his call that often never came. And then, after a few weeks, Sanju called one afternoon to say he was not coming back to England.

She cried, she pleaded, she screamed, she begged for him to return. She told him she wouldn't survive without him. She could hear him breathing heavily, his voice shaking as he said sorry, and then he put the phone down.

She tried to call him every day for the next few days, longing for him to answer, but nothing. It was Jemima, who through some divine instinct had decided to go round one evening, who found her collapsed on the sofa, barely conscious, covered in vomit coagulating across her top and knotted into her blonde hair, with an empty bottle of gin lying next to another on the floor.

Jemima stayed with her the next two months, encouraging Emma into some sort of normality, but each day without hearing from Sanju made her more despondent. She resigned formally from work. She also decided she couldn't stay in that house any longer, made plans to rent out the place and move their things into storage, until the day she hoped Sanju would return, and they could try to restart their relationship.

* * *

Her life took another turn a week before she left the house, with the doorbell ringing from an unexpected visitor.

"Hello, Emma, isn't it?"

"Yes."

"Hello, I'm Marcus, I'm a colleague of Sanju's. We met in Singapore."

"Oh yes, I remember."

"I just moved back to London, and I'd heard what had happened with Sanju, and he's obviously left TDT. Just thought I'd check in to see how he was."

TWENTY-TWO

A person's fears are lighter when the danger is at hand.

Urs, hair gelled, dapper in a plain dark-blue tailored jacket over a burgundy roll-neck, with black corduroys sitting perfectly on tan Chelsea boots, was dealing with some invoices when he noticed Marcus through the office window strolling across to his normal bench, puffing away at a cigarette. He stared, watching Marcus for a few moments half-heartedly reading his emails, and Muttu and Gilbert scraping their spades against the driveway tarmac, piling some mud-stained slush into low walls to the side of the road. Urs would always glean some relatable joy at the thought of how the pushed-around viscous mesh would triumphantly and stubbornly freeze overnight under the open skies, to expedite the slips and slides across the deceptively invisible black ice the next morning.

He stepped into the dining room to make two mugs of coffee before striding outside through the side doors. He could smell from a distance that Marcus, in an off-cream ill-fitting jumper with mismatched red chinos and muddy walking boots, had not showered that morning. Still, he satisfied himself that the scruff would be gone in a few days.

"What's your plan today?"

"I'm going for a walk. Need to clear my head before the call with Pierre. At least it won't be a death trap up to where these guys clear the road."

"Be careful. The wet slush is unpleasant, but it protects from the nasty stuff underneath."

"I'm surprised you Swissies haven't invented anything beyond road salt. You're so fucking into health and safety. Don't you all have a nuclear bunker in every home?"

"Not anymore. But yes, there is always one nearby. I wouldn't put that under health and safety though. One can never be too complacent about risks. Until recently, we had two thousand plus explosives ready to blow up bridges and tunnels on our borders, in case one of our neighbours attacked." Urs' posh English public-school accent was always more enhanced than its Swiss consort in the morning.

"Like whom? Luxembourg, Lichtenstein?" Marcus sneered.

"One mustn't misjudge dangers, Marcus. You never know who your enemy could be until it's too late." Urs paused and looked directly at Marcus and feigned an innocent smile. "Not so long ago, we were all obliged to carry guns – we don't usually use them, but we have plenty of guns here."

Urs could see the tension in Marcus's cheeks after he spoke and stared straight at him as Marcus looked away in discomfort.

"Thanks for the coffee, Urs."

"You're welcome." Urs took the brusque 'thanks for the coffee' to mean the end of the conversation. He turned back to the villa, message delivered.

* * *

Marcus didn't walk far. It was sunny but uncomfortably cold when the wind blew. There wasn't much he could prepare. He would let Pierre speak. He had done what had been asked and spoken to everyone on the management team with, as he expected, no obvious value. Handscombe had been untypically quiet. He had expected a row after he had raised the bullying point at Exco, but Handscombe had chosen not to discuss it, and Marcus chose not to raise it himself. Handscombe also didn't say anything negative about Andrea or any of the sales teams. It was uncharacteristic, and that made him somewhat uncomfortable about what he might be plotting, or what he may be saying to Pierre, but there was nothing he could do about it right now.

It had been difficult to get hold of Shoulderchip, but he was able to catch him briefly at JFK as he returned from another Latin America trip. With his attention elsewhere, and Maley gone, there was not much Shoulderchip wanted to say either.

He played through the potential scenarios for his call with Pierre. If Pierre came out straight and wanted Marcus gone, things would depend on whether he was being accused of wrongdoing and being made a scapegoat. If accused of wrongdoing, he'd need to eke out what evidence and emails they had; if something relatively mild, he could seek to blame others – management, compliance, COO, general market practice, and offer to hang around to help, and perhaps side-step into another role in the bank in due course. He could ask for context around the accusations and try to explain them away.

If it was something genuinely serious, detailed, potentially with direct client action, he was likely done for and, if they let him keep his vested rewards, it was probably best he was out. He just needed to ensure he was free from personal censure from the regulators. That's what he would have to negotiate. Otherwise, he'd have to go on the attack; maybe mention Ashleigh as a starter – perhaps Pierre would blink when he realised Marcus knew about their affair – though probably better to stay silent for now and gather a broader list of things. There were bound to be plenty of skeletons across the senior executives, and getting rid of him was likely to require agreement from a broader and more senior group than just Pierre. His weak point remained the Caitanya affair and that going public and, above all, he needed to know if that had been exposed.

If they had decided to keep him in his role, they were likely to want some changes and he'd just have to go along with those no matter how awkward.

The final scenario was that Pierre had nothing new to report but then Pierre would just have deferred the call to a face-to-face meeting in London next week. No, there must be something. That final thought made him slightly anxious and nauseous. He told himself to stay confident and feel and sound innocent. He took the call in the library.

"Marcus, hello, I've been getting my arse kicked as to why you've been out of the office so long. When are you back?"

Pierre's tone felt ominous even if the question on Marcus's absence had been posed half humorously. "Monday, Pierre. As you know, I've been off sick, and still dealing with everything from here." Marcus spoke confidently and firmly, without engaging in Pierre's semi-taunt.

"Good, then I'm free at two. Let's have a longer chat then. But listen, don't get too fucking uppity, my friend, I've had to work hard to save your skin."

"Pleased to hear that." Marcus still wasn't comfortable about where things were going – he just wanted to get to the detail. "So, where are we at?"

"Well, we've had some internal communication on Epsilon. There is feedback of serious breaches consistent across the regions. The fines are going to be substantial, and we don't know whether there'll be lawsuits with clients but are discussing. That's not good news but our support and transparency in the investigation has been well noted by the regulators. And we do need to show we're making changes and quickly. I've had to fight hard to keep my guys from getting fired and, in particular, as you can imagine, there is a lot of noise for your head, being in charge of sales. One thing in your favour was your suggestion to do a culture audit – at least you were taking things seriously. In short, things are not good, but better than they might have been, particularly for you!" Pierre spoke slowly as if delivering a rehearsed speech with a specific message.

Marcus was about to speak as Pierre gathered his breath, but then kept quiet. The audit was, of course, primarily to shaft Handscombe but he'd take it.

"You're safe as long as nothing new comes out as they finalise the reports." Pierre said 'you're safe' as if it should have been perfectly obvious to both of them that without his support Marcus would have been fired. "But the changes we need to make are not negotiable. I reckon you need to axe a third of your direct reports – that's two of them – and probably a dozen additional MDs across the three regions. We also need some proper management in EMEA. I can't have another situation when you're away and no one is left in charge in one of our biggest regions. So have a think about that but any initial thoughts?"

Marcus just had to accept. He already knew what Pierre wanted about EMEA and knew it would be a disaster. It may also be a ploy to create a succession plan should Pierre want him out a few months later, but he needed to get past this point.

"Well, I'm really grateful for your confidence in me and for backing me up, Pierre. I've been thinking about EMEA myself also, and perhaps having a co-head structure with Guenter and

Eric. It might take a while for them to adjust to each other, being different characters, but they bring complementary qualities." Marcus iterated practically exactly what he knew Pierre wanted to hear.

"I think that makes a lot of sense. I haven't spoken to either of them for a while, but they are grown-ups. I'm sure they'll cope and, if not, we just exit the weaker one in six months."

Marcus felt a short pang of disgust at the blatant lie – 'I haven't spoken to either of them' – but he had to just play the game.

"And what about thoughts on your directs?"

"Well, the EMEA co-heads structure takes two of them out of reckoning. I can't really do anything about Colvin as Maley has gone, so it's two out of Ashleigh, Nick, and Andrea."

"You only have one female direct, so I think it best to leave Ashleigh alone. Guess then the decision is made." Marcus had wondered how Pierre would have gone about protecting Ashleigh. Quite obvious now he thought about it.

"On the MDs, Maley can count. My feeling is that the Middle East and Eastern Europe aren't doing too well. Maybe the guys covering LatAm also. Perhaps get Guenter and Eric to suggest some names with their new responsibilities. What about Simone – am hearing she's been somewhat painful recently?'

"We only just promoted her."

"Come on, this is not the time for sensitivities. We probably did it too early. We're not going to seriously demote her back, are we?"

"A dozen MDs is a lot. It'd be a bloodbath; I know we need to send a strong signal but is it all just my guys in sales?" Marcus felt comfortable enough now that he was safe with that mild challenge.

"Let's make a list of a dozen. We'll start by offering eight or so, including a couple of directs. No, it's not just sales. There's been a lot of trawling of emails and listening to tapes, I have to say, exposing a lot of unpleasantness. You know Hank was talking to Maley about getting rid of Colvin behind his back, and your back, plus fiddling with some of the numbers I was getting. Anyway, he'll be gone."

Marcus took a deep intake of breath. Shoulderchip gone. Wow. That's why he was subdued. Marcus had to maintain his sober tone.

"That's so surprising. I thought he was top-notch. Who do you plan to replace him with?" Marcus spoke seriously, trying to sound sympathetic, but was struggling to contain the howls of joy bursting inside him.

"I've asked Stephanie to go there. She has been doing a stellar job, a future star I'd say. Nice promotion for her and we need to sort out LatAm."

"Anyone else I need to know about?"

"Not really. You were good to mention Starc's bullying. Exited him this morning. I found out from HR that he was drunk on the floor a couple of times too. Glenn tried to cover it up. He's fucked off but I've got no patience for that sort of thing."

Marcus couldn't believe how well things were turning out. It had been a while since he had heard Pierre so relaxed, by now speaking with a tone of Silicon Valley camaraderie. It seemed a good moment to ask a little more about Epsilon.

"A lot of time is being spent on looking at these emails. How far back are they going?"

"They are just looking at sales of specific structured trades, so mostly last five to six years. We don't really have great records before that, so unless some client pipes up with a complaint or a whistle-blower, most of the stuff is since then and done. You haven't got any skeletons lurking, have you?"

"No, not at all, Pierre. I'd tell you straight up if I did."

"That's the right way so we can head it off. Yep, so unless something else turns up, that's the plan going forward. Get your cull list ready and we'll talk Monday at two."

Marcus relaxed and released a long sigh of relief before permitting himself a smile. Shoulderchip gone. Starc gone. Him safe. Sure, he'll have to push out Nick and Andrea, but he would have taken that trade any day. And most of what they've found was over the last five or six years – the stuff with Caitanya was over ten years ago. He sat back in the leather armchair in the library and clenched his fists as if to celebrate a victory. He had managed to work things out. Could he draw a line under it now? Did he really need to share everything with Emma? Probably not. He could rip up the letter. She had obviously been missing him. She had told him she wanted to do what she could to help him. Why not park the other issues and enjoy his time with her? He could learn to deal with his guilt himself – let things evaporate with time – no one was getting harmed now. At least he could try. The last few months had been a nightmare. Perhaps he had passed the point where he could go back to the way things were before, but as a minimum the timing was back in his control. For the moment, he could enjoy life once more, enjoy being Marcus Flint.

The only small niggle was Ayla Finn. Why the fuck would she want to go to Kerala? It had been over ten fucking years since Caitanya left TDT, and Ayla was just her colleague, hardly some lifelong friend. He could just tell Ayla that he didn't have a contact address, but it would be fairly easy to find the family home in Alleppey – he'd managed it himself. Now he'd come this far, after all these months, there was no point leaving anything to chance. As Urs said, 'Don't misjudge any dangers.' He could talk to Ayla himself but that would raise his profile suspiciously. He'd ask Andrea to get rid of her.

Marcus ate on his own that evening, contended, relieved, and enthused about the weekend ahead with Emma. After dinner, he had a brandy with Urs on the terrace – the internal warmth of the Armagnac being exhaled as flyaway spirits into the chilling breeze from the mountains.

They both stared at the meringue-shaped peaks in the moonlight as Marcus updated Urs on the Pierre call.

"You know, Urs, that Tani, she could really have made a problem for me. It wasn't just the money. I think she genuinely loved me."

Urs looked across. This was a man who had never been loved other than by himself, now realising that perhaps he once had. For the first time during his stay, Urs noted, that night, that Marcus hadn't made a visit down to the gym punchbag.

TWENTY-THREE

True love cannot be found where it does not exist,
Nor can it be denied where it does.

Marcus called Emma in the morning to update her that not only was he feeling a lot better, but that TDT had requested that he return to the office as soon as possible; that he was looking forward to seeing her and that he planned to come back with her after the weekend.

Thus, for the second time in his life, he'd be returning to London to renewed focus in settling his life.

* * *

That first time, he had been in a confused, unstable state, still reeling from the hidden angst after the break-up with Caitanya, reignited with career ambition that the transfer back had inflamed, and wrestling with an overpowering, obsessive need for stability and internal peace after the events of the previous few months.

Despite TDT's attempt to respect everyone's desire for privacy, the circumstances of Sanju's son's disappearance were well known across the organisation. The bank had been trying to get hold of Sanju to complete the administration following his departure and arrange for the transfer of some vested rewards. Marcus volunteered to follow up personally with the family, thereby getting Sanju's home address and, ultimately, an opportunity to see Emma.

Their first meeting was short. Emma didn't know where Sanju was and gave Marcus the Kapoors' address in case they knew. They exchanged phone numbers should either have any further news.

He was back two weeks later. The parents had no news of Sanju either, but they had told him what had happened. TDT, and he personally, had a number of contacts in India who knew some influential people, and he offered to touch base with them to see if they could apply some more pressure with the local police, both to help find Anshu and to try to track down Sanju. Some of their wealth management clients also used private security firms who they could contact and would perhaps be more dynamic in their search. Emma listened silently. She did not want to let herself have any new hope only to have to suffer the subsequent disappointment, but she said, of course, any help was appreciated.

Three weeks later, he called to say that there hadn't been any news of Sanju, but although it was a long shot, there had been sighting of a child near the Haryana and Punjab border who matched Anshu's description, where the police hadn't followed up. He had employed members of a local security team to investigate it. Emma's head had started to spin with the news, her heartbeat rose, and her eyes welled up – it was the first time anyone had suggested a sighting. She reacted calmly, almost nonchalantly, controlling her excitement and her hopes.

But she could think of nothing else for the next two days. Nothing other than about Anshu and Sanju. She called Marcus two days later with all the addresses and phone numbers of

Sanju's relatives in Agra and Jaipur, in case they had any news about him too. Marcus promised to contact them and stay in touch with her.

He started to call weekly with an update. They had contacted the chief ministers of both Haryana and Punjab, as well as Rajasthan, and a senior detective had been assigned with a team across the three states. The phone calls became visits. The sighting had seemed genuine with the right clothes and skin colour but was from some months ago. Each time Emma would also ask about Sanju too, for whom there was no news, until one evening she detected that perhaps Marcus was feeling that his efforts on Anshu were not being appreciated, and she apologised that she was always looking for more.

Her hair was short. Every day she would dress in the same pullover and jeans, never wore make-up, and hardly smiled, but for him, her solitary isolation and her vulnerability just made her more attractive. Marcus knew she hardly ever left the studio flat. He desperately wanted to take her to a bar, or dinner, or cinema, but she was totally absorbed in her loss, rarely talking about anything other than the days before Anshu, and then Sanju, left. Indeed, with each interaction by phone or in person, his tacit infatuation was getting irresistibly stronger.

After that evening of the apology, she didn't hear from Marcus with his regular update. She thought to call him but the memories of waiting for Sanju's call and chasing him for updates were too hurtful. She just didn't want to hope on good news, but three weeks later he knocked on the door.

"I have something." Marcus was carrying a parcel that he handed to her to unwrap.

She sank to the floor in tears and muffled screams. Inside was a raggedly torn black-and-white striped top from Gap Kids. She could barely utter the words, "It's his!"

"They found it by an irrigation canal in Punjab. The police

and my guys are searching the area extensively. Obviously, we now have something concrete to go on, on top of the sighting."

Emma held the top to her face, to her heart, unable to stop her tears.

"I know it must be very difficult. Would you like me to stay a while? Maybe I can get you a glass of wine?"

"No, you've done so much, Marcus. I'll call Jemima. She'll be here shortly. I just need some time to let it sink in."

"Yes, of course. I've asked for an update every two to three days and will let you know."

"It was a year ago this week we lost him, and for the first time we have some news he's maybe still alive."

"I'm sure he's out there and will be back in your life soon, Emma. Just keep your faith. I'll let you know as soon as I have news."

"Call me even if you don't have any news, Marcus, please."

He did call or visit regularly but there was nothing to report. All the leads were dead, until, that is, almost a month later.

"Emma, we have some news about Sanju. One of his cousins put us in touch with a family friend who Sanju was close to – he said he had gone to an ashram, just north of Rishikesh. We found out about a week ago and I had hoped to give you some good news, but it seems he joined a group of travelling sadhus about two months back. At that time, they were heading by foot to a shrine in a place called Badrinath. It's a very remote spot in the Himalayas. Right now, I can't see how we can track him until he chooses to contact someone."

Again, there were tears, tears of hope that he was alive, combined with tears of disheartening dismay that she couldn't talk to him and get him back. This time, Marcus stayed and had a glass of wine.

"You've been so kind, Marcus."

"Sanju was a friend of mine too. I hope we'll have a positive outcome. I also hate seeing you, anyone, like this. Perhaps I can persuade you to come out of this flat sometime – maybe for a walk, a coffee, or a drink."

And so, for the first time since the India trip, she went to a pub a week later across the road. Her first impressions of Marcus felt so wrong. She remembered how Sanju didn't trust him at all, and yet here he was, going out of his way to support Sanju's family.

He was now totally besotted with her. It had started as attraction, an infatuation; he wouldn't have described it as lust. And yes, she had been someone to replace Caitanya's loss, someone who could offer him partnership and stability, someone he had felt subconsciously or even consciously would suit his professional career and image. Maybe it had partly been a challenge, a conquest, a desire to have something beyond his reach. But now it was simpler – he wanted her for who she was. Perhaps he even loved her. She had replaced Caitanya and that pain from his mind. He could not take the risk of doing or saying something to lose her. He needed her.

He helped to arrange Emma's finances. After a couple of months, he mentioned that he could perhaps arrange for a death certificate for Sanju so she could accelerate the transfer of his funds, but she point-blank refused.

"No, Marcus. I really dream of having him back."

That night, he tried to fight back his tears, before weeping like a child denied. He had thought not only would it help her financially, but also to get her to move on, but it was far too early. He realised that for Emma he had become just a caring friend, and he dare not tell her how he felt, and that this platonic friendship would continue to feed his internal turbulence. But he could see that Emma's well-being was improving. They would go out once a fortnight.

They had been to a couple of restaurants and a theatre. Nevertheless, her conversation would revolve around Sanju and Anshu and the past in general. He wanted to talk about the present, the future – at some point he would have to make a move.

It had been about six months since they had found Anshu's top. Marcus had agreed with Emma to engage some local friendly journalists to write articles about the abduction, hoping that the publicity may trigger something, but the articles had also created a counter, unfriendly narrative about Western parents not taking care of their child, and abandoning the search for their son. In the end, nothing new emerged and the security teams were running out of ideas.

"Emma, I don't know what more we can do until someone contacts my guys. There has been no ransom demand. I don't know how to say this but maybe he is with another family." Emma looked up. Her eyes were bloodshot red. "I'm sorry, I shouldn't have said that."

"That's OK. You have done far more than anyone could have asked. Yes, please ask the security team to stop now." She burst into tears again. "I'm sorry, it's just that it's Anshu's second birthday tomorrow."

"Oh really? Oh no, I didn't realise." He walked towards Emma. "You look like you could do with a hug."

He saw her body visibly squirm as he approached. "No, Marcus, no. I'm sorry, but no."

"Oh, that came out all wrong." He backed away. "I think I should leave. Will you be OK on your own?"

"Yes, I'm going to *Maman*. Sorry, I didn't mean to... I'm sorry."

Marcus raced home, piqued and disgruntled. He had known it was Anshu's birthday from the papers around the abduction, and yet again he had misjudged the situation. This time he was angry with her as well as himself. He had done everything to help and try to lift her from that cloud.

Emma couldn't reconcile her reaction. It was just an innocent friendly hug meant to raise her mood. Maybe her perception of him had been permanently stained by their first meeting, but that was drunken and a long time ago. Maybe it was discomfort at any physical contact with another male. Maybe it was just her mood at the time.

He knocked on the door a couple of weeks later.

"Listen, Marcus, I'm really sorry about my reaction."

"No, not at all, I was totally out of order. I hope you'll forgive me. I've bought you something that I hope will serve as a distraction." He had a big parcel leaning against the side wall, which they took inside.

She opened it to find a Yamaha keyboard.

"Oh, Marcus, that's so kind, but why? I can't accept this."

"Well, you talked about playing guitar and piano. I thought it could be therapeutic."

"Really, thank you, but you shouldn't have." She got up and put her arms gently around him, fleetingly, before peeling off. "Thank you, but you don't need to do this."

It was a first physical contact that felt uncomfortable for her, but joyously memorable for him.

"Look, not only was Sanju a friend of mine, but I also have a son slightly older than Anshu. I can only imagine what you must be going through."

"Oh really, you have a son, Marcus!" She realised for the first time how little she knew about him. He had never mentioned his family, a wife, or a partner.

"Well, yes, I suppose he has never come up. His name is Ollie." She noticed how Marcus looked coy, clearly not wishing to be insensitive in talking about him.

"And is there a Mrs Marcus?" She was being polite. He

wondered whether the curiosity was due to some interest in him.

"Well, no, just the nanny, but maybe you'll remember his mother. She worked at TDT in Singapore – Caitanya Iyer."

Emma acknowledged that yes, she had met her briefly, but didn't indicate that there was some intense gossip about them. Marcus talked through what happened. He spoke slowly and sorrowfully, taking long pauses as he narrated the story.

The pregnancy was an accident, but once it happened, Tani told her sister and the whole affair was considered a total scandal by her parents and extended family. It didn't help that he was her boss and not from Kerala. She left him, left TDT, and left Singapore a few days later. It took him a while to track down her home address and he went to Kerala to look for her. He wanted to propose, and to meet her parents to try to convince them that he would be a suitable son-in-law, and to apologise for what had happened, but they all blanked him. But she was carrying his child, and he wouldn't give up.

He spoke about his time in India, about the culture, and they exchanged experiences. He visited again just before Ollie was due, but nothing changed. The scandal of a premarital pregnancy had taken its toll on Tani. She looked depressed, detached, and disinterested in the upcoming birth. He just wanted to get her back to Singapore.

At times, he thought it would be easier just to leave them, but he needed to see his child and at least provide financial support, so he went again a couple of months after Ollie was born. The parents again refused to let him go into the house to see either Tani or the baby. He was confused, angry with the situation, anxious about Tani's health, but above all concerned for his child. His eyes welled up as he related that after another two months, he got a call from Tani's sister to say that Tani had passed away resulting from weakness due to complications during childbirth. She hadn't told her parents that she was calling Marcus but wanted to just let him know that his son had been placed in an orphanage and passed him the orphanage address, and that he should never come back to their house again.

He went again to India, stricken by guilt about Tani and his part in the 'scandal', and fear for Ollie. He found out nothing further about her but found the orphanage. Without any help from the mother's family, he had to go through excruciating bureaucracy to file for paternity and make a number of 'payments' over several visits to India to take Ollie home. He gave Ollie his name. Fortunately, he had some business contacts through TDT to help, otherwise who knows what could have happened. It was on one of those visits, passing through Delhi, that he had bumped into Sanju and Emma at the Delhi hotel.

By the end, he was almost in tears. "Anyway, he's lovely; my real hope in this world. Perhaps you'll both meet one day soon."

"I'd love to meet him." She moved across and gave him her second hug as he wiped his moist eyes.

"Anyway, enough of that. I didn't come here to get sentimental. Let's talk about next steps for Anshu. What I'm about to say will not be very nice, but I hope I can be open with what I'm being told, and you won't get upset." She sat down and nodded.

Marcus's feedback was that the feeling of the security team and the police was that, as there had been a sighting but no ransom demand had come forward, it was likely a targeted abduction for a male fair-skinned child, sort of on demand, and that he had been 'sold', probably to a well-to-do family. It meant that Anshu was probably still alive. But he could be anywhere in India or even abroad. They had spoken to other agencies and decided the next best thing would be to place some advertisements in the national press rather than just locally. It had probably been the right thing not to do it earlier and it could create some more negative publicity for her.

She said she didn't care about that – she just wanted him back. In that case, Marcus needed the latest photos she had, and they would create projected images of Anshu, as he may look like as a two-year-old. They'd be as accurate as the technology allowed if she was comfortable with that. He would also need samples for DNA confirmation.

As she sat there listening to Marcus, she again felt that rare hope, with at the same time an anxiety about the potential disappointment to come, but now also having a desire to do something herself and move beyond the paralysis of morose incapacitation that she had suffered over the last year.

"We should also get samples from Sanju's parents. I heard his mother is really unwell and hasn't recovered from losing her grandson, and, frankly, getting no news from Sanju too."

"Marcus, let me go and see her. I need to help with this too. You have been really wonderful helping me get my life back and thank you again for the keyboard. I'll get you some photos of Anshu."

A few days later, they went through the different facial projections for Anshu. She chose a hairstyle, a skin shade as she thought he would be in the Indian sun, and eye colour – a light greyish brown, imagining how she thought they'd have evolved from the original blue. She kept copies for herself which she looked at each day until they, themselves, became part of her memory of Anshu. She stroked his face on the printout and the light black mole on his cheek as tears streamed down her face, allowing Marcus, sitting next to her on the sofa, to place his arm around her.

"I'll send you copies of the advertisements."

"How much will they cost, Marcus? And I need to reimburse you for the security too. I just haven't been thinking about your costs in all this."

"Oh, please leave that with me. Let's get him back." He got up to leave. "By the way, I'm taking Ollie to the Isle of Wight in a couple of weeks. I have a house there. Perhaps you'd like to join us. It would be good company for us; you'd meet Ollie, and nice for you to get out of London." He was speaking hurriedly, rushing to finish his sentence, and let out a small belch. "It's our family home. Well, my father's actually. By the beach, lots of rooms, the nanny will be there, and I thought maybe you could ask Jemima, your sister, to join."

"That's really kind. I'll ask her."

Jemima was very keen to go but mainly for Emma's sake. Emma said yes, but the day before they were leaving, Jemima came down with flu.

"You should definitely go, Em. On your own. You haven't been anywhere for over a year."

"I shouldn't say this, Jem, he's done so much trying to help with Anshu and everything else, but he's a little bit creepy sometimes."

"Oh, don't be silly. He's completely brought you out of your shell into the world. Anyway, the nanny and his son will be there, and it's a big house."

"OK, maybe I'll go for just a couple of days."

"You won't get emotional, will you, Em – his boy is just a little older than Anshu, right?"

"Yeah, hopefully should be OK. I can't go through life avoiding every toddler."

The Flints owned a large house facing the English Channel on the outskirts of Bembridge. Emma took the train down from London. It was true she hadn't been anywhere since returning from India. It was also true that without Marcus she would probably still be in that helpless depression. He had given her her only hope that she would find her son, and then her husband.

Marcus picked her up from the ferry terminal. Ollie was sleeping in his car seat in the back. She took a long look at him – short dark hair, slightly Mediterranean look, but controlled herself from thinking about her own son. He woke up as they arrived at the house.

"Hello, I'm Emma. You must be Ollie."

"Hello. I thought we were going to the beach, Daddy."

"Yes, we will after lunch. The tide is in at the moment. Why don't you show Emma to her room and tell Angie to get lunch ready?" Marcus took Emma's bag out of the boot. "Please make yourself at home. Angie is the nanny. She's very friendly."

That afternoon, they went to walk along the beach from the lifeboat pier. Ollie was wearing green boots over some jeans and a black jumper. Emma was surprised about how outgoing and friendly he was, and immediately comfortable with her.

"Come on, Emma. Can you help me find some crabs? They're in the lock pools."

"Rock pools, Ollie."

"Yeah, Daddy, lock pools."

"Come on then. Are they very big? I might be scared."

"Don't worry, Emma. They're tiny. Anyway, Daddy is here."

He ran off onto the bare wet sand where the tide had receded, towards the low, exposed, flat seaweed and barnacle-covered rocks with pools of stagnant sea water, where seagulls were strutting around, looking for afternoon snacks.

"Hey, wait for me!"

Behind her, she could hear a phone buzzing. "Emma, do you mind if I take this call?"

"Yes, go ahead. We'll be fine."

Ollie ran back and grabbed her forefinger to guide her onto the rocks, asking her to shift some loose stones in case there were crabs hiding underneath. They could see Marcus sitting on the boulders near the grassy coastal bank, engaged in deep conversation. After a few moments, Ollie released Emma's finger and ran along the beach and across a spread of large pebbles. He squealed in laughter as Emma pretended to chase him, turning to see if Emma was close behind, and bursting into laughter again as she stretched forward pretending to catch him.

"Oh, you're too fast for me, Ollie." Emma stopped, only to see Ollie veer sharply and trip against some embedded stones in the sand, and land in a tidal puddle. The laughter stopped, to be followed by a second's silence, and then a big cry.

"Oh no, are you OK?" She picked him up and he clasped his arms around her neck, sobbing loudly. "Oh, you're all wet. Let me see if Daddy has a towel or spare trousers."

Marcus was running towards them across the beach.

"It's OK, Marcus, just that he's wet. I'll get these boots off."

"I've got some spare jeans and a jumper in the bag."

Ollie was still clutching onto Emma when Marcus arrived. "Let's get these dry trousers and top on, shall we?"

"I want Emma to put them on." He had stopped sobbing.

"I can do it." Her heart was beating fast as she tried not to well up with Ollie in her arms. "Oh, you have a little graze there." She tried to distract herself. "I'm sure we can put some cream on that when you get home, and you must be a brave young man; I can see quite a few scars from falls."

"Actually, some of them are old burns – happened a while ago with his nanny in the kitchen in Singapore. He was just a baby then." Marcus was looking at Emma as she changed Ollie's clothes.

Emma looked at the little white marks on Ollie's legs, a couple on his left arm and one on his cheek. She stroked them gently with the back of her forefinger, wiped away his final lingering tear, but could feel the moisture and vulnerability in her own eyes.

Marcus continued quickly, "The scars should fade and, anyway, we can do a skin graft when he's older, but he's a solid lad considering his start in life at the orphanage, and then being burdened with me."

Ollie still had his arm around Emma as he sat on her legs, and she put his boots back on. "There we go. Let's get back to hunting for those crabs."

Over the next few weeks, Emma couldn't resist spending time with Marcus and Ollie. She started to meet them on Sundays in the park and then going round for dinner. They would discuss any developments in India on the search, but although the advertisements had raised a lot of responses, nothing material had come to light. Most of all, Emma enjoyed spending time with Ollie. Her anxieties and depression had eased significantly, and she had the two of them to thank for that.

Marcus, on the other hand, could think of nothing but being with her, thinking of ways to see her more often, leveraging her clear affection for Ollie, realising how obviously he had come to fill the void that Anshu had left. But he continued to struggle to take their relationship another step beyond that platonic friendship. He knew moving too quickly could result in rejection again, yet with each moment, the desire and uncertainty around the outcome continued to become more tortuous.

He asked her again to come to the Isle of Wight with them for the May Bank Holiday weekend. She immediately said yes. This time, there was no nanny, and the weekend passed as if they were the fun-loving family that he had envisioned in his dreams. He had planned to say something on the Saturday evening but decided that could make things awkward the next day, so waited until they got back, choosing to drop Ollie off first with their nanny against his pleas, before taking her home.

"Thank you for a lovely weekend, Marcus."

"Look, Emma, I wanted to say something. I really enjoy our time together. I've grown very fond of you." He spluttered out the sentence.

Emma could feel her body tense. It had caught her off guard. "Marcus, you've been lovely to me. I couldn't have recovered from where I was without you, and your help with Anshu has given me so much hope to live. But I'm married to Sanju and I'm sorry, I really don't think I could be with anyone else." She could see him trying to hide his face flinch.

"That's fine, but I needed to say it."

"Can we still be friends as we are, Marcus?" She stayed in the car, looking at him.

"Yes, of course." He got out to get her bag from the boot, handed it to her and, without looking back, got in the car and drove off.

She walked slowly inside, at the same time slightly shocked, slightly guilty, and slightly disappointed about what had happened. She called Jemima to tell her.

"What did you think – that he was doing all this for you just as a favour?"

"I never thought of it like that. He's a good friend of Sanju's!"

"Sanju is not coming back, Em. You haven't heard a thing for two years. And even if he did, do you think he'll be the same after wandering round the mountains for years?"

There was silence. "I'm sorry, Em. I shouldn't have said that. Look, he's probably very nice. He's brought you back to life. You love his boy. Why don't you think about it? You don't want to be alone for ever."

Emma wondered whether Marcus would call again, when she would get an update on Anshu, and when she would get to see Ollie again. Normally he texted or called every two to three days, but a fortnight had passed before she called him.

She wanted to sound upbeat – she asked how everyone was, what Ollie was up to, if there was any new news from India. He said he'd been really busy in the office and hadn't had a chance to update her, but everything was fine, a couple more leads in India but nothing major to report.

"Marcus, I just wanted to say, you've been so good to me, and thank you again for inviting me to Bembridge and spending time with your wonderful boy. I was, er, thinking, maybe, I could cook you dinner one evening, if you're not too busy." She hadn't cooked or entertained for years and never in her tiny flat.

Marcus agreed straight away, and they met two days later. He spoke about his childhood and how he found it hard to be a father. He mentioned Tani a couple of times, and she sensed he still had strong memories of her. He would continue to talk about her a lot over the years. She tried hard not to speak too much of Anshu, and particularly Sanju. He got up to leave after they had finished their second bottle of wine.

He said goodbye at the door, and she leant forward and kissed him on the lips. He seemed genuinely surprised but immediately shuffled back towards her, making her take a long step back out of the way.

"Goodnight, Marcus. Give my love to Ollie." She spoke firmly, clearly signalling for him to leave, and shut the door.

The contact was dry, uncomfortable, and felt unclean as she wiped her mouth. She walked up to her bedroom, took out a photo of Sanju, held it tightly to her heart and whispered,

"I'm so sorry, Sanju, I so wish you were here," and burst into tears.

The next day she received a big bouquet of flowers.

He would soon realise that there would be affection but little passion in their relationship, but, for him, he had stability, he had a partner to help with Ollie; he had a fit for his career. His plans had slotted into place.

For Emma, it was an escape from the nightmare that had lasted over two years. She struggled to find Marcus physically attractive. She was grateful to discover she couldn't have any more children, but she was completely enamoured with Ollie and couldn't spend a day without him.

There was to be no further news about Anshu or Sanju.

TWENTY-FOUR

The end may justify the means
As long as there is something that justifies the end.

"Hey, *ciao*, Marcus. You are the greatest. You did it!"

"Tell me about it, Andrea. You sound hoarse. What happened?" Marcus had put on his managerial tone.

"Was going to call you last night but we've just had the most fucking amazing party. So Starc got marched off the floor around four, and the whole place just stands up and bursts into applause, and nearly everyone then walks off to the bar."

"Don't burn your bridges, Andrea. You never know where he may land."

"It won't be in Singapore, my friend – the guy is so out of the money – it was his birthday last week, someone bought him some cake; I mean someone in his team spent money getting him a cake, fucking arse-licker, not that that shit was grateful. Anyway, listen, the next time, if ever, he gets a chance to celebrate his birthday in an office in Singapore, it will cost them more to buy the candles than the cake!" Andrea burst into a raucous laugh. "That's Zhao Kun's joke, not mine."

Marcus briefly joined in the laughter, more at Andrea's joy than the old joke itself. "Handscombe must be pissed off."

"*Si*, big time. He's been busy wrapping up stuff on Epsilon for Pierre, but no he wasn't at the party, and haven't seen him at all today."

"Pierre is under pressure to get rid of people. Show the world we're doing something about Epsilon. Not sure Starc was much to do with me, but there will be others going soon."

"That sounds unpleasant."

"Yep, and on that note, I'll need some names from you – a couple of MDs and three or four other seniors."

"Shit – that many?" Andrea's tone quickly lost its earlier exuberance. "Obviously you know it's tougher here – if they have no job, the expats have to leave. I'd have nowhere to go, for example."

"Yes, yes, I know."

"OK, good. I knew I could trust you."

Marcus reflected momentarily on how Andrea had been desperate to leave Europe, supposedly having become estranged from his family. He never found out exactly the reason why, but there were rumours that his ex-girlfriend had some connections to Columbian drug cartels, who, having realised Andrea's position in Italian society, had started to intimidate and threaten him to assist in their business. Things had started to become public, and it seemed rather than provide protection, the family were keener for him to ditch his girlfriend and leave London, seemingly more concerned about their reputation than his well-being. Anyway, there was nothing he could do. He had saved Andrea once, and if Andrea had to leave Singapore once he fired him, frankly, that was not his problem; he wasn't going to fucking babysit him again, but before that he needed a return favour.

"Listen, Andrea, you remember you told me about Ayla going to Kerala to see the Iyers, yeah?"

"*Si.*"

"Well, that can't happen." There was a pause during which Andrea didn't speak before Marcus continued. "I'm sure you remember why but let me remind you."

Marcus's tone was serious – he raised his volume and intonation, clipping his words into short sentences to reflect his obvious annoyance and irritation around what he was relating. "Caitanya. She left Singapore. She left me. She left my baby, our baby, in an orphanage. I tried to bring her back. I've told the world that she died in childbirth. I've told my boy that. I didn't want him to grow up and start thinking about the mother that dumped him, dumped us. I didn't want him wondering who she was – where she is!"

There was another pause. "So, what happens when Ayla goes to Kerala and comes back and tells TDT that Tani is alive and well? Do you understand what happens then?" Marcus finished off almost shouting down the phone.

There was another, longer pause, as Marcus waited for his little soliloquy to sink through.

"You need to fire her, so she's away from TDT, and goes back to New Zealand or wherever," Marcus continued.

"Fire her for what? She's one of our best. She herself hasn't done anything wrong. Anyway, she'll easily get another job here."

"Andrea, if you want to stay my senior Asia guy, you really need to grow a couple. Go through her expenses – there's bound to be something odd. Do a review. Anything. I'll make sure she doesn't get another job in Singapore or in banking for that matter. I want it done this week."

After a final pause, Andrea cleared his throat. "You know, Marcus, I heard a story about this Neapolitan aristocrat in the eighteenth century who got into arguments about who was the better poet, Dante or Ariosto. He fought twenty duels on the topic and killed fourteen people. Why? Who knows? Surely the issue wasn't that big. Maybe it was a desire to put down others, or maybe he was covering some other darkness, but fourteen people died until, eventually, he took on one too many, only to reveal on his own deathbed that he'd never read either man's work."

"Oh, just fucking do it, Andrea. This week! They deserved to die. No one has ever heard of Ariosto."

* * *

Marcus spent the rest of the week surreptitiously working on the cull list with his directs, who, despite their outward confidence, were still comforted by the reassurance in Marcus's tone that they were safe, despite the size of the upcoming changes.

He passed the afternoons walking around the villa where, in spite of the thaw, remnants of ice patches still needed to be tackled with caution. The path behind Villa Traxler went up a hill, which provided a broader view of the Teiflaubach gushing below towards the Meiringensee, turning right just a few hundred metres before the lake, eventually crashing into the edge of the valley, and veering left into the large pool of water. It was on that headland bordering the turns that the village of Weisenberg now stood, and Marcus watched and wondered how long it would be before the erosive forces of the river cut off the village from its chapel, and whether the village, or even humanity itself, would survive to that day.

He took time to explore the woods away from the marked paths, seeing, one afternoon, the small holes that had been dug by Gilbert, causing him to vomit violently against a large tree.

The villa had become a hub of activity as empty rooms were being prepared for the guests arriving the following week. Marcus would take time to talk to Urs, showing interest in the types of well-to-do guests that came: tourists, those who needed to relax, and others looking for escape.

"We wanted to provide a full range of services here, Marcus, beyond tourism, or the restaurant, or the spa services. Next week we have a lady needing psychiatric help. She will stay here, and the psychiatrist will visit, and we may put him up in the village to be nearby. Another gentleman is suffering intense pain and pondering an assisted death and wants to spend some days with his extended family to make a decision. Interestingly, in Switzerland, we can legally help those with unbearable physical pain, but not unmanageable mental anguish from guilt, for example, or trauma, or from something else they can't share, whatever."

"Well, there used to be the foreign legion or the church for those people."

"True, but those options are not for everyone and, in many cases, perhaps only provide a short-term diversion. Look, ultimately, the source of their anxiety will eventually catch up with them."

"Yeah, I suppose some things just need to be stored up, unspoken, even if they're eating you up inside – who wants to risk losing their family, or end up in prison by opening up voluntarily, eh?" Marcus sighed distractedly.

"Exactly, so, here, I thought why not offer options for escape. Oh, the delivery people are calling me. Please excuse me."

Marcus waited for Urs to walk away before muttering under his breath, "And I suspect some of those 'escapes' are not totally voluntary."

* * *

Marcus's gentle slumber in those spring days in the Swiss hills came to a dramatic end the day before Emma was due to arrive. It was a call from Pierre on his private mobile.

"Hello, Pierre, this is a surprise."

"Yes, it is a fucking surprise." Pierre's tone was angry and confrontational, as it had been at the Exco. Marcus wondered if the stress of the regulatory reviews were taking a toll, but in that instance, he feared something worse, and he was right in his discomfort. "Do you remember, as I'm sure you fucking do, Caitanya Iyer?"

"Yes, she worked for TDT about ten years back." Marcus tried to stay calm but, with a sharp gasping intake of air, let out a quiet burp.

"Marcus, don't fuck with me! Her name has come up as she was selling the same Epsilon structured products, and it seems you were more than distant colleagues."

Marcus wondered how they had gone back so far. A whistle-blower. How could Handscombe have stumbled across that – he had only joined the bank three years ago? Surely it couldn't have been Andrea. He had to think quickly.

"Can we talk about it on Monday? I don't know absolutely everything that she was selling. She was quite junior, and it was a while ago."

"On Monday, Marcus, we'll be discussing with HR what the fuck you were doing with her, and the circumstances around her departure." Pierre stressed each noun and pronoun in the sentence.

Marcus's pause was overly prolonged. Unable to think of anything else, he went on the attack. "Oh, come on, Pierre, you and I know I'm not the only one who has had a passing liaison in the office, don't we?"

"Really, Marcus, I'd encourage you not to fuck with me!" By now, Pierre was almost shouting down the phone. "There isn't a whole megabyte of emails concerning anyone else's 'passing liaisons'."

"This was a long time ago. Over ten years ago. No one knows or needs to know. No one is interested. It has been quiet this long. It can stay quiet." Marcus reverted to a calmer tone.

Marcus heard Pierre sniff. "Well, it seems, as of now, plenty of people do know, and plenty more will be interested. The regulators will be asking questions about our culture. The management will be asking how the same fucking head of sales that I saved, under whose management these products were being sold, was at the same time fucking the staff, both literally and metaphorically."

"They'll only be interested if they find out. Personally, I'd be more interested in ascertaining who is spreading these rumours and damaging the bank. We have NDAs in place."

"They are not fucking rumours, Marcus. Her emails, file notes, dealings with clients, whatever they could find, have been sent to the MAS, but they come with saucy interactions between the two of you. It's inconceivable that they will not take note of, and focus on, your shenanigans, particularly given what is filed in our HR archives. There will be questions to our management. You will be suspended while we review. People will start to talk. That's when the broader world will hear. I'll give it a couple of weeks before journalists start to gather outside your house, NDAs or not, and are seeking you out, and then Ms Iyer, for comments."

"Oh, fuck off, Pierre. If I go down, I'm going to bring you and the others with me. Ashleigh—"

Pierre interrupted him brusquely. "Marcus, friend, that's not the approach I would take. I would calmly reflect and think hard and fast over the weekend about what, if any, mitigating circumstances you have for the way forward; that is to say, what story you can come up with, and come and see me Monday morning." He hung up.

* * *

Muttu bought Marcus lunch, having watched him spend the rest of the morning shuffling between the cigar room and the library, moving uneasily and looking uncomfortable in both, sombre and totally uncommunicative. He had asked for a ham sandwich with piccalilli, his favourite comfort food as a child, even though he said he didn't feel hungry.

Urs returned to the villa early afternoon, and immediately went to see Marcus, who had clearly been drinking. They were still engrossed in conversation two hours later when Muttu brought them coffees. Various papers were stretched across the desk. Marcus had moist, bloodshot eyes. Urs stood serious next to him with his hand on Marcus's shoulder. It was the first time Muttu had seen Urs show any emotion towards a guest.

"What would you like to eat this evening, Marcus? We'll get it prepared."

"Why don't we let Muttu pick something? It's our last evening, just the three of us together."

"Of course, are you happy to eat on the terrace? It's calm although a little cold."

"Yes. We'll need some warming drinks, Muttu."

Muttu stared as Marcus forced a smile hiding the pain – the sort of smile he was so familiar with himself. Marcus had had his hair cut in advance of Emma's arrival, but he looked old, a decade older. There had always been tension in his face, but now the shoulders were slouched, the posture aquiline, and the stomach resting on his belt.

Marcus turned to Urs. "OK, let me get my laptop and make those changes, and then I'd like to call Ollie, and perhaps go down to the gym before dinner."

* * *

"Hello, Emma, are you all ready for your flight over?"

"Well, almost, I need to take Ollie across to Jemima. We're having dinner, then I'll come back and finish off the packing. Really looking forward to seeing you."

"Won't be long now. Anyway, I thought I'd have a quick word with Ollie before you go."

"Yes, of course. He's here."

"Hello, Daddy, I'm so excited you're coming back."

"Listen, Marcus, can I leave you two? I'm running late and need to get his weekend bag ready. See you in the morning."

"Bye Emma, love you."

Emma left them talking, feeling excited like a young child before Christmas – it had been so long since she'd seen him, and now it was just hours before she'd be with him, and in a couple of days they'd be back together in London, and she could take care of him. From the other room, she could hear Marcus talking to Ollie and hear their intermittent giggles. They hadn't spoken for this long for a long time and she could feel how keen they were to see each other again.

Marcus managed to maintain his joyful demeanour for the whole call but burst into tears as soon as he put the phone down. He had been away too long. He hadn't managed to resolve anything, and now the moment had arrived to face the consequences.

* * *

The mood was solemn as Muttu brought in two glasses of pre-dinner Calvados for Urs and Marcus.

"Let's lighten things up a little. I'll put some music on. What would you like, Marcus? And, Muttu, can you put the outside lights on and bring some wine, maybe an Aussie Shiraz – bring the Grange?"

"I don't mind, Urs. How about something like that loud dance music from the '90s, like The Prodigy?"

"It's not a genre or group I'm familiar with," Urs retorted, but managed to find a track, 'Breathe', and turned up the volume. "It's early evening so I think we can get away with a little noise, even in Switzerland."

"I don't know anything by them either, but I remember the graduates talking about them when I was in London. It'll make me feel younger!" Marcus stood up and started gyrating his arms wildly like a drowning man signalling to a distant lifeboat. Urs joined in with a gentle rocking of his hips, moving his knees like an ageing piston and giving the appearance of a dinghy struggling in rough waters. The two were joined by Muttu, holding three glasses and the bottle of wine, but still able to swirl his shoulders, taking long strides left and right in a bhangra procession towards the table. The three were out of breath before the track finished, but their moods had lifted. Urs changed the music to a playlist of '80s and '90s hits that they all recognised.

They exchanged the same banter and laughs over tacos and Lebanese kebab canapés that had enlivened their conversations over the past weeks, with Marcus talking loudly and drinking aggressively, and Muttu hardly at all.

For the main course, Muttu had made Rogan Josh with aubergine *bhurta*, served with naans and rice.

"It's gorgeous but I sense a little more heat than normal, Muttu."

"Not too much to dampen your enjoyment, I hope."

"No, it's lovely." Marcus suddenly lowered his voice and became more serious as if about to share something highly personal and confidential. "You know, you guys know almost everything about me, but I know very little about you guys, and virtually nothing about you, Muttu."

"You've mentioned this before. It really shouldn't bother you. There is really not much to know," Urs interjected with a mild playful dismissiveness.

"Well, let's say I'm curious. I had a bit of time this week, so I thought I'd do a bit of research, getting the brain cells warmed up for the office again. Why don't I run what I found by you?"

Urs and Muttu were quiet. Muttu took a small sip of wine and kept the glass notably in front of his lips, keeping any facial expressions hidden.

"You were from near Valvetti-something – a village on the Northern coast, right? I googled it. Pretty place. But it also comes up as a bit of a hotbed of Tamil nationalism. I saw there was a very unpleasant massacre there around the time you must have been growing up, and then another mass shooting with the Indian peacekeepers. It must have been tough for a young guy. I guess that's why your parents were keen to get you out of there to Bangalore."

"It's true. I was a child when those things happened. Wars are not pleasant, and we are a peaceful family." Muttu spoke seriously, sounding pensive, but also noticeably slightly apprehensive.

"Yeah, but there must have been a bit of pressure for a young man to join the movement when things kicked off again. There were undoubtedly guys wanting young men like you for the fight, and your peaceful parents wanting to keep you out of trouble – no?"

"As I say, sir, I was far away in Bangalore." Muttu now answered with a terser 'let's not go there' tone.

"The thing is, I read that in amongst those innocent students getting away to India were also young fighters escaping across the Palk Strait, hiding undercover of studying as it were, so difficult to tell who was a genuine scholar or an escapee terrorist," Marcus continued, ignoring the tension building around the table.

"Terrorist is a loaded word, sir. Maybe 'freedom fighter'?"

Marcus was looking straight at Muttu, and felt sure he had just seen Muttu flinch, momentarily ruffling that smooth and composed aura.

"Oh, come on, Marcus. What are you getting at? Relax. It's our last evening," Urs interrupted again.

"Yes, I'm sorry. Freedom fighters. One freedom fighter, thought to be underground in India, who particularly caught my interest was a Karthik Shivathamby – hope I said that right – but who went under an alias, Alpha. He was originally from near your village, and about the same age, so I guess you must know who he was. He was relatively junior but had built a reputation with LTTE commanders." Marcus, ignoring Urs, was speaking a little faster now, extrapolating from his hosts' reaction that perhaps he was, as he had assumed, truly onto something.

"Marcus, let's move on!" Urs had raised his voice.

"No, please, sir, let him finish. I'm interested in what he has to say. Yes, of course, we had all heard of Alpha around that time."

"During the war there were Sri Lankan agents trying to track down those Tamil Tigers all over India, but even after the troubles ended, these agents would often be in India for military training, visiting friends and connections, or perhaps even looking to settle old scores. And it was during the peacetime, although there was normally nothing noteworthy to report, that there was the death of a Colonel Kulasinghe, who was a fit military man, but died suddenly on one of those trips in Chennai. He would have been a high-ranking target for the Tigers as he was supposedly involved in a number of attacks against Tamils, including the civilian massacre in a library near your village. But at the time nobody really suspected anything odd about his death, as most of the Tiger assassinations would be using landmines or suicide bombers, and all this guy had before passing away was a bad stomach and vomiting."

"That's very interesting, sir. Obviously, I don't know anything, but you've done a lot of research. I remember the name Kulasinghe vaguely. Nasty man, if I recall correctly. Forgive me, though. I'm missing your point."

"I'm very curious, like a cat." Marcus couldn't resist a little wink at Muttu, recalling his use of that expression. He had, of course, used various security contacts in India who had managed to get access to some archived files. "I'm coming to the point. You see, I think if they had done a post-mortem, they would have discovered that he had been poisoned."

"Really, why? I'm sure that would have been big news. Post-mortems can be expensive affairs and rarely conducted unless you have a strong suspicion of wrongdoing. We used to hear stories of many people in that part of the world die from taking the kernels of something called the pong-pong tree. Their slightly bitter taste can be easily hidden in spicy food, so they are frequently taken for suicides, or even murders, but seldom confirmed as such because the post-mortem, being so expensive, would require a strong inkling of foul play and would need to be specific. And, as you say, there was no cause for suspicion here."

Marcus could see that Muttu had engaged in the story, perhaps to see how far it would go, but, most importantly, Muttu's clear interest was helping to confirm his hypothesis.

"Well, I think we should stop there and get some rest." Urs was now starting to look very agitated.

"Actually, I wanted to say a couple more things."

"Go ahead, sir." Muttu was looking even more serious now but continued to speak calmly. "Interested to hear the end of your tale."

"Well, one of the professors of chemistry at the Institute of Science in Bangalore, a VJ Sripavan, it turns out, had settled in India, having married a fellow Indian lecturer, but was originally from the north of Sri Lanka. In fact, also from near your village. You would probably have met him in your studies."

"I know that name also, sir."

"It turns out that the professor's sister married a chap called Shivathamby back in Sri Lanka – coincidentally the same surname as our Alpha freedom fighter. Could it be too much to think that this Alpha was the professor's nephew, supposedly studying under him at the university?" Marcus paused for a second to let the point sink through.

"Well, I couldn't find anyone studying there around that time under the name Shivathamby, but there was a Sri Lankan Tamil student there by the name of Pradeep Etrandaar. Intriguingly, this Etrandaar disappeared without completing his master's at around the time of the death of the Sri Lankan agent.

"You see, where I'm getting at in my little imagination is that Alpha escaped to Bangalore to become a student at the university with the help of his professor uncle, changed names to Pradeep E, was involved in the assassination of our Sri Lankan colonel and then disappeared."

"It is very imaginative, Marcus, but you said the death of the colonel rose no suspicions, so why would he need to disappear?"

"Because, you see, the Indians did suspect something and did a post-mortem. He was poisoned, confirmed, but they kept the results quiet so as not to reignite tensions. Probably that news was leaked to our freedom fighter."

"I still don't see where this tale is going. You started by saying you were curious to know more about us." Urs spoke deliberately, more calmly now, but his demeanour was of someone expecting an uncomfortable conclusion.

"Let me continue, Urs. Interestingly, another of Professor Sripavan's students was Hamid Aljawahiri. Yes, part of the same family as the previous owners of this villa and one of your clients, Urs. It's a small world." Marcus looked at Urs before turning back towards Muttu. "And despite all my digging, as with the name Shivathamby, I didn't find any record of any student there called Muttu Murali. I don't think I need to spell out what I'm thinking." Marcus looked at the other two gentlemen in turn again and smiled contentedly like Poirot concluding a particularly difficult case.

There was an awkward silence before Urs spoke. "That's all very interesting, Marcus, but, tell us, have you shared your thoughts with anyone else?"

"Obviously not, and of course piecing together where we came from is much easier than seeking to find where we have gone." Marcus nodded once at Urs, concurrently noting and wishing to alleviate any concern.

"Sir, I'm a private person. That's the only reason I keep my past to myself. It is true I grew up during the civil war, but my family were very focused on education so sent me to India. I am ashamed to say I was not bright enough to complete my degree, which is probably why you found no record, but I became a chef in a local restaurant, then in a global hotel. That is where I met Mr Aljawahiri. Really nothing more to it than that, sir."

"You know the guys in the village said that when Ishmail left here and boarded his private jet, he was not looking good and vomiting profusely."

"There are some very strong leaps of deduction in your story, if I may say, Marcus, and I will add you are moving onto some highly unpleasant assertions." Urs raised his voice again.

"Urs, I'm not in any fucking position to make any judgements, and I'm not doing so but I am, and have been, very curious." Marcus matched Urs' volume.

Muttu leaned across the table for the first time, imposing his body language noticeably against the other two, like the provoked alpha male. "Despite your denials, I do think a judgement is being positioned, sir, but, as you know yourself, context is important, and that can often go missing in these superficial piecemeal accounts. You used the word 'assassination', sir. A glorious term for both the victim and the killer, I may say; maybe it was manslaughter in self-defence, maybe a justified revengeful murder; both cases could generate more sympathy than a cold-blooded pre-planned kill. Perhaps the victim knew he was at risk and was seeking glory in rooting out an enemy. We see taking life as an ultimate sin, but I sometimes think that it is less sinful than creating situations that make others' lives a living hell, wouldn't you agree, sir?" Muttu ended with a raised intonation and was looking directly across at Marcus.

"I'm really not seeking to make any judgements, Muttu." Marcus spoke calmly, keen to de-escalate the conversation.

"A person who grows up in a childhood constantly seeing death in front of him, and as a youth constantly feels death creeping up on him, no longer fears it as an adult; no longer tries to define the circumstances, so no longer reflects too long before pulling a trigger or administering a fatal dose; lives on that vague edge of life and death himself. His life becomes a temporary base for his soul, his names are just labels, but it is what is deep inside his soul, in context, that he hopes will be judged, not his life." Muttu stopped, noticeably perturbed.

"Ishmail bought disrepute to the family and disappeared. Was that really deserved? What context justifies that?" Marcus asked the question with a tone not to challenge, but as someone wishing to genuinely understand.

"Again, I have already said, he left our establishment peacefully and comfortably. And you are making more judgements. Like many others, Ishmail was struggling. There were many expectations on him, and all he wanted to do was to read and write poetry. Bringing disrepute to the family was a step too far for him, maybe for them too, but certainly for him, and well, as I say, he is very comfortable now." Urs took a long sip of wine.

There was another long silence.

"People will make judgments about me, Urs. They will not have the full context." It was a melancholic comment.

"But you have made a judgement about yourself, Marcus, and you do have the full context, or at least a better one than anyone else."

"I'm really not sure," Marcus muttered to himself before raising his voice. "Anyway, it's time to finish this wine." Marcus took a big gulp and poured himself the rest of the bottle. "Tell me: with these pong-pong kernels, is the end very painful?"

"Not necessarily. The technical term for the plant is *cerbera odollam*, and, locally, it is called the suicide tree. For those who take the ground powder voluntarily, first, any pain from dying is more comfortable than their pain living, and mostly they just fall asleep and don't wake up again."

"And I guess they are available globally now?" Marcus made a passing glance at Urs.

"Let's clear the table, Muttu. It is getting chilly. Bring the cheesecakes into the cigar room, and Marcus and I will have a cognac."

They did not stay up too long.

"Do you have everything you need, Urs?"

"Yes, I do. Goodnight, Marcus. It's been a pleasure to have had you stay with us." They hugged the sort of hug that grown men give after a drunken night, as they are starting to sober up.

"Goodnight, Urs. Goodnight, Muttu." Marcus placed his arm around Muttu and brought him close. "Hey, I wasn't making any judgements. You're a good friend."

"Goodnight, sir. Sleep well."

"By the way, is the taxi booked for Emma at the airport tomorrow?"

"Yes, sir."

Urs and Muttu watched Marcus go up the stairs to his room.

"Do you think he may have shared that story with others, sir?"

"No, I don't think so, but it's a lesson learnt for you, I hope. You need to smile more and talk less."

Urs noticed the light was on in the basement gym. He went downstairs to find the usual curled-up scraps of paper where Marcus had been venting with his fists. He picked them up to put in the bin but couldn't resist unfurling one. There, splattered with specks of blood on the A4 was a picture of him, of Marcus Flint himself.

TWENTY-FIVE

There are only two tragedies in life;
One is not getting what one wants, and the other is getting it.

The problem is that Tani was, like everyone else, doing what she was told to do, and also selling those structured products. Her sales were a long time ago, and I had hoped that that would put them well before the time frame for these reviews, and so leave her emails and other correspondence untouched, and any details of our liaison left uncovered. And if the worst happened, I had hoped to find some answers. Well, her emails, like everyone else's, are being dug up and being sent to the regulator.

The affair will be frowned upon, as she was a junior in my division, and more so as I was her mentor, and also ultimately the decider of her promotion and compensation, which was elevated because she was a good salesperson, nothing else. But it will form part of a narrative around our culture and, in particular, my behaviour. When TDT are looking for scapegoats, it'd add to the case against Marcus Flint for that much alone; another easy scrap to throw to the regulatory dogs, but they are likely to stumble across other things that are much more damning, for which today I have nothing, as I say, but the deepest regret. Why did I do what I did? I don't know what to say. I was trying to protect my career *that massaged my ego, that fed my greed and ambition, and that had leveraged my propensity to move from the half-truths and deceptions, that had served me so well, to blatant dishonest lying. I was wrong. But the story will leak, and will no doubt titillate the media and their readers from whom I really had hoped to protect us.*

That affair should never have happened, but it did, and these things do happen. I had thought it was a bit of fun, you know, between consenting adults and all that, but something to keep quiet in the office, something that would undeniably have been career-threatening for me if it had ever become public. I even tried to end things at the beginning, but I couldn't, we couldn't, and we drifted into this secret relationship, and during which, to be totally fair, she was utterly discreet. My previous relationships had never lasted more than a few weeks – I simply hadn't been able to commit to anyone nor, I suspect, could anyone have been committed to me. But with Tani it had definitely started to feel different, deeper, and I know now that I was truly in love – something I would not have recognised or had ever experienced before.

You know after the distant childhood I'd had, the dysfunctional family, the expulsion from school, the drugs, my career at TDT in London was the best thing that had happened in my life. It had become my passion. It was how I defined and valued myself, how I gauged myself against others until, because of that shithead Dietmar, I got shoved off to Singapore. I already mentioned the bitterness I felt. All I did there was to work my balls off to try to get my career back on track – I became Asia sales head, but away from the main TDT centres in London and New York, there really wasn't anyone to take notice. Frankly, Tani was the only really good thing that happened to me out there.

Of course, when I thought about it, a secret love affair with a junior wasn't going to work with my career and life aspirations, and it definitely caused me an internal tension, not just because she was a junior, but also when I would see Sanju and you, or other beautiful ideal couples, mixing freely and networking with the upper tiers at TDT like with Prasad and his wife, it was something I couldn't do.

Yet my 'internal tension' would have been nothing compared to what Tani must have been going through, keeping us secret from her friends and her family. For them, and their conservative world, it would have been bad enough that she was having an affair, but it was with her boss, who was not even Indian, let alone a Keralite. She had family, and with it, the loves and pressures that I had never known.

After simmering for several years about how my career had been thrown off the rails, and effectively sidelined in Singapore, I finally got my break. I was offered the role to return to London as the global head for distribution, to sit on our executive committee, and who knows where that might have gotten me to next, career-wise. It was everything that I had wanted and aspired to at that time. I could face my peers and friends, and say, look I'm back! All I needed was for Tani to stay quiet about us. My 'internal tension' about our relationship had finally come to a head and I needed to resolve the situation one way or the other. I had thought that I could persuade her to get a job elsewhere, and we could pretend the affair started after she left. Maybe we could also have become the 'ideal couple' like you and Sanju.

That's the context, not an excuse, for what unfolded.

I had just gotten back from a business trip when she told me she was pregnant. Of course, she had told her sister. I was furious about that – going 'public', I mean – and I really don't know what came over me the next few days, but at that time, I just felt I simply couldn't risk our affair leaking and jeopardising that promotion. I didn't want to discuss it. I just wanted to close it out and blank it out.

Tani's sister told her parents, who were devastated, scandalised, ready to disown her, and just in those hours when Tani needed me, I disappeared, refused to answer her calls, and worse.

I went to see our HR head, this guy, Roy, who I had recruited into the firm a while back, and who owed me something of a big favour. I made up some cock-and-bull story about how she had been my mentee before, and it had come out that she was suffering from some mental issues affecting her confidence and her self-esteem, which led to counter bursts of delusion resulting in angry fits with herself and others, so I had offered to see her a couple of times out of hours to talk about it. One of those chats was after someone's drunken leaving do, where one thing led to another, and that it was just a one-night stand, after which I had asked her politely not to see me again. But she had become spiteful and angry, telling me how I had totally destroyed any ego she had left, and now was saying that she was pregnant with my baby and threatening to go public, and so effectively blackmailing me. I told Roy that I had no idea what to do as she was getting totally out of control, stalking me, and calling incessantly.

I was pretty sure no one had ever seen us out of the office, apart from Andrea who wasn't going to say anything. No one checked any emails or anything in those days. I had no idea what I would have done if they had looked into our phone call records or those emails, but Roy and I agreed to offer her a settlement. I don't know what he said to Prasad, you know the Asia regional head you knew, but he got it signed off. But they're looking at those incriminating emails now.

You know Tani didn't say a thing during her meeting with Roy. She didn't even negotiate – we reckoned she could have got maybe double or treble what we had initially offered as settlement. She just signed the non-disclosure agreement and walked out of the office. I remember Roy and I drinking champagne in a quiet dark corner of a bar that night, celebrating a trade well done.

Tani left Singapore the following day without seeing anyone. That's the real reason she left; not because she was leaving me because of any scandal or pressure from her family.

But when the dust settled, her departure left a far bigger hole for me than I had anticipated. It started with the lonely weekends. It was like a mild pain, but it grew – I started to miss her laughs, her touch, her smell, her everything, like I had never missed anything before – the pain started to become all-consuming. I tried to dismiss it by throwing myself into my work, drinking, having random nights with other women, but while the pain was ripping through my heart, the guilt of how she had departed was gnawing and crippling my mind. And on top of that, she was pregnant with my child.

The first time I flew to Kerala, I had no idea what I would say. I sought forgiveness from her. I wanted her to marry me, be with me. I would do what I needed to prove myself to her parents. We would sort out the mess with TDT and, if necessary, I would leave and find work elsewhere and she would come with me to London. She was the stability and life companion I needed.

Emma, I hope you're not getting upset with me talking about her like this – it was a long time ago. I want to be open about this like I have never been.

But she refused to see me. I sat in a taxi near their house for a week hoping to catch her somewhere outside, but I had absolutely no joy except on the last day before I had to leave. I was able to speak to Lavi, her sister, who passed on a letter I had written.

I went back a few weeks later, and in that week she met me once for a coffee. I cried, I pleaded for forgiveness, for hope for us, for another chance, notwithstanding what had happened. I went another four times on the same mission, and on the last trip she told me her parents had arranged her marriage to a local businessman, who had been happy to have her as his wife despite her 'life's scandal'. That was the last time I saw her. I was totally distraught. It was just before I bumped into you and Sanju in Delhi.

'Notwithstanding what had happened'. Over that first coffee, she told me she had aborted our child, a little girl. I often think of her in my darkest hours, my only child, and in my mind, she even has a name. Her name – Olive.

TWENTY-SIX

Sometimes it's not the people who change,
It's the mask that falls off.

It was a beautiful morning. The Meiringensee glistened under the cloudless sky. The sun reflected its celestial hue onto the heavens above, and its bright rays pierced through like shimmering static, into the deepest nooks and crannies of the woods, sprawled like an unmade emerald quilt over the valley banks.

Urs left his office as he saw a taxi climb up the driveway. He timed his arrival just as the driver was opening the door and Emma was getting out of the car, dressed immaculately in a flowery blue cotton dress under a fitted denim jacket and black ankle boots, with her sunglasses perched to hold back her soft, short blonde hair from falling across her face. She was every bit as beautiful as Marcus had described, and Urs could not help but feel surprise and regret about how she could be with that slouch of a guest that had stayed at his villa these last few weeks.

"Hello, Emma Kapoor, I believe. Welcome to Villa Traxler. I'm Urs Waelchli. It's very nice to meet you."

"Hello, what a lovely place and location. I have been so

looking forward to seeing it and meeting you." Emma put down her leather weekend bag to shake his hand.

"Thank you, but where is Marcus?"

"Marcus! Not with me. I thought he was coming to the airport but assumed something had changed. I couldn't reach him on his phone." She sounded only mildly irritated like someone who had become accustomed to another's last-minute change of plans and didn't want to let that spoil the excitement of their reunion.

"I had understood that too. I have not been around this morning and just got back. Let me find out where he is. Can I get you a tea or coffee or something else?"

"Just some water, please. What a beautiful view!" Emma sat on the same bench where Marcus would normally settle in the morning and lowered her sunglasses onto her face.

Urs returned a few moments later with Muttu carrying a tray with a glass of water.

"This is Muttu. Marcus must have mentioned him."

"Hello, Miss Emma." Muttu had his white halo smile, sparkling even more than normal under the bright sun.

"Yes, of course. Hello, Muttu. Marcus talks a lot about you. Have you found him? I thought he'd be rushing out to see me." She giggled but it was obviously to obscure a higher level of irritation.

"Well, it's a little odd. Marcus told Muttu that he had some urgent work to do this morning for Monday, and he didn't want to ruin your weekend together, so asked the driver to collect you while he finished things off."

"OK, but where is he now?"

"Actually, we don't know. He's not in the library or the gym. It's strange but when the cleaners cleaned your room, they saw he had mostly packed, even though we thought you were staying until Monday."

"We are staying until Monday. That is a bit strange. Maybe he was hiding his mess from me!" She took off her sunglasses and managed a slightly disconcerted smile.

"And there was this envelope addressed to you."

"An envelope for me, from Marcus?" Emma now looked visibly perturbed.

"Yes. I'm going to call one of my guys, Gilbert, to have a look and ask around in Weisenberg, to see if he's there or if anyone has seen him. Muttu, can you go and have a look along that path behind the villa? He really can't be anywhere else. Emma, please make yourself comfortable while we find him. Would you like to come inside? I can show you round."

"No, I'm fine here enjoying the sun. It's a bit odd, this envelope. Do you mind if I take a look?"

The taxi drove off back down the hill. Urs and Muttu walked off in different directions, as Urs took out his phone to dial Gilbert. They heard the faint ripping of Emma opening the envelope and then inside, another letter.

A few minutes passed before there was a wild scream, the same wail as the sound of the sati widows in the Rajasthani desert all those years ago, now reverberating across the verdant Swiss hills and that sunlit view, echoing through the woods where Muttu reflected how the shrill of living torture could be stronger than the cries of certain death in a burning library in Valvettithurai, and Gilbert heard the fading sound down in the valley standing next to the Weisenberg chapel.

Urs watched Emma from his office window, shaking uncontrollably, sunk to her knees on the ground where a magpie had once ripped open a helpless mouse.

TWENTY-SEVEN

There are three gates to self-destruction hell –
Lust, anger and greed.

I flew to Delhi straight after seeing her, completely lost and confused, and again I did what I always do when I feel the world is against me – I threw myself into work and drink, and in this case at the Leela Palace hotel, simultaneously. The guys who offered you a free stay at their new hotel, the Trivedis, were looking for a financial deal with TDT. They were desperate and therefore generous with their favours. Perhaps they also thought I'd be more amenable to their request if they plied me with alcohol – honestly, in that mood, I needed no second invitation. Over the course of the evening, they offered me straight cash, a villa in Goa, and even to arrange an attractive Indian wife – that's when, in my drunken stupor, I started to talk about Tani. It was very unprofessional, but, as much as the drink, I needed to talk.

It started as jokes and banter as they tried to cheer me up – 'it was good that things had come to an end, an Indian wife would have come with a large family of Indian in-laws, and I would need a cook, a maid, and goodness knows what else'. They couldn't help noticing how I had been looking admiringly at you, Emma, and detected the sickening envy I clearly had for Sanju and your relationship. They started to tease me about how I had soon forgotten Tani when you turned up. Of course, I said you were beautiful, intelligent, charming, ticked every box, if I can say that, but taken. "Out of your league," they teased.

"Not at all," I retorted – had you been single, they could have watched me in action.

"Everything is possible in love if you know how."

It was all boys' talk, Emma – unpleasant to write but I want to set the scene.

If I'm honest, I don't remember much detail about our discussion during that fourth bottle of whisky, but there was plenty of witty ribbing, repartee, and the conversation drifting between financial details of their business, Tani, my emotional well-being, and a lot of time spent talking about you. I remember we were still there in the early hours. I was tired. I remember saying we should wrap up. I had an early flight. We hadn't spoken enough about their business, which is what we were there to resolve. We had spent too much time talking about me, a problem that wasn't solvable. That's when the conversation quietened. One of them leaned across, I don't remember who, and whispered, "Everything is possible in India if only you know how."

And that's how fate brought us together – they, looking for financial security, and me, emotionally drained and distraught – and a deal was struck between someone who had been born and lived life used to getting everything he wanted, and those who had learnt the means through life to achieve everything they needed. But it wasn't in any way fated or preordained – it was cruel, immoral, driven by greed and behaviour that had never been shown enough red lines – it was, and is, utterly unforgivable.

Greed. Isn't the power of greed like the power of lies – the more you get, the more you want? A symptom of what you have and what you don't, and as you grow older, the more you see of what is possible, the more you don't want to miss out?

The following days are still a haze for me – I spent most of my time drinking in the flat in Singapore, thinking only about what might have been with Tani, and clearly not enough about what was coming, and by the time I was sober enough to process what had happened, it was too late to go back.

A week later, I heard about Anshu's disappearance. Of course, there were doubts, anxieties and guilt about what we were doing, but at that time they would be subsumed both by my elation at the thought of being with you and the planned perfect future, and the pain of my split with Tani. It was also too late to change. We had no direct contact or link with the abductors. They worked in a secret chain of local gang networks – no one knew anyone other than their direct contacts along the chain. When I asked, at a particularly angst-driven moment, if it was possible to reverse what had happened – maybe leave the child at some police station – we actually didn't know where he was being kept and by whom, and the risk would have been too great that the kidnappers, if they suspected we were backtracking, would simply 'dispose' of him. Look, I have inflicted a lot of suffering on people, but the death of a child, no, that was not something I would countenance. There was discussion upfront about physically hurting him, to deliver some physical deformity that could help to hide his identity – again, thankfully, it was a firm no from me – but the conspicuous birthmark on his face was too great a risk for his recognition. I don't know how they did it, but the facial burn scar is there to hide that, and then the scars on his arms and legs were more burns added to give the accidental burn story more credibility. So many times, over the years, I have looked at those scars and swelled up with guilt, anger, and self-hatred about what has been done to that poor boy.

I collected Anshu in Mumbai. All his papers had been prepared for him to come to Singapore as my son – forged release papers from an orphanage, birth certificate, passport, everything.

At that point, I could have done something – left him in the hotel lobby, in a temple, or church, anywhere. I think back, and I cannot understand why I carried on, but it had been made far too easy. My dread about what I was doing one minute would be countered the next with an 'everything-in-life-is-a-means-to-an-end' philosophy that is so ingrained in me. I would tell myself this is life's cycle, the sorrowful break-up with Tani being countered by the happy coincidence, and hence this opportunity, that we both would have had an Anglo-Indian mixed-race child about the same age.

Emma, I confirmed Ollie's DNA all those years ago in London when I took your sample and Sanju's parents' – Ollie is 100% Anshu, your son.

I arrived in Singapore and hired a nanny and went to work on my part of the plan. I told everyone that Caitanya had died, that Ollie was rescued from an orphanage, and that ensured that no one from Singapore would try to contact her, and I was pretty sure she would not be looking to call anyone the other way. By now, I was too far in – I had a visible child, but over the next few weeks and months I actually fell totally in love with Ollie, and the increasingly frequent pangs of guilt and shame at having taken him away from his rightful parents had started to traumatise me, and just made me even more desperate that the plan of connecting with you just had to succeed. I still hadn't fully gotten over Tani and the lingering depression from that continued to cloud my thinking, and on top of that I had my new dream career move. It was in that turbulent state that I arrived in London.

When we met at your flat, your relationship with Sanju had, as anticipated, started to deteriorate, and he had left TDT. If it hadn't or we hadn't 'connected', I had thought maybe I could have taken Ollie back to India, thought of some story to tell, and he would have been 'discovered', but if that had seemed impossible before, now with each week he got older, each week that he was with me, each week that he started to mature and learn to talk and relate, this had become even harder. Things moved frustratingly slowly. Your pining for Sanju was stronger than I could have imagined. I had no guarantee that, despite all I was doing, that you'd eventually fall for me. I had to carefully pick the moment you met Ollie and, as you know, probably that was the moment that the plan eventually started to come to fruition.

It helped that the printouts we made of Anshu's facial development were doctored so as not to look anything like Ollie, but they became, in your mind, the image that you had of Anshu growing older. And that picture was so embedded in your head that you couldn't see the real Anshu, right there, standing in front of you.

My security guys also found Sanju. He had not become a wandering sadhu. He had jumped into the Ganges but was saved by a local, and, after another attempt, he joined an ashram. He believes that Anshu is dead and has cut himself off from the world – all his family and his closest friends – but I understand he's well. He's still there near Garuda Chatti, just by Rishikesh. His address is in the other envelope as well as the contact details of his closest friend, who doesn't know about his well-being but can help you get to the ashram.

Many times, I have wondered about coming clean, many times, but I consoled myself by questioning 'what would that have achieved?'. When you are so far from the truth, so comfortable with your lies, your life becomes a comfortable falsehood, and maybe you can't tell the difference between fact and fiction anymore yourself. As I write this, I realise that, for me, telling the truth is more uncomfortable than telling lies is for others. These last few months in Switzerland have made me realise clearly what I am, and what I have done, and the pain caused.

You're probably thinking that if it hadn't been for Epsilon and the knock-on effects, this story would not have come out. Perhaps, but as I said earlier, the truth has been slowly crumpling me, the guilt tearing me from inside. I would not have been able to keep it all suppressed. Someday, the truth would have exploded into our lives. Yes, it should have happened a lot earlier.

You will have realised that I have gone, left the villa. Please don't waste time looking for me.

You will be a cauldron of anger, but when you return to London, you will have Anshu, and, I hope, soon you will be able to reconnect with Sanju too. You may feel the need to go after the Trivedis. Emma, they are powerful, ruthless and protected – I think you'll achieve nothing other than more anguish by trying to get justice for this crime. They have done a lot worse than this with no repercussions. And remember, the biggest responsibility for what has happened lies with me.

In the other envelope are also all the details to transfer my assets to you. Urs will be able to help you – he's trustworthy, knowledgeable, and discreet. All his bills have been settled for my stay. There is also a flight booking for you to go back to London tonight.

Please give my love to Ollie. I truly love him. I don't know how you will explain this but at least he'll learn that his true father is an honourable man. He won't and should never think of me as his role model. The immoral path, ultimately, somewhere, comes laced with pain. I hope he'll not become too cynical of the world, too untrustworthy, though after this who could blame him, but all I think that delivers is a bitter loneliness. I hope he'll seek to recognise people's different motivations – the good, the dark, the extremes, and their histories, with their truths and their lies, and perhaps that will help him find his direction to happiness and success without comprising the values I know you will distil in him.

Emma, I truly love you. I'm not deserving of either of your loves. I am not deserving of any of your forgiveness.

I think, for the first time in my life, I have laid out the truth. And the context. I hope when judgment is made about me, at least for a moment, people may reflect on that too – the context.

All my love

Marcus

ACKNOWLEDGEMENTS

I'd like to thank a few people.

First, let me start by thanking YOU for taking the time to pick up this book and giving this story a chance.

Secondly, I'd like to thank all my friends, acquaintances and colleagues, and the life events and memories that we have shared, that have inspired the characters and incidents in this book. Some people, perhaps sitting somewhere on a trading floor, may see a little of themselves in a character, in an incident, but just to dispel any presumptions – this is a work of fiction, there's nothing in here about you.

Next, I want to say particular thanks to those who have participated with me on this, my debut book-writing journey: reading the drafts, guiding me through the publishing process, helping with the book cover design, drafting the marketing blurb, etc. I could name you all, but you know who you are; you are all so very close to me and I am truly grateful to you. I am, however, going to single out my long-time best man, GAC, who has been dragged through so many iterations over the last three years, for sharing his thoughts and opinions, and, despite my sometime reluctance, for taking a firm cull to the more outlandish metaphors.

My literary journey began before my parents, with my

grandmother, but I'm going to fast-forward to London and my mother. My mother, who had the energy to work all hours and then more, still had the time and patience to spend each evening with her seven-year-old son, teaching him English, reading the one book we had, *One Thousand and One Nights*. I remember getting upset once when, despite her best efforts, I couldn't understand the expression 'broad' shoulders – why broad, I asked? Surely the correct word should be big, or wide, or round, but the explanation was right there in front of me – my parents, theirs were the broadest shoulders of all. They, who left their beloved families and came to England and stayed, once my father had completed his PhD, for my better life, and loved and suffered. Sadly, they are not here today for me to thank in person, but I hope and pray that the pairs of peacocks I see on the lawns and the riverbank can somehow read this, and, if they like it, I could say everything that I am is them.

And on that journey, I also must mention my late aunt, my mami, an author herself, who once gave an overly mathematical teenager a copy of *One Hundred Years of Solitude* and opened his eyes not only to the world of literature but to art itself. I know she'd be smiling at me now.

My boys, the A team, their friends and cousins, provided the inspiration for this story. As they look forward to their career journeys, and in a world of seemingly increasingly questionable dynamics, I wanted to share some of my own experiences and insights into corporate and political behaviours – behaviours with their underlying motivations and sometimes apparent contradictions – in the hope that understanding these contexts will allow them to manage and maintain their own ethics and integrity while working with those who so easily sacrifice theirs on the altars of ego and ambition.

Most importantly, I want to thank my wife, head of the A team, my fire, my granite, my calming soothing sea, who encouraged me to write during the newfound spare time during Covid, cajoling me to carry on when the doubts flooded in, and the words drowned. Without her, there would be no words. Without her, no world.

And finally, thank you to Troubador Publishing for taking me from the script to the final product.

ABOUT THE AUTHOR

Dark Pools is the debut novel by Alexander DuCharme. Alexander, writing under a pseudonym, has worked for many years in financial services, predominantly in investment banking.

This book is printed on paper from sustainable sources managed under the Forest Stewardship Council (FSC) scheme.

It has been printed in the UK to reduce transportation miles and their impact upon the environment.

For every new title that Troubador publishes, we plant a tree to offset CO_2, partnering with the More Trees scheme.

For more about how Troubador offsets its environmental impact, see www.troubador.co.uk/sustainability-and-community